ASK MY

Mood

Ring

HOW I FEEL

ASK MY Mood Ring

HOW I FEEL

BY DIANA LÓPEZ

LITTLE, BROWN AND COMPANY
New York · Boston

Also by Diana López:
Confetti Girl

Little, Brown and Company

Hachette Book Group
237 Park Avenue, New York, NY 10017
Visit our website at www.lb-kids.com

Little, Brown and Company is a division of Hachette Book Group, Inc. The Little, Brown name and logo are trademarks of Hachette Book Group, Inc.

The publisher is not responsible for websites (or their content) that are not owned by the publisher.

First Edition: June 2013

Library of Congress Cataloging-in-Publication Data

López, Diana.
  Ask my mood ring how I feel / by Diana López. — 1st ed.
    p. cm.
  Summary: When thirteen-year-old Erica "Chia" Montenegro finds out her mother has breast cancer, she makes a promise to God to raise money for breast cancer awareness and discovers that when family and friends work together, miracles can happen.
  ISBN 978-0-316-20996-0
  [1. Fund-raising—Fiction. 2. Promises—Fiction. 3. Cancer—Fiction.
4. Family life—Texas—Fiction. 5. Friendship—Fiction. 6. Christian life—Fiction.
7. Hispanic Americans—Fiction. 8. San Antonio (Tex.)—Fiction.] I. Title.
  PZ7.L876352 Ask 2013
  [Fic]—dc23
                                                                                    2012029856

10 9 8 7 6 5 4 3 2 1

RRD-C

Printed in the United States of America

To Amabel, Marina, and Soli

9 BIKINIS

I spent the entire month of May waiting for summer—for waking up when I felt like it and not when the alarm told me to, for wearing cool skirts and no shoes, for spending time with my friends at the park and pool, and for our family vacation—this year a trip to Carlsbad Caverns, a giant cave system in New Mexico—and on to Roswell, where aliens once crash-landed. Of course, I knew aliens were a hoax, but I looked forward to Roswell anyway, if only to see how many people could be fooled by such a silly story. So when Mom said she was going to shop for bathing suits, I didn't think twice. Sure, New Mexico was a desert, but every vacation spot had pools—not to mention the Texas coast, which we visited two or three times a year. And when she brought home nine bikinis, I thought it was odd, but only for a second, because Mom did funny things sometimes, like making potato chip pancakes or talking in a computer voice inspired by *Star Trek* shows.

"Come look, Chia," Mom said, waving me into her room. "You too, Carmen."

I stepped in, my nerdy little sister following.

"What do you think?" Mom asked, arranging the bikinis on the bed with the care of someone setting the table for Thanksgiving dinner. Their colors were bright like piñatas. One bikini top was striped, another polka-dotted, a third checkered. One had tropical flowers, and another, little palm trees.

"They're very pretty," I answered.

"Yeah. Real pretty," Carmen said. "Are these for vacation?"

Mom shrugged. "You could say that. I bought one for each day of the week."

Carmen's finger pointed at each as she counted. Her math brain always counted things. "But there are nine bikinis here," she said. "Does that mean we're having a nine-day vacation?"

Once again, Mom said, "You could say that."

Mom took the bikini bottoms and threw them into the small wicker basket she used as a trash can, then folded the tops and stacked them neatly in her lower dresser drawer.

"What are you doing?" I asked. I could totally understand potato chip pancakes, a computer voice, and buying nine bikinis, but throwing away something new was beyond me.

Before she could answer, my two-year-old brother walked in. "Gimme, gimme, gimme," he said, grabbing a bikini top. When I tried to take it away, we got into a tug-of-war match.

"Let go, Jimmy!" I cried.

"It's okay," Mom said. "Let him have it. He'll give it back after he's had a good look." She ran her fingers through his hair, but he was too interested in the bikini top to notice. Then she lifted him, hugged him tight, and said, "My baby, my beautiful baby," even though he wasn't a baby anymore. When Jimmy wriggled free, Mom grabbed Carmen and me for a group hug, and she said it again, "My babies, my beautiful babies."

"Is everything okay?" Carmen asked.

"Of course. I'm just showing a little affection."

"But you're acting weird. Right, Chia?"

"Maybe," I said.

"What do you mean by 'maybe'? She *is* acting weird."

Truth was, I *did* think Mom seemed a bit…off…but there were a lot of things I'd rather do than take Carmen's side—like sleep on a block of ice or drink tomato sauce with crushed Oreos.

3

"It's not weird," I said. "Mom doesn't need a special occasion to hug us or call us her babies."

Mom said, "You're so sweet," and kissed the top of my head.

Carmen hated to be wrong, but more than that, she hated for me to be right. She glared at me. If her eyes were claws, I'd have a dozen scratch marks on my face.

"Okay, girls," Mom said. "Why don't you go to the other room? It's time for Jimmy's nap."

"Gimme nap. Gimme nap," Jimmy said, climbing onto the bed and grabbing a pillow. Carmen and I left him there and made our way to the kitchen.

A long time ago, Mom and Dad had bought us matching desks and placed them side by side in the den, but we preferred to hang out in the kitchen because it was huge and had a table as big as a stage. Besides, it usually smelled good in there—sometimes like Mom's *charro* beans or beef stew, other times like biscuits or coffee—and when we were lucky like chocolate cake. Today, though, it didn't smell like anything, but it would as soon as Mom started dinner.

Carmen and I sat on opposite ends, the rest of the table like a long hallway between us. Carmen made a skyscraper of library books about dream interpretation, Egyptology, and renewable energy. I had to roll my eyes. I mean, she wasn't in college—*yet*. Besides, it was summer. Who spent the summer studying? Only *my* sister begged for a trip to the library each week. No thank you. I'd rather hang out with my friends or watch TV than read boring books.

Speaking of friends, I flipped open the laptop and spotted an e-mail from Iliana, with "Park?" in the subject line. "Hey, guys," she wrote to me and a few other friends, "want to meet at the park tomorrow?" We all lived in the same neighborhood, and the park was a short walk from our homes. It had lots of shade, skateboarding ramps, swing sets, and a pool.

"Mom!" I called out. "Can I go to the park tomorrow?"

"Sure," she called from the bedroom.

I hit the "reply" button and wrote, "I'll be there."

After checking the rest of my messages, I glanced at the shipping information for the Endless Band Mood Ring, the one Dad ordered for me after I said "please" a dozen times. Mom mentioned having one when she was a teen, and when I learned that mood rings change colors according to your emotions, I had to get one, too. My friends always wanted to know how I felt, and pointing to a mood ring seemed a lot easier than having a whole conversation about my feelings. It was scheduled to arrive tomorrow. Good. I needed to make sure I was here because the last thing I wanted was Carmen stealing my übercool ring, and she'd do it. No doubt in my mind she would.

"Did you know," Carmen began, "that when Egyptians were turning dead bodies into mummies, they sucked the brains out through the nose?"

"I wonder if they used a sippy straw?" I said.

"And then they took out the intestines and put them in jars."

"Imagine seeing that in a pantry—not strawberry preserves but gut jam."

She ignored me. "They put *all* the organs in jars. Except for the heart. Do you know what those jars were called?"

I took a second too long for a comeback.

"They're called *canopic* jars," Carmen said, all proud of herself.

"I knew that," I lied. "I was just testing you. Now, quit being a show-off." I crumpled a napkin and threw it at her, but it missed.

Her way of knowing a bunch of useless details really bugged me, especially after I learned that she'd be joining me in middle school next year. She was supposed to be in the fifth grade but she got bumped up to sixth. So when she started acting like the narrator of a Discovery Channel show, I did my best to make jokes or ignore her. I didn't want Carmen to know how dumb she made me feel. She'd never stop teasing me if she did.

Forget her, I told myself. I had my own intellectual pursuits. Carmen liked ancient civilizations and math equations, but I liked to mind-travel—that's what I called it when I let my imagination take me somewhere else, somewhere far from my pesky sister. I loved to visit Google Images. Today, Mom's bikinis made me think of the ocean, so I typed "seaside" in the search box. So many pictures came up—peaceful coastlines with water as blue and clear as marbles, busy boardwalks with roller coasters right over the ocean, resort towns with rows of condominiums, and places where waves splashed against giant rocks. I finally settled on a crowded beach. Every inch seemed full of people in lawn chairs or on blankets, their coolers beside them, their umbrellas providing shade. The sand was dotted with footprints. I mind-traveled and felt the wind, the sun, and the gritty sand. I heard gulls, waves, laughter, and flapping towels. I tasted the salty air and an ice-cold—

"Gimme Chia. Gimme Chia," Jimmy said, interrupting my "vacation." He had walked in, dragging a pillow and bikini top across the floor. He dropped them and pointed at the baker's rack. "Gimme Chia. Gimme Chia," he said, reaching for our SpongeBob Chia Pet. Chia Pets are clay figurines with little holes, usually where hair or fur belongs. When you water them, grass grows through the holes. So instead of pies and cookies on the baker's rack, we had green-haired characters. On the top shelf were actual Chia

Pets—a cat, a puppy, a lamb. Then we had the patriotic shelf with George Washington, Abe Lincoln, and Barack Obama. Below that, we had SpongeBob SquarePants, Scooby-Doo, Homer Simpson, and Dora the Explorer, all with green hair. In the middle of our collection was a picture of me when I was one. I had thick curly hair back then, so for my first Halloween, Mom and Dad painted it green, put me in a Onesie the color of terra-cotta, and told everyone I was a real live Chia Pet. That's why they call me Chia now. It isn't my actual name. My actual name is Erica. Erica Montenegro. By the time I was three, I had long straight hair, but the family called me Chia anyway. In fact, I didn't know I was Erica till I started school.

I never asked for a Chia Pet, *ever*, but after Mom and Dad framed that Halloween picture, my aunts and grandparents, and later my friends, bought them for me as Christmas or birthday gifts. So the surprise wasn't what I was getting, since I knew a Chia Pet was in the box, but which one. When I complained that I was getting too old for Scooby-Doo and Dora the Explorer, they started to buy me historical figures, even though I really meant "no more Chia Pets." Then I said, "I'm not really into politics," so they started buying animals. I didn't bother to complain because I knew they'd just discover another Chia Pet category. In fact, I absolutely loved my collection. In a way, the

Chia Pets were like a timeline of my life, a happy timeline since they mostly came gift wrapped at a party.

"Gimme Chia!" Jimmy said again. He looked so cute with his wide, innocent eyes. I almost forgot how destructive he could be until I noticed a blank spot on the shelf.

"Gimme!" he insisted.

I tried to break the news gently. "I can't. You'll break it. Remember what you did to Garfield last week?"

"But I wan' it! I wan' it!" He started to cry. Jimmy didn't know about sniffles or sobs. When he was upset, he went straight to bawling.

"Sorry," I said. "I don't want you to get in trouble."

This time, he added stomping to the tantrum.

Carmen whined. "I can't concentrate with all this noise. Where's Mom? She's the only one who can handle Jimmy."

"I can take care of him, too," I said, heading to the pantry because a snack was a great way to calm him down. I offered him a cookie. He slapped it away from my hand.

"No cookie!" he yelled.

"Will you be quiet?" Carmen said, scolding him. "Where's Mom? Can't she hear him?"

I wondered too, especially since pep rallies were quieter than this.

"Maybe she's sleeping," I guessed.

Just then, Dad got home from work.

"What's going on?" he said as he stepped into the kitchen. "I can hear Jimmy from outside."

"He wants to play with SpongeBob," I explained.

Dad stooped down to Jimmy's level. "Is that right, little buddy?"

Jimmy nodded and stomped again. "Gimme Chia!"

"Okay, okay," Dad promised.

"Dad, don't!" I warned. "He'll break it."

"We're just going to touch it, right, Jimmy? We're not going to play with it because it's not a toy."

Jimmy nodded again. Then Dad picked him up and let him pat SpongeBob's hair. After a minute, Jimmy said, "Down now." He was perfectly quiet again. He picked up the bikini top and the pillow and headed to the hallway. I made a mental note: when cookies don't work, just give Jimmy what he wants.

"Where's your mother?" Dad asked.

"Asleep," we said.

He looked toward their bedroom. "Okay. We'll let her rest awhile longer."

He took off his coat, tie, and buttoned-up shirt. His undershirt looked funny with his pressed slacks and shiny black shoes, but we were used to seeing him like this. He worked at USAA, a giant insurance company and one of the biggest companies in San Antonio, so he had to wear a suit every day, what he called his straitjacket. He couldn't wait to take it off when he got home, especially in the summer when it was so hot.

After he got comfortable, he opened the fridge and took out ground beef, lettuce, tomatoes, and cheese. Then he opened the pantry and took out a package of corn tortillas. After that, he pushed aside all the cans and boxes and reached *way* back into the pantry. He scratched his head a minute, then opened all the cabinet doors, even beneath the sink where we kept cleaning supplies. Then he peeked on top of the fridge, behind the microwave, and under the toaster.

"What are you looking for?" I asked. "You look like a kid on an Easter egg hunt."

"I'm looking for that packet of spices for the tacos," he said. "I want to start dinner."

"We ate tacos last week," Carmen answered. "Mom hasn't been to the store since then."

His shoulders slumped. "I guess we'll eat *migas* instead."

Migas was our favorite Tex-Mex dish—a mix of corn tortillas, eggs, tomatoes, onions, and cheese. We loved the recipe. Thing was, *migas* were for breakfast, not dinner.

In a way, it made sense for Dad to make them because he always cooked breakfast. After all, my parents believed in "division of labor." Dad made breakfast, Mom made dinner, and Carmen and I cleaned the kitchen at the end of the day. We used to wash dishes together, but since we kept fighting over who washed and who dried, who cleared the table and who swept the floor, Mom and Dad came up with a new "division of labor" plan. Carmen would clean on the odd-numbered days, while I cleaned on the even-numbered. Sounded great to me. Of course, Carmen quickly pointed out how unfair it was since months like January had thirty-one days, which meant she'd have to clean two days in a row because the next day was always the first. So to make things *exactly* equal, Mom or Dad cleaned when the last day of the month ended with an odd number.

"We can't eat *migas*," Carmen complained. "That's for breakfast."

Dad took out the cutting board and started to chop an onion. "The only dinner recipes I know are tacos and barbecue. Anyway, who says breakfast is just for the morning? We might have to get used to eating breakfast at night now."

"Why?" Carmen asked. "Is Mom going on strike or something?"

Dad stopped a moment, closing his eyes tight. I thought he was going to cry, but that was silly. Dads didn't cry. Must have been the onions he was chopping.

"Well?" Carmen said.

Dad didn't answer. Instead he said, "Jimmy's too quiet. Go check on him."

When Carmen didn't move, I said to her, "He means you."

"No, he doesn't," she sassed back. "It's your job to baby-sit. You're the oldest. Whoever heard of the *second* oldest taking care of little kids?"

"Girls," Dad said "Not now. Why don't *both* of you check on Jimmy?"

We still didn't move.

"One, two," he began.

"Okay, okay," we said. The last thing we wanted was Dad to hit three. Once he hit three, we hit some kind of punishment. Usually he took away our iPods or computer privileges for a day. But we never knew. Punishment could mean pulling weeds or dusting baseboards. It could mean writing a five-paragraph essay about the possible consequences of our bad behavior. Like, what if we *didn't* check on Jimmy? What's the worst kind of trouble he could get into? I'd heard stories about little kids sticking their fingers in sockets and getting electrocuted or swallowing small toys and choking. That was the last thing I wanted for my brother, even if he was a pest sometimes.

I bolted from my chair and sprinted past Carmen, who hadn't budged an inch. Once again, I had to look after Jimmy, while Carmen got to stay with her precious books.

I searched all over the place, even called his name. He never answered back. I finally discovered him in the coat closet where we kept our tennis shoes and hiking and work boots. He'd taken out all the shoelaces, so now they were in a giant tangle. How could he make such a mess in fifteen minutes?

I picked up a shoelace, and it was wet with saliva. "Gross!" I said to Jimmy. "Did you put all these in your mouth?"

He laughed. Then he said, "Gimme!" as he opened and closed his hand.

I didn't hand it to him. Instead, I ran the shoelace over his face, tickling him.

"Let's clean this up," I said.

He shook his head to say no, and then he ran back to the kitchen. That brat!

I grabbed my cell phone from my pocket and wrote to Iliana. "Can we trade bros?" A few seconds later, she replied, "Let's." If only it were that simple. Iliana had twin brothers in high school. They were super cute and athletic. They were smart too, and polite. And they were exactly identical. Sometimes I wished I were their girlfriend because if the first one couldn't take me to the homecoming dance, I could ask the second one. It'd be like having two iPods with the same playlists. That way, when the battery ran out on one, I could switch over to the other. My dad always said it was good to have a backup plan. Twin boyfriends and twin iPods sounded like good backup plans to me.

I shook the wishful thinking from my mind as I untangled the shoelaces and threaded them through the tennis shoes and boots. Then I returned to the kitchen and found Jimmy tearing paper towels into tiny pieces, while Dad spooned *migas* onto our plates and Carmen set the table.

"Thanks for helping," she told me, all sarcastic.

"No, thank *you* for helping *me*." I could be sarcastic, too.

"You're the one who snuck off to text Iliana so you wouldn't have to work in the kitchen."

"Well, *I'm* the one who had to clean up Jimmy's mess after Dad asked *you* to check on him."

"He didn't ask me. You're the oldest, remember?"

"*¡Por favor!*" Dad said. He still had the spoon in his hand and was clenching it so tight. I could see the muscles and veins in his forearm. "I just want to have a nice dinner for Mom. A nice, peaceful dinner. She had a really hard day, understand?"

Carmen and I glanced at each other. Why did Mom have a hard day? As far as we could tell, she went shopping and got a good deal on bathing suits. Something was up, and we both knew it. We'd never admit that our brains were hooked on the same idea, but they were.

"Take your seats," Dad ordered. He picked up Jimmy and placed him on his booster chair. "All of you stay put. And don't say a word till I get back."

We obeyed, but it was tough. Staying quiet was impossible for my little brother and sister. Jimmy kept blowing bubbles through the straw of his sippy cup and Carmen kept tapping her fork against her glass. I could see her lips moving, which meant she was counting. Later she'd tell me exactly how many times she tapped her fork, plus whatever else she'd counted. She couldn't help herself, and Jimmy couldn't help making a mess, even with his spill-proof sippy cup. I loved them, but I couldn't stand it sometimes, couldn't stand *them*.

Finally, Mom and Dad stepped in. As soon as she saw the table, Mom said, "What's this?"

"I made dinner," Dad announced.

"And I set the table," Carmen added.

"But I could have made dinner," Mom said. "I was planning to. I *always* make it, don't I?"

"Just wanted you to have a day off," Dad said, all cheery.

He pulled out her chair. He could be a real gentleman, but since he pulled out Mom's chair only at fancy dinners or weddings, this was weird. Mom must have thought so too, because she hesitated before sitting down. Then Dad went to his seat and told us to dig in. We did. Quietly. For once, Carmen wasn't acting like a know-it-all and Jimmy wasn't begging for something to hold. It was a perfectly quiet dinner like Dad had wanted, but it sure wasn't peaceful.

Finally, Jimmy broke the silence. "Gimme juice!" he said, holding out his sippy cup..

Mom scooted back her chair, but Dad said, "I got it."

"That's not…" she tried.

"It's my pleasure," Dad said. "You get Jimmy's juice every night."

She crossed her arms. "That's right. I do."

"So let the rest of us help," Dad said. "There's no need for you to do everything."

"And there's no need for me to do *nothing* at all."

I felt totally confused. Dad was acting super nice, but Mom was acting mad. "What's going on?" I had to ask.

"Your father's treating me like an invalid," Mom said.

Carmen jumped in. "Chia doesn't know what that is. You have to define it for her."

"I know what 'invalid' means," I protested.

"What does it mean then?"

"An invalid is what you're going to be after I break your legs because you're such a brat all the time."

"Quit fighting, girls," Dad scolded. "You're upsetting your mother."

"They're not upsetting me. I'd rather see them fight than see you cater to me. Their fighting is normal. It's… it's *energetic*."

That was a strange thing to say. My dad thought so too,

because he stared at my mom for a long time—she stared back—whole paragraphs passing between them. The entire time, Jimmy kept saying, "Gimme juice. Gimme juice." But Mom and Dad were motionless. Finally, Mom stood up, and then—she pulled off her shirt! She was wearing a hot-pink bikini top, and she straightened her shoulders to show it off.

"You can't walk around like that," Dad said.

"You're *not* going to make me cover up."

"But we're not at the beach!"

Mom laughed. "Well, I can pretend. I've got nine days to pretend."

"Mom? Dad?" Carmen's voice cracked a little, and then Jimmy started to cry. Maybe he was tired of waiting for juice, or maybe he was scared like Carmen.

"Is this how you want to tell the children?" Dad said. "While they're all upset?"

"Tell us what?" Now *my* voice cracked. Once again, my parents stared at each other. This time, whole chapters passed between them, while a dozen scenarios ran through my mind. Were they getting divorced? Were they going bankrupt? What secret were they keeping from us?

"Your mother is sick," Dad said calmly.

"What kind of sick?" I had to ask because I knew this was bigger than a stomachache or the flu.

Mom took Jimmy's cup and refilled it. I could tell she was stalling. When she handed it to him, she kissed the top of his head. Then she returned to her seat, grabbed her fork, and pushed the remaining *migas* around her plate. And finally, without looking at us, she said, "I have breast cancer. I'm going to have a mastectomy in nine days."

5 ROBINS

The next day, Iliana stopped by my house so we could walk to the park together. Like me, she was skinny and had brown eyes, but Iliana wore gobs of mascara, so sometimes her eyelashes looked like spider legs. Our hairstyles were different, too. I had long brown hair, usually in a ponytail, while Iliana had short hair with lots of curls.

"OMG," she said (she loved to speak text sometimes), "my brothers' friends are so cute."

"Your *brothers* are cute," I said.

"To *you*, maybe. To me, they're a pain. They are so protective. I have to tell them everywhere I'm going to be and when I'll be back and they'll probably still check up on me. They're stricter than my parents. And they *torture* me!"

"How?" As far as I could tell, they were the nicest brothers in the world. At least she didn't have to live with a walking encyclopedia.

"First, they invite their friends over to play video games. Did I mention how cute their friends are?" She didn't let me answer. She just kept going. "Then, they shut me out. Literally. They close the door to their bedroom and tell me to stay out. So there I am standing with my ear to the door, just listening to all the video game sounds and to these really cute guys cheer after shooting some monster or who knows what, and then..."

I didn't mean to tune out. Normally, I loved hearing about Iliana's brothers, but how could I get excited about video games and cute boys when Mom was scheduled for surgery next week?

Suddenly, Iliana yanked me off the sidewalk, seconds before a skateboarder whizzed by.

"What planet are you on?" she said. "Didn't you hear the skateboard? Didn't you hear Chad call 'Sidewalk!' right before he almost bumped into you?" She held up two fingers to show me how close he'd been. "You have to pay attention because knocking a cute guy off his skateboard is not the best way to make a first impression, even if it is a close encounter of the fourth kind."

"Close encounter" is how we describe our relationships with boys. We got the idea after Iliana did a report on space aliens and learned that scientists call UFO sightings "close encounters." They even have different categories depending on whether you saw a vague shape in the sky or an actual life-form. Since boys seem as strange as aliens, Iliana and I decided to invent our own categories:

- Close encounter of the first kind—boy knows you exist.
- Close encounter of the second kind—boy talks to you, but only at school and only about boring school stuff like "Can I borrow a pencil?"
- Close encounter of the third kind—boy talks to you *and* sends you text messages about interesting stuff like favorite video games or funny YouTube videos.
- Close encounter of the fourth kind—actual physical contact!

I still hadn't experienced a close encounter of the first kind with Chad, which was disappointing because, with his blond hair and perfect tan, he topped my Boyfriend Wish List, along with Forest Montoya, Alejandro Guzmán, Lou Hikaru, Jamal Grey, Derek Smith, and Joe Leal.

I shrugged. "Chad's never going to notice me," I said. "I'm like that crack in the sidewalk that he jumps to avoid. I'll have to become a skateboard ramp or a pair of Vans before he notices me."

Iliana punched my shoulder. "Stop it, will you? Of course he's going to notice you. You've got nice, silky hair and a cute figure."

I had to disagree. "A lamppost has more curves," I said, pointing to one.

She laughed. "Only because of the way you're dressed. What's with the baggy, uninspired outfit? Even your T-shirt seems depressed."

I glanced at it, a faded brown V-neck. Usually, I wore T-shirts with punch lines or funny cartoons, but I couldn't laugh when Mom was sick. I shouldn't be going to the park, either. I should have stayed home and helped her. I offered, but she got mad just like the night before. She said, "Don't start acting like your dad by treating me like an invalid," and she ran me out of the house, even gave me extra money.

"You're not listening to a word I say," Iliana complained. And she was right. I had no idea she'd been talking.

"I got some really bad news," I explained, immediately regretting it. Sometimes, I didn't want friend-to-friend counseling sessions. They made me feel…weak. I could take care of myself, thank you.

23

"What happened?" Iliana wanted to know.

I shrugged. "Nothing. It's no big deal. I shouldn't have said anything."

We turned a corner and the park came into view. I sped up, nearly jogging.

"Wait!" Iliana reached for my arm but missed. "Don't you want to talk?"

"Sure," I called back. "Let's talk about boys."

"That's not what I meant," she said.

I pretended not to hear. "Hey, look. There's Patty waving us over."

We headed toward a picnic table with the Robins, our special group of friends. We have five members: me, Iliana, Patty, Shawntae, and GumWad, whose real name is Roberto. He had a purple tongue today because of his grape bubblegum. He really grossed me out sometimes. And to think that without the gum, he could be a decent-looking guy. He wasn't athletic and he didn't wear anything more interesting than T-shirts with sports logos and jeans. But he had a cuddly type of body like a teddy bear and dimples when he smiled. Too bad the dimples were on either side of a rainbow-colored mouth.

The Robins were my best friends, though we didn't choose one another—not at first. Our second-grade teacher put us together. Her classroom had four big tables, and in the center of each was a nest with a stuffed bird—one with a cardinal, another with a mockingbird, and another with a blue jay. Our table had a robin. When you squeezed its belly, it sang—*cheerily cheer-up cheer-up*. We'd have contests. Whoever finished an assignment first or made the highest grade got to squeeze the bird's belly. It seems silly now, but in second grade, squeezing the bird was a big deal.

As we approached the table, Iliana and I gave our friends a big Texas "Hi, y'all."

"Hey," they replied, hardly missing a beat in their conversation about some movie. This time, I tried my best to pay attention, especially since Iliana had already forgotten about my bad news. After a while, though, I started to feel really hot. In San Antonio, the temperature regularly hits the nineties, and the humidity made it feel like a hundred degrees. I grabbed a rubber band from my pocket and gathered my hair for a ponytail.

"You look hot," GumWad announced.

"Ooh, Erica," Shawntae teased. "Roberto thinks you're hot." She made a sizzling sound.

"That's not what I meant," GumWad said. "She's not sexy or anything…just hot, like overheated, like there's sweat running down the back of her neck."

"Gee, thanks," I said. "You sure know how to flatter a girl."

"I was just noticing you were hot. I wasn't trying to flatter you."

"Obviously," I said.

Shawntae punched me. "Leave the poor guy alone."

"You started it, Shawntae, with all those sizzling sounds you made."

"Yeah," GumWad said, taking my side. "You started it. Erica's not the only one who's sweaty. We all are. Look." He lifted his arms to show us round, damp splotches on the underarm parts of his T-shirt.

Patty pinched her nose. "Quit giving the skunks competition."

"Do I smell that bad?" GumWad said, full of dismay.

Patty, Shawntae, and I nodded, but Iliana said, "Don't listen to them. They're picking on you because they don't have anything better to do."

"I can think of something better," Patty said. "Let's go see who's skateboarding."

Her suggestion reminded Iliana about our close encounter with Chad earlier, and as we walked toward the ramps, she told the group about it. We reached the skateboarding park and sat on some bleachers just as she finished her story. Then we scanned the cement hills before us. "There's Alejandro," Iliana said, pointing.

In fact, several cute guys from school were showing off

grinds, kickflips, and ollies. We had fun watching them, giggling when they stumbled or fell and sighing when they took off their shirts. At one point, Forest stopped by. He said, "Hey, girls," and we said "Hey" back. Then he turned to GumWad, "Where's your board?"

"Left it at home."

"You should bring it next time."

"Sure thing."

When Forest skated off, Patty hit GumWad's shoulder and said, "You don't have a skateboard."

He shrugged.

"So why'd you lie?"

He shrugged again and glanced at me. He seemed embarrassed to be caught in a lie, but I could totally understand.

"I know why," I said. "It's a lot of trouble saying 'I don't have a skateboard' to a guy who thinks skateboarding is life. Then you have to explain *why* when there isn't a reason. You have nothing against skateboards. They just don't interest you. But try telling *them* that. They'll think you're weird, which can cause all kinds of awkwardness. So it's best to pretend, get them off your case."

"Yeah," GumWad said as grateful as someone who had just been rescued from an overturned ship.

Just then, we heard bells from the *paleta* man, a guy

who hauled an ice chest between the back wheels of a three-wheel bike. He stored *paletas* in there, frozen fruit bars. They cost one dollar each.

"You want one?" GumWad asked me, but before I could answer, the other Robins were handing him money.

"Thanks for offering," Iliana said. "You are so sweet," she cooed.

Shawntae jumped in. "Yeah, you're as sweet as...as sweet as..." She snapped her fingers, my cue to finish the sentence.

"As sweet as a cookie dough pizza topped with chocolate chips, marshmallows, and caramel."

Everyone smacked their lips as they imagined it, except Patty. She rolled her eyes and said, "You'd have to run ten marathons to work off all those calories."

Patty looked like the sweetest girl on the planet with her freckles and blue eyes, but if she won a million dollars, she'd focus on the extra taxes instead of the extra fun she could have.

"Well, I guess I could get some for all of us," GumWad said, taking the not-so-subtle hint. We told him which flavors to buy, and he took off. The skateboarders and kids from the playground and pool had already formed a long line in front of the bicycle. That *paleta* man knew exactly when to show up.

While GumWad waited in the line, Shawntae, Iliana, and Patty went on and on about boys, which was usually my favorite topic, but I couldn't stop thinking about Mom. How could she be sick? She seemed perfectly normal, full of energy. I couldn't imagine cancer eating away part of her body, especially when she hadn't complained about pain. Maybe it didn't hurt till it was too late. Maybe cancer was like a termite, silent and invisible until you noticed the walls falling down.

"Erica!" Iliana said. "This is the second time you totally ignored me."

"I ignored you?"

Patty explained, "You didn't answer when Iliana asked who was cuter, Alejandro or Chad. You were looking right at them, but your mind was somewhere else."

Just then, GumWad returned and passed out the *paletas*. I had ordered banana, but the other girls got strawberry, while GumWad got mango.

"Fess up," Iliana said. "Time to tell us about your bad news."

"What bad news?" Shawntae wanted to know.

"It's private," I said.

The Robins stared at me, silently eating their fruit bars and waiting. If I didn't tell, they'd spend the whole day pestering me.

"Okay," I said. "If you really have to know." I paused, secretly hoping they'd let it go but knowing they wouldn't. Taking a deep breath, I said, "My mom has breast cancer."

If I was scared about cancer before, I was more scared now, because all of them stopped eating, stopped *breathing*, it seemed. They were as frozen as the *paletas* we held in our hands, but like the *paletas*, their initial shock was quickly melting away. "When did you find out?" they asked, and "How serious is it?" and "Is she in the hospital?" and "Is she...is she...is she going to die?"

"I don't know!" I said, throwing my *paleta* to the ground. "This is why I didn't want to tell you guys. I knew you'd have a million questions that I can't answer." I got a lump in my throat, the one that meant tears were on their way, so I swallowed hard and breathed deeply. I was *not* going to cry. Sure, these were my friends, but that didn't mean I should act like a baby around them. "All I know for sure," I said, more calmly, "is that my mom's going to have a mastectomy."

"What's that?" GumWad asked.

"It's an operation," Patty said. "They cut off your breast."

Iliana, Shawntae, and I winced and crossed our arms over our chests as we imagined the pain. GumWad winced and crossed his arms, too.

Then he said, "My uncle had an operation last year. He had a stone in his gallbladder."

"How did he get a stone in there?" Shawntae asked.

"I don't know. He didn't swallow it, if that's what you're thinking. It's something his body made." He blew and popped a bubble before going on. I couldn't believe he was chewing gum while eating a *paleta*. "They took out his gall-bladder," he went on, "and then they put the stone in a little jar with some formaldehyde and gave it to him—like a souvenir. He keeps it by his computer and he named it Bob."

"That is so weird," Shawntae said.

"No, it's not," I said. "It's like having a pet rock."

"Yeah!" GumWad smacked a little more quickly. "You're the first person to get it!"

Maybe I understood pet rocks because of the Chia Pet zoo in my kitchen.

"Is your uncle okay now?" Iliana asked.

GumWad nodded.

"See?" she said to me, putting her hand on my shoulder. "Lots of people have surgery, and they come out okay. I'm sure that's how it'll be for your mom."

"But it makes you wonder," Patty said. "What do they do with the breast after the operation?"

"Patty!" Shawntae punched her. "That's so rude!"

I shivered, suddenly feeling cold even though it was

ninety-plus degrees. The image of Mom's breast displayed in a jar on someone's desk was freaking me out. But Patty had asked a good question: When ladies had mastectomies or when soldiers had arms or legs cut off, where did the body parts go? Were they sent to some crazy scientist's lab? Or were they thrown away, like garbage? And was that what we became when a part of us died or when our whole body died? I looked at the fruit bar I had thrown on the ground, how quickly it was melting, how the banana had been plucked from its tree.

We sat silently for a while. The Robins knew my mom and were probably feeling worried like me. Soon the skateboarders returned, and I focused on the sounds of their wheels, how they rolled and thudded after jumps.

Finally, Shawntae leaned forward and said, "You're not going to believe this, but..."

"Not another dream!" I moaned, because this was the one thing that bugged me about Shawntae.

"I can't help it," she said. "I have psychic powers. You guys are just jealous because you can't predict the future like me."

"It's not a prediction," Iliana explained, "when you tell us your dreams after the fact."

"This isn't after the fact. I had the dream last week."

We knew she'd tell us about it, so we slumped in our seats and sighed. Only GumWad seemed interested.

"So what did you dream?" he wanted to know.

Shawntae straightened her shirt and smoothed back her hair like an anchorwoman with a news flash. "I saw Erica's mom wearing a bikini, but she had a thermometer in her mouth. Who wears a bikini and sticks a thermometer in her mouth? So I thought she was at the beach and the thermometer was a symbol of how hot it was. But now I get it. The thermometer meant she was sick. Like when the nurse takes your temperature."

"You didn't have that dream," I said. "You're just repeating stuff from our conversation. That's what you do. You take a few clues, and you make something up."

"I *did* have that dream. Last week."

"Why didn't you tell me then? This is serious, Shawntae. My mom has cancer. What's the point of seeing the future if you can't warn your friends?"

"That's not how psychic powers work."

I stood up. "How many times do we have to tell you? You do *not* have psychic powers!"

I stomped away, heading to my house, but Iliana caught up to me. "Don't be mad," she said. "We're just trying to help."

"Then tell me why my mom's sick." When she didn't answer, I repeated myself. "Why is she sick, Iliana?"

"I don't know."

"That's right. Nobody does," I said, realizing that I wasn't angry about Shawntae's dream. I wasn't angry with my friends at all. What bugged me, what *really* bugged me, was that no one knew the answer to the most important question: Why did cancer choose my mom? After all, cancer had always been the big, scary end to bad habits. If you smoked, you got lung cancer and a hole in your throat. If you drank beer, you got liver cancer and yellow eyes. If you went to the pool without sunscreen, you got skin cancer and a dark mole creeping over your body. But what bad habit made breast cancer?

As far as I knew, Mom lived right. Several times a week, she pushed aside furniture and did a step aerobics tape. She drank eight glasses of water each day, and when she felt like coffee, she drank the decaffeinated kind. She didn't eat doughnuts or chocolate bars or syrupy pancakes. She never sped past the yellow lights or told lies or cheated or cursed or stole.

And every night—every single night—after saying "sweet dreams" to Carmen and me and singing lullabies to Jimmy, she made the sign of the cross, clasped her hands, and prayed.

30,000 PEOPLE

Most people slept late on Saturdays, but I had a brother who thought he was the six o'clock alarm. Jimmy Gimme's room was next to the one Carmen and I shared, so I piled pillows over my ears, hoping to drown out his cries. No use. Even if Jimmy were miles away, I'd still hear him scream.

"What's the matter, *mijo*?" we heard Mom say. "You've got no reason to cry. Everybody loves you, don't they?"

She must have lifted Jimmy from his bed because he calmed down. I rolled over and found a comfortable spot, hoping to get back to my dream about the guys on my Boyfriend Wish List. But six o'clock was my normal wake-up time, so I was awake, wide awake. That was okay. Daydreams were just as good; even better, since I could put myself into a pretend situation—like imagining Alejandro

Guzmán on crutches after breaking his leg while skate-boarding and me pushing his wheelchair to the park, then him realizing how sweet and dependable I could be, unlike the girl who dumped him as soon as he wasn't a cool skate-boarder anymore. I was just about to imagine the good part, when Alejandro looked in my eyes, whispered sweet nothings, and leaned in close, then closer, and then...

"Wake up, sleepyheads!" Dad called, stepping into the room and tugging at our feet.

"But it's Saturday," I said.

"Yeah." Carmen yawned. "And we're still tired."

I tried to hide beneath the blankets, hoping Dad would feel sorry for me. No such luck. He started to sing. *"Hi ho, hi ho."* He marched like one of Snow White's dwarfs, the whole time singing and stomping.

"Stop it!" I cried, covering my ears for the second time this morning.

"Hi ho. Hi ho," he kept singing.

"He won't stop till we get out of bed," Carmen said. She was right. This wasn't the first time Dad had tried to annoy us with cheesy Disney songs.

"Okay, okay." I threw back the covers and sat up. "We're awake now."

"Bueno," Dad said. He stooped over to kiss Carmen's

forehead, and then he kissed mine. "After you get dressed," he told us, "I want you to pick something special for Mom."

As soon as he mentioned something special, I thought about my Chia Pets. Then I thought about the brand-new mood ring that had arrived in the mail yesterday.

"Why do we have to pick something special?" Carmen asked.

"Because of her operation," I said, glad to know an answer before she did.

Dad nodded. "That's right. We've got big plans today. We're going to the valley."

The valley was at the southernmost tip of Texas. Carmen and I glanced at each other, both of us wondering why we were driving more than two hundred miles to go there.

"We leave in forty-five," Dad said. Then he stepped out, and a few minutes later, I heard him tickling Jimmy.

I sat on the edge of my bed for a minute. Carmen and I shared a big room, split in half by an imaginary line that was as real to us as that bold yellow line down the middle of a street. To the left was my side, and to the right was Carmen's. We had our own furniture and our own style. Above her bed, Carmen had tacked a poster of the human body labeled with interesting facts like how many miles of blood vessels we had and how many times we blinked each day.

Above my bed, I tacked posters of my favorite movies. I updated them periodically, but right now, I had posters from *Twilight*—one with the guy who played a vampire and another with the guy who turned into a wolf every time the girl of his dreams was in trouble. Carmen didn't like them since they weren't educational. But she left them alone because of our invisible line. It was our lifesaver, and we respected it. The only time Carmen crossed to my side was to get to the closet, and the only time I crossed to hers was to get to the door or to wake her up, something I had to do nearly every morning.

I fixed my bed and washed up. Carmen still hadn't moved. I nudged her. She groaned. I nudged her again. And one more time. If it weren't for me, Carmen would lie in bed till noon.

"Hurry up!" I told her.

She mumbled, but she managed to sit up. After stretching a bit, she made her way to the closet, while I picked out my own outfit. Today, I selected a T-shirt that pictured a chicken and an egg with legs racing through victory tape, a photo finish, with the caption, "Which came first?" I modeled it for Carmen, but she wasn't impressed. Why did I even try?

Carmen put on jeans, but instead of blue, they were

pink—only Carmen said they were fuchsia. And she wore a T-shirt like me, but she wore it inside out. On purpose!

"What's wrong with you?" I asked.

"I'm a nonconformist," she announced. "And in case you're wondering, it means I don't follow rules."

"I *wasn't* wondering," I said, even though I was. "And besides, you follow rules. I can think of a trillion rules you follow."

"Really? A trillion? Do you even know how many zeroes that has?"

I pulled my hair. I actually pulled my hair! It was too early for this. "Stop it, already! Don't you get it? I'm exaggerating."

"Where I come from, we call that 'hyperbole.'"

"And where do you come from? Please tell me. Because last time I looked, you and I came from the same place."

"That depends on how you define 'place.' It doesn't have to be a physical location. It can be—"

"Mom!" I yelled. "Dad!"

"What is it?" they called from the other room.

"Carmen's getting on my nerves!"

"Just ignore her."

Easier said than done. Even though I could never have the last word with Carmen, I could have the longest, most intense stare. So that's what I did. I stared at her, and she stared back. We were two growling dogs waiting to see who'd back down first. Carmen might have a dictionary, a calculator, and the entire Wikipedia in her head, but she was still my little sister. No way could she outlast my stare-down. Finally, after the longest two minutes of my life, she looked away. Gotcha!

Okay, quit wasting time, I told myself. Find something special. It's for Mom.

"I guess I'll pick one of my awards," Carmen said, studying a bookshelf where she kept trophies, ribbons, and binders with every assignment from every teacher she'd ever had in her entire life. "This one's special, don't you think?"

She held out her spelling bee trophy. Last year, Carmen was the best speller in the district. Our whole family followed her to Austin for the state competition. She made it all the way to finals before the word "eidetic" tripped her up. It sounded a lot easier to spell than "confabulation," which she got right, no problem, so I was surprised she missed it. Then I learned that "eidetic" meant having a super-duper memory, which cracked me up. Imagine a girl with an almost perfect memory missing the word "eidetic" at the spelling bee. I made a joke about it, and she cried. I felt horrible. Sure, my sister really got on my nerves, but when she cried, I went into big-sister guard-dog mode. Same with Jimmy.

"You should pick an award, too," Carmen said. "Oh, I forgot. You don't have one."

I was about to point out the bike rodeo ribbon I won in third grade, but she beat me to it.

"That one doesn't count," she said, "since it's for participation. They give those so people like you won't feel bad. It's to help your self-esteem."

"At least I signed up," I said, remembering how I knocked down every cone on the obstacle course. "At least I tried."

"That's about *all* you did."

I threw a pillow at her. She caught it and tossed it back. I threw it again, this time harder and with a secret wish that instead of a pillow, I'd thrown an ink balloon. That's right. A balloon filled with ink instead of water.

"Don't get mad at me," Carmen said. "It's not *my* fault you don't have something special." For a second, I thought about asking her to spell "eidetic"—just a friendly reminder to put her in her place—but if I knew Carmen, she had memorized the spelling by now.

She walked out cradling her trophy. That brat. Maybe I didn't have any awards, but I did have something special. I had a whole baker's rack of Chia Pets. But with so many to choose from and so little time, I knew I had to pick something else. I had my new mood ring, but I hated to give it up, especially because I still had to learn what the different colors meant. I searched through my jewelry box, not the top shelf, where I kept my earrings and bracelets, but the secret compartment beneath. This was where I kept the spearmint gum wrapper from a piece that David Bara once offered me. I had a crush on him last year. I also kept a pencil with Alex Herrera's tooth marks. I'd saved it after he left it on his desk one day. I'd had a crush on him, too. And I'd had a crush on Allen Gibbs, so I stole one of his homework assignments when the teacher accidentally gave it to me. It was stuck behind my paper. I noticed it right away, but I didn't say anything when Allen said, "Hey, where's *my* assignment?"

I looked lovingly at each of these "souvenirs," but I wasn't planning to give Mom a gum wrapper, a chewed pencil, or a strange boy's homework. I had something else in mind, so I picked up an envelope that Iliana had given me last spring.

"This made me think of you," she'd said. "We're supposed to pass it along."

Inside the envelope was a pink note card that said, "Friends are forever." The envelope also contained a black pebble, a small crystal, and a "kindness" coin with a happy face that said, "You made me smile! Pass this smile along!"

I don't know why I kept it instead of following the directions. Then again, I liked remembering that Iliana chose me over all the other people in the world, over all the Robins too, and it made me feel special. Special like Mom.

I put the envelope in my pocket and went to the living room, where I found Carmen pulling crayons from Jimmy's hands while Dad complained about Mom's rainbow-striped bikini top.

"You're not wearing that today," he told her.

"Yes, I am. I explained already. I bought one for each day before my surgery."

"But, Lisa, we're going to a church."

"I know. I'll put a shirt over it when we get there."

Carmen finally freed the last crayon from Jimmy. "Why are we going to a church all the way in the valley?" she asked.

"We're going to a shrine to say special prayers," Mom said.

"Can't we say special prayers here?"

"Yes, but this is different."

"Why?"

"Quit being a pest," I told her.

Dad sighed. I thought he was going to scold me, but instead he answered Carmen's question. "Because a miracle happened at that church. There used to be another church there, but it was destroyed when a man crashed his plane into it. Over a hundred people were at mass when the church burned to the ground, but no one, except for the pilot, got hurt."

"There's another part," Mom went on. "The statue of La Virgen de San Juan was also spared. La Virgen has healing powers. She's helped many people in my family over the years."

Even though I thought the story was amazing, I wasn't convinced it was a miracle, but since it meant so much to Mom, I didn't say anything.

"Now let's get going," Dad said. "You girls take Jimmy to the car while your mother changes into something more appropriate."

"I *am* wearing something appropriate!" I heard Mom say as Carmen and I chased Jimmy, who had run out of the house screaming, "Gimme bye-bye! Gimme bye-bye!" as soon as he'd heard "car."

Jimmy liked going bye-bye, but he hated the car seat. In order for us to strap him in, Carmen had to hold down his arms while I buckled the straps.

Finally, Mom and Dad came out. Mom must have

won the argument because she was still wearing her bikini top. She looked beautiful, in my opinion, with her long flowing hair, curvy jeans, high-heeled shoes, flat stomach, firm shoulders, and breasts as full as the ones on Victoria's Secret models. I wanted to look like her someday. I wanted her hair, face, legs, and stomach. But did I want her breasts? I would have said yes a week ago, but now I wasn't sure.

The drive between San Antonio and the valley was nothing but flat land and cows. We finally reached the shrine around noon. For some reason, I thought it would look like the Alamo, but it was much bigger and more modern. The first thing I noticed was a giant mural facing the highway. It pictured Jesus in a blue robe, standing over the Virgin Mary. Her robe was also blue and was spread out like a triangular tent. She wore a crown and stood on a gold crescent moon.

"That's her. That's La Virgen de San Juan del Valle," Mom said when she caught Carmen and me stretching our necks to get a better look.

Dad found a parking spot and told us to grab our special items. Then we jumped out of the car and found ourselves near a fountain between the church and a group of buildings that included a school, a convent, and a gift shop. Many flowers surrounded the walkway. We pointed so Mom and Dad could tell us the names—blue plumbago, pink bougainvillea, and yellow esperanza. Carmen repeated the names as if prepping for a quiz. I'd probably forget which plant was which by tomorrow, but Carmen would still remember in twenty years. Mom put a shirt over her bikini top and told us to wait while she went to the gift shop. As soon as she left, Jimmy ran to the fountain. "Gimme money!" he said when he saw the coins there.

"You can look but you can't touch," Dad told him as they leaned over the pool. "See how shiny the money is?" Jimmy opened and closed his hand, so Dad reached in his pocket and gave him a penny. Jimmy looked at it, then threw it into the water.

"Hey, you're supposed to make a wish," Carmen said, holding out her own hand. Dad gave her a penny. She closed her eyes, took a deep breath, and tossed it in. Then Dad handed me a penny, keeping one for himself. We closed our eyes, made our wishes, and tossed the coins. All of us kept our wishes secret, but I felt certain that we had asked for the same thing.

Mom returned a few minutes later. She had bought a stuffed puppy for Jimmy. He was so delighted. For the rest of us, she bought candles. They featured La Virgen on one side and a prayer with *"ayúdame"* on the other. I couldn't speak much Spanish, but I knew that *ayúdame* meant "help me."

"When we get there," Dad said, pointing to the church before us, "we're going to pray."

"Then we're going to make *promesas*," Mom added.

"What's a *promesa*?" I asked.

"A promise, just like it sounds," Mom said. "Only this is a different kind of promise. A 'thank you' promise."

"What are we being thankful for?" I said.

"We're going to ask God and La Virgen to help your mother," Dad explained, "and in return, each of us is going to do something special."

"Like what?" Carmen asked.

"That's up to you," Mom said. "Some people promise to say extra prayers every day. Others promise to work for charities or do something for the church."

"I heard of a man," Dad added, "who promised to run a thousand miles."

"All at once?" Carmen sounded totally amazed.

"No. But every day he ran and recorded how far he went till he got to a thousand."

"And I had an uncle," Mom said, "who promised not to cut his hair for two years. This was in the 1950s, when men weren't supposed to have long hair."

"So it's like a bribe," I concluded. "We're bribing God to help us."

"No," Dad said. "We're *thanking* Him."

"But He hasn't helped us yet."

"But He will."

"Because of our prayers and *promesas*?"

They nodded, all of them, even Carmen. Apparently, I was the only one who thought this was a bribe. It just didn't make sense. Weren't you supposed to say "thank you" *after* someone helped you?

We entered the church and stepped into a giant, fan-shaped room with a floor that sloped down like in a theater. High above the altar stood the legendary statue of La Virgen de San Juan, an exact copy of the mural outside. I was expecting a giant statue, life-size, but this was a small doll with a dark brown face. She stood in a nook surrounded by a huge wooden frame that reminded me of an Aztec sundial with its ring of hieroglyphics and shapes that looked like snakes and leaves.

Mom and Dad led us to a chamber behind the altar, where hundreds of candles flickered and dozens of people knelt to utter prayers. As I overheard their different accents, I realized that they had come from all over the United States and Mexico to visit this shrine.

"Here's where you light the candle," Dad said. "Say a prayer and make your *promesa*, okay?"

Carmen and I nodded. Then the whole family filed into an empty section of the kneeling pad. I placed my candle in a slot, lit it, and said the Our Father and Hail Mary. I didn't know what else to say, so I added the Act of Contrition and asked to be forgiven for all the times I fought with Carmen. Then I was done feeling guilty, but when I glanced at my family, they were still praying, so I pretended to keep praying too, though I was actually thinking about Mom's surgery, like how she would sleep on a cold, metal table surrounded by strangers wearing masks and gloves. I thought about the medical dramas on TV, how they always showed clamps on the patient's chest while doctors gave one-word orders like "scalpel" or "suction," and how something bad always happened. The doctors would snip an artery or inject the wrong drug, which made the patient have a heart attack. Then the doctors would call, "Code blue!" as they charged paddles to jolt the patient back. Sometimes the heart monitor would bleep again, but other times, it stayed flat till someone said, "Call it," and a frustrated doctor announced the time of death. I trembled as I pictured the scene, though I knew TV wasn't real life. Sometimes, though, the fake world of TV actually *did* happen, and that's why I got so stressed, and the only way to deal with stress was to ... well ... to think about the boys on my Wish List. I knew it was totally wrong to think about boys in church, but I couldn't help it. My mind just went there.

Enough of that, I told myself. Think of a *promesa*. I silently brainstormed, but I had absolutely no inspiration, so I felt even *more* stressed. I considered Mom and Dad's examples, but I couldn't concentrate enough to say extra prayers, and I couldn't grow long hair because my hair was already long, and I couldn't run a thousand miles—at least, not in one lifetime.

"What are you going to do?" Carmen asked.

I shrugged. "What about you?"

"I'm going to clean the bathrooms till Mom gets better."

I had to admit, Carmen had a great idea—practical but also a real sacrifice since cleaning toilets was so gross.

"Look it! Look it!" Jimmy said, showing me his fingers, black from squeezing the tips of burned-out matches.

"Mom," Carmen tattled, "Jimmy got ashes on his fingers. It's all Chia's fault."

I elbowed her. "No, it isn't."

Mom glanced at me and jerked her head, a signal that meant "get him out of here." I couldn't believe it. I got in trouble even when I was praying.

"Come on, Jimmy," I said, happy to get away. I led him to a doorway, where I found a basin with water. I lifted him. "Wash all that black stuff off your hands."

He splashed his hands, getting himself and me all wet.

"Hey," a lady hissed. "That's holy water."

I set Jimmy down. "I didn't realize," I said, but she just glared at me. She must have thought I was the most sarcastic teenager. After all, I was in a church. Of course it was holy water. How dumb could I be? Maybe I shouldn't go to church at all. I seemed to get in more trouble here than in the Land of Temptation outside.

I grabbed Jimmy's wet hand and took him through a hallway, hoping to find a way out before I'd have to say more Acts of Contrition, but instead, I discovered the most amazing room. It wasn't very big, but it was filled, ceiling to floor, with flowers, wedding veils, communion dresses, locks of hair, jewelry, car keys, cards, toys, empty prescription bottles, letters, rosaries, shoes, braces, crutches, postcards, newspaper clippings, dog tags, expired licenses, eyeglasses, helmets, and pictures. Lots of pictures. Not an inch of the room was bare.

Jimmy's mouth opened as if he wanted to swallow the whole scene. I'd never seen him look so astonished. His eyes widened as they glanced across the room. "Gimme?" he said, for the first time not knowing what to ask for.

I picked him up so we could look at some of the letters on the wall. Most were in Spanish, but I did find a few English ones. One read:

Dear Virgen de San Juan del Valle,
Thank you for your intercessions. When my husband fell off a ladder last summer, he suffered a serious head injury. The doctors said he would never talk again, or if he did, he wouldn't make sense. But thanks to you, he's talking now. And he makes sense. Escúchame, Madre. Your generous heart has made this possible. For this, and for all the kindnesses you have shown to my family and to all those throughout Earth and time, I thank you. Please accept my humble offerings. I have planted roses in your honor and will make rosaries from its petals for patients at the hospital where my husband stayed. In that way may I share your message of love and hope.

All the letters were about the sick, injured, or those at war. They gave thanks for people who survived or requested blessings for people who had died.

"They're testimonials," I heard Dad say. He took Jimmy from me, and immediately my brother put his head on Dad's shoulder, since this was when he usually took a nap. "This is *el cuarto de milagros*, the miracle room," Dad continued, "where people share stories and make offerings." He nodded toward Mom. She had removed one of her bikini tops from her purse and was placing it on a table. Then she took out a notepad and started to write a letter. Carmen was with her. She seemed reluctant, but after a few seconds, she decided to leave behind her trophy.

"Do you have your special item?" Dad asked.

I reached into my pocket, pulled out the envelope, and showed him the pebble, crystal, and coin. Then he reached into his pocket and pulled out two movie tickets for *Back to the Future*.

"From my first date with your mom," he explained. "I kept them all these years. Isn't that silly?"

"Not at all," I said, remembering the "romantic" mementos in my jewelry box.

We placed our special items beside one another, right next to a newspaper article from the *San Antonio Express-News* with a picture showing a giant mass of people by the Alamodome, almost all of them in pink shirts, and a caption that read "Over 30,000 Race for the Cure." I read the first paragraphs of the article and learned that they were participating in a fund-raiser for breast cancer research. Wow! I thought to myself, wondering what it was like to be with thirty thousand people, all walking in the same direction and wearing the same colored shirt. I couldn't help it. I mind-traveled. I put myself right in the middle of the crowd, imagining people lightly bumping into me as we walked, and everyone chanting the names of their loved ones with cancer. I imagined myself peeking over shoulders and looking for breaks in the crowd so I could make my way through, stopping at the water stations for a drink, and waving to the people on the sidelines. But mostly I imagined the energy, the positive energy, and the joy. If I actually *did* the race, then I wouldn't have to mind-travel about it. Maybe the race could be my *promesa*. Then again, it was only five kilometers. It didn't come close to being a thousand miles, and if it wasn't a thousand miles, would it be good enough to cure Mom?

45 BILLION BEES

The next Wednesday, Mom went in for surgery. When my parents were gone for an hour or two, they let me babysit my brother and sister, but since Dad would be at the hospital the whole day and Mom even longer, Grandma came over to be with us.

As soon as she arrived, Carmen said, "Did you hear about the honeybees?"

"No, sweetie. What happened to the honeybees?"

"They have a disease called colony collapse disorder. I read about it in that magazine you ordered for me."

Last Christmas, Grandma had given Carmen subscriptions to *Discover Magazine* and *National Geographic*; she gave me barrettes.

"That sounds awful," Grandma said.

"It *is*," Carmen agreed, "and it killed around forty-five billion bees last year."

I knew bees lived in hives the way people lived in cities, so when I heard that number, I pictured downtown San Antonio totally abandoned. I saw the city going dark because no one was around to fix the electricity. I saw the boats slapping against the edges of our famous River Walk. I saw parking lots like empty seas. Then I pictured other big cities, like New York, Chicago, and Houston, all of them completely silent with no people around.

"Imagine forty-five billion *people* dying," I said.

"That's ridiculous," Carmen told me.

"It could happen," I insisted.

"No, it couldn't." She snapped. "Not when there aren't forty-five billion people on the planet."

Grandma patted Carmen's head the way a trainer pets a dog that jumps through a hoop and fetches a stick. Why did I even try to join the conversation?

In order to distract us, Grandma kept us busy. First we baked cookies. Then we played Monopoly. Carmen won— but only because I had to keep Jimmy from grabbing the pieces. For lunch, Grandma took us to Alamo Cafe, one of our favorite restaurants, and after, to a shopping center that had a bookstore for Carmen, a toy store for Jimmy, and a T-shirt shop for me. I bought a shirt with a teddy bear wearing a feathered hat and reading from a scroll. According to the caption, his name was Shakesbear. I thought it was totally cute, but I couldn't get excited. I didn't even feel like sending a picture of it to Iliana. Grandma meant well, but her plans to distract me weren't working. In fact, I felt worse. I couldn't stop moping or thinking of some doctor putting Mom "under the knife." And why did we use that word, "under," when we talked about surgery? It made me think of "*under*ground," as in graveyards. I knew I shouldn't think the worst, but my mind kept going there.

Soon after we got home, GumWad called. "Hey," he said. "How's it going? Is your mom still in the hospital? Today's the day she's having that operation, right?"

"Yeah," I said. "But you don't have to sound all cheery about it."

"I'm not cheery. That's just how my voice is." He paused a moment. I could hear him smacking on the other end and wondered what color his gum was today. "How are you holding up?" he asked, using a totally fake low voice.

I couldn't help laughing.

"What's so funny?" GumWad wanted to know.

"Your voice," I explained. "When you make it deep, you sound like a frog with a serious sore throat."

He sighed. "I guess I can't win. I'm either too cheery or I sound like a sick frog."

"That's okay," I said. "I shouldn't have snapped at you. But all this waiting while my mom's in surgery is driving me nuts." I glanced at my new mood ring. The stone was black, which, according to the mood ring color chart, meant I was severely anxious.

"You have to think positive thoughts," GumWad said.

"That's tough for a girl who's wearing a T-shirt that says, 'I used to be a pessimist, but now I just think the worst.'"

He laughed. "I love your 'I used to' series."

"My what?"

"You have a lot of shirts that start with 'I used to.'"

"I do?"

"Yeah," he said. "Like 'I used to be doubtful, but now I'm not so sure' and 'I used to be infallible, but now I'm perfect.'"

"'I used to be a loner,'" I added, "'but now I hang out with myself.'"

"And 'I used to be apathetic, but now I just don't care.'" He laughed again, still managing to smack his gum.

When he settled down, he said, "I stopped by your house but no one was there."

"We went to Alamo Cafe. Why did you come by?"

"To drop something off. It's in your mailbox, okay?

There's no stamp on it or an address because I put it there myself. I mean, it's no big deal. Just a little something. But don't read it when people are around, okay?"

"Are you nervous?" I asked.

"No. Why?"

"Because you're saying 'okay' a lot. You always do that when you're nervous."

"Ha-ha." He laughed, smacking extra loud now. "Okay, gotta go." He hung up before I could say good-bye.

I went out the front door, reached into the mailbox, and pulled out an envelope. It had my name on it and a blue smudge, probably from GumWad's gum. I was about to open it, but I heard a loud crash, followed by Jimmy's screams, so I stuffed the envelope in my pocket and rushed back inside.

I found everyone in the kitchen.

"Jimmy was climbing the counter, trying to get at the cookies," Carmen explained. "He dropped the plate, and it broke. Now all the cookies are on the floor. They're all dirty and mixed up with the broken plate, so we can't eat them after all." She started to tear up. "And I really wanted one!"

This only made Jimmy scream. Grandma was holding him and saying, "Now, now," as she kept him from grabbing the cookies on the floor.

"This wouldn't have happened if Mom were here!" Carmen whined. She was really crying now, which upset Jimmy even more.

Grandma looked at me and said, "I'm getting too old for this."

Poor lady. I could tell Jimmy was wearing her out. He really wanted the cookies, but how could he eat them without swallowing a piece of glass?

First things first, I told myself. Remove the temptation. I grabbed a broom and started to sweep. Step two, find another temptation. "Hey, Jimmy, isn't it time for your favorite cartoon show?" I winked at Grandma. "Don't you want to see it? If not, let me know because I've got a lot of shows I want to watch."

"No!" Jimmy said. "*My* TV!"

"I don't know," I went on. "As soon as I finish cleaning up, I'm going to watch the afternoon news. Whoever gets there first gets to choose."

"Gimme TV," Jimmy said, pointing to the living room. "Gimme cartoon!"

"Are you finished crying?" Grandma asked.

He nodded, so Grandma took him out. A few minutes later, I heard cartoon music in the other room. Meanwhile, Carmen hadn't moved. She kept sniffling, while I swept the mess into a little pile. As I cleaned, I got more and more frustrated. The least she could do was help. But no. She just stood there, watching, not lifting a finger.

"Why don't you go read a book or memorize some vocabulary words if you're not going to help? They're just cookies, anyway. They probably tasted gross."

"I'm not Jimmy," she said. "You can't lie to me and act like today's a normal day, because it isn't."

With that, she kicked the pile of broken cookies and glass, respreading them across the floor. "Hey!" I shouted. I wanted to pinch her, but she ran to the backyard, slamming the door behind her. Fine, I thought. Let her melt outside. It had to be over ninety degrees today.

I was prepared to let her stay outside all afternoon, but the last thing I needed was for Dad to discover a badly sunburned child. He had enough on his mind with Mom's surgery. Since she'd probably ignore me, I asked Grandma to call her in, and we all sat in front of the TV. For the next hour, I put on a happy face as I watched cartoons with Jimmy, but every few minutes, I glanced at my watch. All this waiting was torture.

At last, the phone rang. Grandma rushed to answer it. She kept saying, "I see" and "okay" and "uh-huh." Finally, she hung up and said, "Your mom's out of surgery. She's doing okay."

The knot in my stomach relaxed a bit. I could finally

ignore my watch. And maybe, just maybe, the stone on my mood ring would change to a color that was happier than black.

An hour later, Dad picked me up. "Tomorrow, we'll all see Mom," he said to Carmen and Jimmy. "But she's really tired today, so I'm only taking Chia."

Carmen pouted. "I'm the one who should go. Chia needs to take care of Jimmy."

"Grandma can take care of him just fine," Dad said.

I knew he was right, but I also knew that Jimmy would cry as soon as Dad and I stepped out the door. So I asked Grandma to take him to the backyard. That way, we could sneak out while he was on the swings. When we heard Jimmy laughing outside, Dad and I quietly left the house.

Once we rolled out of the driveway and turned the corner, I spotted a group of kids from school, including Lou Hikaru. What a heartthrob! Iliana and I had been trying to engineer a close encounter with him, but no luck so far. Wait a minute. Why was Lou walking so close to Paula Wilson? Were they an item? Oh, no! They *were* an item. He'd just grabbed her hand. This was not good. Lou was a top pick on my Boyfriend Wish List. We hadn't moved beyond nodding hello and good-bye, but that didn't keep me from hoping. After all, he was the star of our baseball team. Then again, Paula was a pep squad captain, so they made total sense as a couple. I shook my head. I'd have to text Iliana to tell her that Lou was on the Currently Unavailable List.

Luckily, Forest Montoya was with the group, too. With him, I actually had a chance because last year, we paired up for a science project, and in front of the whole class, we demonstrated how potatoes conduct electricity. When the teacher gave us an A, Forest gave me a high five. I secretly cheered. Physical contact, at last! Okay, so it wasn't exactly *romantic* contact, but I still put it in the close encounter of the fourth kind category. And he did say hello when he spotted me at the skateboarding park last week.

"You like him?" Dad asked, nodding toward Forest.

I covered my face, all embarrassed. I couldn't believe Dad had caught me staring at a boy.

"No," I said. "Well…yes…maybe a little."

"So what's his name? What's he like?"

I squirmed. "I don't know."

"So you like a total stranger?" he teased.

"He's not a total stranger. I mean, we had a class together last year, so we kinda know each other, a little bit."

"Oh, yeah? Which class were you in? Did he get good grades?"

"Stop with the twenty questions," I pleaded. "I can't discuss boys with you."

"Why not?"

"Because you're my dad. It's...it's..." I glanced at my mood ring, the stone a yellowy orange, which meant my emotions were..."unsettling. It makes me feel unsettled."

Dad glanced at me. "Unsettled" wasn't one of my usual vocabulary words.

Dad finally drove out of the neighborhood and onto the major road. He didn't ask any more questions about boys. Instead, he turned up the volume for his favorite radio talk show, *All Things Considered*, and we listened to people from NASA discuss the space program. Dad usually shared his opinions about the stories, but today he was quiet. I couldn't tell if he was *really* listening. With Mom in the hospital, he was probably too preoccupied to pay attention.

We finally reached the Medical Center, a section of San Antonio crammed with hospitals, clinics, and the University of Texas Health Science Center, where people learned to be doctors, dentists, physical therapists, and researchers. Mom was at Methodist Hospital, but instead of going there, Dad parked at Baskin-Robbins.

"What are we doing *here*?" I asked.

"Getting ice cream, what else?"

Even on the worst days, I wasn't the type to turn down ice cream, especially when I had a chance to enjoy it without Carmen and Jimmy around. Come to think of it...I hardly *ever* had one-on-one time with Dad. I liked pretending that I was the only child sometimes, a totally spoiled only child who could order whatever she wanted.

"Can I get whatever I want?" I asked.

"Of course," Dad said.

I got two scoops, Rocky Road and Chocolate Chip, Cookie Dough, in a chocolate-dipped waffle cone. Dad ordered two scoops too, Chocolate and Vanilla, but he asked for his ice cream in a cup. I shook my head. Sometimes, adults have no imagination.

I was halfway through my dessert when Dad said, "I wanted some alone time with you before going to the hospital. We need to discuss a few things."

"Like what?"

He took a spoonful of ice cream and stared at it. "We need to discuss your mom," he said. "Today's surgery is a very important part of Mom's treatment, but the doctors need to make sure they get rid of all the cancer cells. They're worried the cancer might have metastasized."

"What does that mean?" I asked, glad Carmen wasn't around to supply the definition.

"It's a fancy word for 'spreading.'"

"You mean the cancer traveled outside the breast?"

"Maybe, but to make sure it doesn't grow into tumors, your mom is going to have radiation therapy."

"That's good, right?"

"Yes, but the treatment has a lot of side effects, so your mom's going to be under the weather for a while."

I moaned.

"What is it?" he asked.

"I hate the word 'under,'" I explained.

"Why?"

"Because it's so negative. I was thinking about it this morning—how we call anesthesia 'putting the patient under' and surgery 'going under the knife'—and now you're telling me Mom's going to be 'under the weather.' What does that mean, anyway? If the weather is something that happens in the sky, then aren't we *always* under it? If being 'under the weather' means we're sick, then being above the weather should mean we're feeling healthy, right? But think about it. No one ever says 'above the weather.' They might say they're on 'cloud nine,' but that's not the same thing. And why cloud nine, anyway? Why not say you're on cloud five or cloud sixteen? Who came up with the number nine? Did someone look at the sky one day and count?" I didn't mean to go on and on about weather and clouds, but when I feel nervous, I tend to ramble. Okay, I ramble a lot, but usually I don't ramble out loud.

Dad took my hand and squeezed it. I guess I had an "off" switch on my palm because I immediately hushed. Usually when Dad silenced me this way, he let go of my hand right away, but this time, he kept holding it. He bit his lower lip, and I knew that if he had a mood ring like mine, it would be black, too.

"I just don't know why your mom got sick," he said. "It's not fair."

"Lots of things aren't fair," I said, thinking about how Carmen was so smart without even trying, while I broke a sweat every time I opened a textbook.

Dad smiled and released my hand. "You're right, Chia. We can fill a whole book with things that aren't fair. Lots of people, for example, don't have a nice house like we do. They don't get new clothes every season. They don't go to places like Baskin-Robbins for ice cream. Lots of them are alone in this world." He paused a moment because his voice was starting to tremble.

"It's okay, Dad."

"Nobody asks to be sick," he went on. "It just happens and all we can do is deal with it."

I nodded, wishing I had the perfect words to comfort him. But all I could say was "it's okay" again.

I looked into my ice-cream cone. The last bites had melted, making the cone all soggy. Why did all the good stuff melt?

Soon, we left the ice-cream shop and headed to the hospital. The lobby had an information desk and signs to the cafeteria, the gift shop, and a chapel, but Dad walked straight to the elevators and pushed the "up" arrow. First, the elevator beeped, and when we got to Mom's floor, beeps from call buttons echoed through the hall. The doctors' and nurses' pagers beeped too, and so did heart and blood pressure monitors and the intercom before every announcement. All that beeping reminded me of items being scanned at the grocery store. Who knew hospitals were so loud? And how could anyone rest with all that noise?

"She's in here," Dad said, leading me to a door.

When I thought about Mom in the hospital, I pictured a dozen machines attached to her body and a tube stuck down her throat and a bloody bandage wrapped around her head. Of course, this was ridiculous. Mom's head was fine. I must have watched too many hospital scenes on TV. Luckily, she looked okay. She was asleep, her hair spread upon the pillow. Her lips were pale but only because she wasn't wearing lipstick. She had an IV and a splint on her finger with a red light to monitor her blood pressure. With the sheets tucked in at her armpits, I couldn't see her chest, but I could tell it was bandaged.

Dad took the chair beside her bed, reclined it, and stared at the newscast on TV. The sound was muted, so we had to read the headlines: "Burglar Caught on Tape," "Car Accident on Loop 1604," and "Local Unemployment on the Rise." How depressing, I thought. No wonder I hated to watch the news. I walked to the window ledge to examine a vase of roses. I smelled them and touched their velvety petals. The card said, *"Abrazos y besos"*—hugs and kisses—followed by all our names. I recognized the handwriting—Dad's. He'd also brought a present from Mother's Day, a photo of Carmen, Jimmy, and me in a frame that said, "World's Best Mom."

I turned to him. "You're really sweet, Dad. These are the perfect things to cheer Mom up."

He nodded. "Maybe we can buy her a big balloon tomorrow. Jimmy would love to pick it out, don't you think?"

"He'll want to keep it for himself," I said, and Dad had to agree.

Then he pointed to an empty chair. "Why don't you sit down?" he suggested.

I nodded an okay, and when I sat down, I thought about my *promesa* again. Would a 5K be enough? Maybe I could promise to do it two times in a row?

Dad had closed his eyes for a nap, so the room was quiet. How could he relax when I was feeling—I checked my ring—still unsettled? Then I remembered the blue-smudged envelope that GumWad had left in our mailbox. I pulled it from my pocket and opened it. Inside was a card with a kitten clasping a branch, its legs hanging free. The front cover said, "Whatever you fear, you can overcome," and inside, it said, "because you are not alone." The inside picture showed the same cat, but this time a pair of hands reached to catch it. There was a personal note, too. "Just wanted you to know," GumWad wrote, "if you need help with anything, you can count on me. Your friend, Roberto."

Leave it to GumWad to mess up. *I* wasn't the one who needed a "get well" card. He meant this for my mom. She's the one who called him "Roberto," anyway. I shook my head as I stood the card beside the roses.

That's when I heard someone whisper my name.

I turned. Mom's eyes had opened. Her fingers weakly waved me over.

"Hi, Mom," I said, taking her hand and kissing her forehead. Some hair had fallen near her eyes, so I brushed it aside. "How're you feeling?"

"Woozy."

"Want some water?"

She nodded. I filled a glass, lifted it to her lips. When she finished drinking, she turned her head aside, and then she clenched her lips and blinked as if fighting back tears. That's when I saw the ninth bikini top. She must have worn it to the hospital.

"Chia," Dad said, his voice startling me because I thought he was asleep. He nodded toward the dresser. "Can you put that away?"

I picked up the bikini top. "I'll take good care of it," I told Mom. "I'll hold it for you, okay? Just for a little while."

She smiled. "You can have it, *mija*. You can have all of my bikini tops. Take them from my room when you get home, okay?"

"Okay...but...they don't fit."

She laughed a little. "They will, Chia. Someday soon, they will."

50 PAIRS OF SHOES

The next day, Dad promised to pick us up around dinnertime so we could see Mom. In the meantime, Grandma was spending another day with us. She took Jimmy outside before it got too hot, while Carmen and I sat at the kitchen table, me with the Sunday tabloid and Carmen with the laptop. I loved glancing at pics of movie stars with and without their makeup, especially when they were doing normal things like buying groceries or pumping gas.

"Did you know," Carmen began, "that there are different kinds of surgeries for breast cancer?"

I shrugged. I was not in the mood for one of Carmen's lectures.

"A mastectomy and a lumpectomy," she explained. "Do you know the difference?"

I lifted the tabloid to block my view of her.

"I figured you didn't," Carmen said. "And you probably don't know what 'sentinel lymph nodes' or 'immuno-therapy' are or what the word 'metastasize' means."

"It means 'spreading,'" I said, remembering the conversation with Dad yesterday.

"And the others?"

I put down the paper. "I don't care, Carmen. You're not my teacher. You're my little sister, which means you're supposed to do what I say. And I say quit being a pest right now."

"You're not my boss," she snapped back.

"Am too."

"Are not."

We locked eyes for a stare-down. I was not going to blink first. Who cared about the strand of hair tickling my temple or the ceiling fan drying out my eyes? Carmen might be smarter than me, but she wasn't tougher.

After a few intense moments, my phone pinged. Carmen blinked.

"Gotcha!" I cheered.

She just shook her head and went back to her computer screen.

I glanced at my text message. It was from Shawntae to all the Robins. "I'm totally bored," she wrote. "Anyone free? If so, come over. Save me, plz!"

I peeked into the backyard to ask my grandmother if I could visit my friend for a while. "I'll put Jimmy down for a nap first," I said, so she wouldn't have to worry about him crying.

"Sounds like a deal," she answered.

So I texted back to Shawntae. "CU in an hour." Then, I went back to the tabloid. I was just starting to read about the strange names stars gave their kids when Carmen interrupted.

"Did you know that the mastectomy rate in the United States is fifty-six percent?"

"I'm not a doctor," I replied. "Why would I know something like that?"

She ignored me. "The rate in Central and Eastern Europe is seventy-seven percent," she went on. "And in Australia and New Zealand, it's thirty-four percent."

I had to admit, I was a little interested. After all, this related to Mom. But what did it matter? All those percentages were meaningless to me. What did Carmen expect me to do with those numbers? When I thought about breast cancer, I didn't see an equation. I saw a picture—Mom in a light blue gown, her hair spread upon the pillow, and a quiet tear when she realized that she wouldn't wear bikinis anymore.

I folded up the paper and scooted back my chair.

"Where are you going?" Carmen asked.

"I'm going to get Jimmy. It's almost time for his nap."

"But don't you want to learn more about breast cancer?"

"When you can tell me why *our* mom got sick," I said, "I'll listen." With that, I headed out the door.

An hour later, I was at Shawntae's. She lives on the next street over. Her bedroom is an explosion of color—bright yellow walls, a rainbow-striped bedspread, and a tall bookshelf for her pumps. She has *so* many pumps. She organizes them by color. Lots of people wear black, red, or gray pumps, but Shawntae has orange, green, and pink, too. She has pumps with animal prints and some with bows or buttons. She must have more than fifty pairs! I imagined she slept with them because the only time I saw her bare feet was at the pool.

When I stepped in, she said, "Thank goodness you're here. I'm *dying* of boredom. Feel this."

She held out her wrist, so I touched it.

"I don't feel anything," I said.

"You see? No pulse! Like I said, I'm *dying*."

"Sorry to burst your bubble, but I heard heaven's boring, too. You don't get to chase boys, and heels are useless when you're walking on clouds. Plus, the only instruments they have up there are flutes and harps."

"That does sound worse than being cooped up in my room all day," Shawntae admitted. "At least I have a computer."

I put my hands on my hips and cleared my throat.

"And cool friends like you," she added.

"Thank you," I said. "It's nice to be remembered. So who else is coming over?"

"Iliana and Roberto are busy," Shawntae said, "and Patty..." Her phone rang. "Patty's calling right now."

She turned to answer it, so I decided to mess around with my own phone while she talked. I went to a screen saver site. I found one called "ribbons," bands of color running across the screen like shooting stars or glow-in-the-dark eels. Another screen saver had glowing light like the aurora borealis, and another had fireworks. I finally settled on a screen saver with bubbles. They changed colors—pink, blue, and yellow. They floated and bounced against one another. I picked one and followed its trail across the screen.

"I don't believe this!" Shawntae said, looking over my shoulder. "I *dreamed* about this."

"You dreamed about the screen saver?"

"No. Yes. Kind of." She took a minute to compose her

thoughts or, rather, to make up one of her silly after-the-fact predictions. "In my dream, you were in a giant bouncy ball. It was see-through, like a bubble. You were screaming because you wanted to get out, but you couldn't. There wasn't a door, only air holes. And you were bouncing down the street. Sometimes you hit the side of a building and sometimes you bounced right on top of a car. When I woke up, I thought you were going to join the basketball team, but now I see that my dream was actually predicting that you would stare at the screen saver."

I didn't feel like arguing, so I said, "Hmm...very interesting." Then I went back to looking at the bubbles.

"Wake up!" Shawntae said, snapping her fingers in my ear. "Why are you acting like a zombie?"

I sighed. "I can't help it."

"Because of your mom?"

I nodded. "She's still in the hospital. She was so weak yesterday. She could barely open her eyes. It was like her eyelids were bricks or dumbbells or boulders. That's how heavy they were."

Shawntae put her hand on my shoulder. "I know it's tough, but you can't mope around all day. She'd feel awful if she knew you were moping around."

"And the other thing that's stressing me out," I went on, "is my *promesa*."

"What's that?" Shawntae asked.

"It means 'promise.' I'm supposed to do something or make a sacrifice in honor of my mother. That way, all the angels will know she needs help. It's like giving thanks. My sister's cleaning the bathrooms, and I decided to walk a 5K, which is a bit lame, but what else can I do?"

"Maybe you can plant a garden," Shawntae suggested.

"Maybe. But if the plants die, I'll think it's a sign."

"Then write a poem every day."

"I would if I could, but I'm not smart enough to write poems."

Shawntae thought for a minute. "That's it!" she blurted.

"You have a good *promesa* for me?"

"No, but I totally understand my dream now. It wasn't about you staring at a screen saver. It was about you feeling trapped and hopeless. It's like you're bumping into things, with no control over where you're going."

"Gee, thanks," I groaned. "I feel a whole lot better now."

"Don't blame me," Shawntae said. "It's not my fault you're stuck in a bouncy ball. I gave you some good suggestions."

"Suggestions for what?" Patty asked as she stepped into the room. She slurped through the straw of a giant Slush from Sonic, took a big swallow, and said, "Major brain freeze." Then she kicked off her flip-flops and plopped on the bed. "Well?" she said, all impatient.

"Erica has to walk five whole kilometers for her mom," Shawntae explained. "It's so the angels will hear her."

"It's called a *promesa*, which means 'promise.'" I glanced at my feet, imagining them in tennis shoes. "I wish I were more inspired."

"I told her to think of another promise," Shawntae said.

"It has to be some kind of sacrifice," I explained.

"A *painful* sacrifice, huh?" Patty said, thinking about it. I nodded, even though I hadn't mentioned pain. "Why don't you promise to walk over broken glass or hot coals? I saw some guys do that on TV once. They didn't even get hurt. You just have to put *mind over matter*."

I shook my head, remembering how walking barefoot on the hot cement made my feet blister.

"How about fasting?" Patty said. "Or you could ask your dad to drop you off in the middle of the desert and then you can find your way back. That's what the Indians did, and they always returned with the answers to the universe."

"I don't want the answers to the universe," I said. "I want my mom to get better."

"She had the operation yesterday," Shawntae explained. "And Erica's all stressed."

Patty slurped from the giant cup again, and then said, "So have you seen your mom's chest? Did it creep you out?"

"Don't ask that!" Shawntae scolded.

Patty just shrugged. "Feeling creeped out is a normal reaction to something like this, right, Erica?"

I nodded. "Just thinking about it creeps me out."

"So have you seen it yet?" she asked again.

"No. I visited my mom, but she was all covered up."

"It's not like she's going to ask her mom to take off her shirt," Shawntae said. "Things like that are private."

I shivered as I imagined women without breasts. I didn't want to think about it, but I also had this weird desire to know what it looked like.

Patty took another long slurp. Then she turned to me. "Your mom has joined a warrior tribe of women," she announced.

"Because she's fighting breast cancer?"

"Yes. I mean, that, too. But I also mean a *real* warrior tribe of women. Have you heard of the Amazons?"

"You mean the rain forest?"

"No, I mean Amazon women. Back in ancient times, they decided to live without men."

"No guys?" I felt scandalized. How could you have a Boyfriend Wish List when there weren't any guys around?

"Sounds like a good idea to me," Shawntae said. "I like guys, but sometimes they're overrated. This world would be a better place with more women as mayors and presidents."

"That's what the Amazons thought," Patty said. "But the men kept trying to take over. So they had to learn to defend themselves, and their favorite weapon was the bow and arrow."

"That's cool," I said, imagining arrows arcing across the sky.

"But there was a problem," Patty added. "The Amazons had big breasts that got in the way."

Shawntae stood up, pretended to pull back on a bow. "I guess it'd be hard if you had giant boobs."

"You want to know how they solved the problem?" Patty asked.

Shawntae and I nodded.

"They cut off the breast. Can you imagine a whole group of women walking around like that? But it worked. They were the best archers around."

"They weren't sick?" I asked.

"No, they weren't sick at all. They volunteered to do this, and it made them stronger."

I imagined a tribe of women warriors in the forest. They had long hair, muscular arms and legs, and white tunics, one side flat. But they were wrestling, swimming, and running through obstacle courses. And Mom was with them, doing all of those things—not sick but strong.

180 TILES

A few days later, Mom returned from the hospital.

"Be careful," Dad said as he helped her sit at the kitchen table. "You're still recovering."

As soon as she sat down, Carmen and I gave her hugs and took the seats beside her. Dad poured her a cup of coffee and then went to the sink to rinse dishes, while Jimmy rolled a ball across the floor.

"How are you feeling?" I asked Mom.

"I'm tired, but I'm glad to be home."

She wore a shirt that buttoned down the front. I couldn't help glancing at her chest and noticing that the right side was flat now, just like an Amazon. Mom must have caught me looking because she said, "I'm going to get a special bra. A prosthetic."

"What's that?" I asked.

Carmen turned into Little Miss Factoid again. "It's a replacement part, like a fake leg or a fake arm."

"That's right," Mom said. "I'm going to have a fake boob." She was silent a moment, and then she laughed. She winced as if the laughter hurt a bit, but the chuckles kept coming. Soon, Carmen and I were laughing, too. Even Jimmy joined in.

"Okay," Dad said, his voice stern. "Quit laughing at your mother."

"Oh, lighten up," Mom told him. "They're not laughing at me. We're just having some fun. You have to admit that a bra with a fake boob is funny."

"No, it's not." Dad turned from the sink to face us. "There's nothing funny about cancer, about having to get…"—he glanced at Carmen—"replacement parts."

Mom frowned. "I'm the one who's sick," she said, "so *I* get to decide what is and isn't funny about *my* body. Isn't that right, girls?"

Carmen and I didn't want to take sides, so we kept our mouths shut.

"I'm just saying…" Dad began.

Mom held out her hand to hush him. He stared at it for a second before turning back to the sink. When I looked across the table at Carmen, I caught her biting her lower

lip. I almost bit my lip, too. That's how tense the room was. I wanted to lighten the mood, change the subject, talk about something fun and easy, like boys or Jimmy's cartoons. I wanted to suggest we eat ice cream, fly a kite, or go to the movies. But when you're sitting beneath the gloom of cancer, everything that's *not* cancer seems silly. You wonder why boys or ice cream or kites ever mattered in the first place.

Dad finished the dishes and left the room. A few minutes later, I heard him vacuuming the den.

"Can you refill this?" Mom asked me, tapping her coffee cup.

I brought the pot over, poured the coffee. Mom lifted it, a bit awkwardly. She spilled some on her shirt. "I don't believe this," she said, all frustrated.

"Why are you using your left hand?" Carmen asked—a good question because Mom was right-handed.

Before she could answer, Jimmy walked to her and climbed onto her lap. He hugged her tight, making Mom grimace.

"Careful, Jimmy," I said. "Mom's sore, remember?"

She hugged him back but with her left arm only, and since Jimmy wiggled a lot, he slid off. He tried climbing onto her lap again, but she waved him off.

"Up, up," he told her.

"I can't, *mijo*. At least, not right now."

"Up!" he cried.

Mom looked at Carmen and me. "My right side's weak," she explained. "When they took my breast, they took some muscle tissue too, so I won't be using my right side for a while."

Mom looked like an Amazon, but she didn't feel like one. Not yet. I still hoped, though, that soon she'd feel stronger.

Jimmy reached for her again. She leaned over and kissed him. "I can't carry you, but you can sit right next to me."

"Gimme Mommy," Jimmy said as he started to bawl.

Now it looked like Mom wanted to bawl, too. "Chia," she said, her voice a little choked, "will you take him? I'm going to the bedroom to rest."

As she walked out, Jimmy kicked her chair. "Mommy's mad!"

I picked him up. "No, she isn't," I said. "She really wants to carry you, but she can't right now. She's sick, remember?" His whole chest shook with sobs. "She'll get better," I went on, "and then she'll hug you and carry you and never let you go. I promise."

At that, Carmen said, "I'm going to clean the bath-

room," and she hurried off. Carmen never volunteered to clean, so I thought an alien had taken over her body. Then I remembered her *promesa*. She was going to clean bathrooms till Mom got better. My sister could be a real brat sometimes, but once in a while, she did something nice.

I decided to follow her example and work on my *promesa*, too. I told Dad I was going to start training, and since he was so busy cleaning, I offered to take Jimmy. He loved being pushed in his stroller, even though he was getting too big for it.

"Come on, Jimmy," I said, and he happily joined me.

We walked down the block, and by the time I reached the next street, sweat was dripping into my eyes and stinging them. My hands were swollen, too. I could tell by how tight my mood ring felt. And my T-shirt, this one with beetles and ants over a caption that said "You're bugging me," was getting damp. Was I crazy? No one exercised when it was near one hundred degrees. Then again, the *promesa* was supposed to be a challenge, so I walked on, refusing to turn back until I reached the major street at the end of our neighborhood.

When I got home, I took a shower in the sparkling clean bathroom. Carmen probably spent a whole hour polishing the counters and floors. I couldn't blame her. Even

though I felt tired, I went to the laundry room, sorted the darks and lights, put in a load, and dusted furniture while I waited for the wash cycle to end. In a strange way, cleaning made me feel like I was accomplishing something. Carmen and Dad probably felt the same way because they were doing extra chores, too.

Later that night, I heard Carmen turning pages in a book. The lights were out, and since she didn't have her book lamp on, I knew she wasn't reading.

"What are you doing?" I asked.

"Counting the pages."

"What for?"

"I like counting things," she said. "Did you know," she went on, "that there are one hundred eighty tiles around our bathtub?"

"I can't believe you stood there and counted tiles."

"At first, I multiplied the number of tiles in a row by the number of tiles in a column. Then, I double-checked my calculation by counting each and every tile. And then, I triple-checked. If you don't believe me, you can count them yourself. You'll see. There are one hundred eighty tiles."

"That's amazing," I said, my sarcasm as thick as the cheese on the pizza we ate for dinner. "I always wondered

how many tiles there were. How can I ever thank you for enlightening me?"

She didn't reply, but a few seconds later, I heard the rustling pages again. How annoying!

"Will you stop that?" I said.

"I'll stop when I get to the end of the book."

"Why on earth are you counting pages when they're already numbered?"

"I told you," she said. "I like counting."

"But it's ridiculous. No one who's sane counts pages in a book."

"Then I guess I'm not sane," she said, getting out of bed and heading to the door. "Don't worry. I won't be bothering you anymore. I'm going to the living room to count in peace."

She stepped out, and I almost said "good riddance" because without the sound of rustling pages and mumbled numbers, I could finally fall asleep. At least, that was the theory. For some reason, though, I couldn't relax. Sure, Carmen got on my nerves with all her counting, but at least she had cleaned the bathroom. I spent a while resisting the urge to call her back, but eventually, my guilty conscience got to me.

I found her in the living room. The porch light's yellow

glow came through the window. Carmen was asleep with the book open on her chest. I shook her.

"Hey, Carmen," I whispered. "Come back to the room."

She opened her eyes partway, reaching for the book and mumbling, "Not finished yet."

"You can finish tomorrow," I said. "If you start early enough, you can count all the pages before you fall asleep."

She nodded, and without saying another word, she followed me to our room.

1 BELLY FLOP

Because of Mom's weak arm, I had to put away the heavy pots and pans, carry the baskets of laundry, and vacuum. She didn't ask me to do these things, but when I caught her wincing at the chores or giving up, I decided to do them myself, but secretly. That way, she wouldn't feel like an invalid. And when things were settled at home, I'd go walking. After a while, I could walk around the whole neighborhood without feeling tired, even though I still had to deal with sweat and swollen hands. I kept thinking a 5K wasn't enough, but since I had no other ideas, it would have to do.

I kept in touch with my friends, though I wasn't seeing them very much. They invited me to all their outings, but I felt too guilty to go when I had so much to do at home. So

when Iliana called to invite me to the pool, I said, "I wish I could go, but I hate to leave my mom. She's still not one hundred percent."

"Go where?" I heard. I turned around and spotted Mom at my bedroom door, eavesdropping on my conversation. She held out her hand. "Give me the phone." When I handed it to her, she said, "Who's this?" and then, "Oh, hi, sweetie." She quietly listened for a while. "Of course, I'm fine. Getting stronger every day. You know Erica. She tends to worry over nothing." She listened some more. "Of course she can go. She can't spend the whole summer moping around here. It's not healthy. She'll be ready in thirty minutes. I promise." She hung up, handed me the phone, and said, "Time to put on your bathing suit."

I should have felt excited about seeing my friends, but I felt angry instead. "Why did you tell Iliana that I'm all stressed out and worried? That I'm moping?"

"Because you are."

I glanced at my mood ring, wondering if Mom knew how to interpret the colors. "No, I'm not," I lied. "But even if I *was* stressed out, it's none of Iliana's business."

"She's your friend, so it *is* her business."

"But that's the problem," I complained. "She's going to tell *everybody* and they're going to feel sorry for me, and instead of having fun, they're going to give me useless

advice, like the kind you find on a cheesy card, because even if they *really* try to understand me, they don't. Then I'm going to get mad. But if they think everything's fine, I *won't* get mad because instead of talking about me, we'll talk about other things."

"So tell her I was exaggerating," Mom suggested. "That way, you can have some fun." She pointed to my dresser. "Now get ready."

"But I'll have to—" I stopped myself.

"You'll have to what?" Mom asked.

I hesitated, not sure I wanted to finish my sentence. "I'll have to wear a bathing suit."

Mom crossed her arms. "Is that the *real* reason you don't want to go?"

I shrugged.

"So how many times have you turned down a trip to the pool?"

I shrugged again, not wanting to admit that my friends had invited me three times already. "I don't want to hurt your feelings," I said instead. "If you see me in a bathing suit, you'll think about having cancer."

She sighed. "*Mija*, I think about it anyway. I feel worse knowing you're avoiding fun because of me. Now get ready. That's an order."

She left me alone in my room, shutting the door behind

her, so I hunted in my drawer for a bathing suit, finding one of Mom's bikini tops instead. I decided to put it on. It sagged because I wasn't developed enough. I made fists and put them inside the cups, so I could see what I'd look like as a *real* woman and picture my body as beautiful as Mom's...as Mom's *used* to be. I took my hands out of the bikini top. I made a fist again, placed the other hand over it, trying to form the shape and size of Mom's breast and then imagining that part of her body being cut away. How could she stand it? Didn't it hurt? Didn't she hate looking at herself in the mirror now that she wasn't whole? If she did, she never mentioned it. But that was Mom, strong and brave. She didn't feel sorry for herself. Or maybe she did. Maybe she kept her true feelings inside, wearing a brave face for the rest of us, because that's how mature people acted. They *handled* things.

So in the spirit of handling things, I went to the pool. It was at the neighborhood park, on the opposite side of the skateboard area. The pool was fenced in, and you had to sign a guest list before going in. Behind the entrance was a covered patio with picnic tables. Mostly parents sat there, reading magazines or visiting as their children played in the water. The pool itself was a giant rectangle, three to ten feet deep, with black swim lanes painted on the floor. Life-

guards sat upon high perches beneath colorful umbrellas, and high school girls tanned on the chaise lounges.

"Over here, Erica!" I heard the Robins call. I spotted them, waving to me from the five-foot section of the pool. I went over and jumped in. The water felt cold. I shivered, but it felt so refreshing, a perfect cure for the heat.

"Iliana says you're all depressed," Patty told me. "That you aren't sleeping because you're worried about your mom."

"You do have bags under your eyes," GumWad said, his mouth full of red gum today. When I touched the area beneath my eyes, he said, "I didn't mean that in a bad way. Baggy eyes are pretty."

"She does not have baggy eyes," Shawntae said. "You're imagining things. But"—she turned to me—"you do look skinny. Have you been eating? I heard depressed people lose their appetites."

"It's true," Iliana said. "They don't feel like doing anything like going to the pool. I just hate the thought of you feeling too sad to come to the pool. You have to get out and *do* something."

I thought about how busy I'd been—helping with the chores and walking around the neighborhood to train for my *promesa*, things you can't do while sleeping—so if I looked a bit skinnier, it was because I'd been working, not because I'd been skipping meals. I probably had bags under

my eyes because Jimmy woke up at six o'clock every morning. Mom slept right through his cries for attention, and even though Dad was awake, he was too busy getting ready for work. So I had to help Jimmy instead. And although Carmen cleaned the bathroom, that's *all* she did. My friends didn't have younger brothers or lazy sisters. How could they possibly understand?

They circled, waiting for me to share a true-confessions moment. When I didn't say anything, Iliana put her hand on my shoulder to encourage me to talk. This is exactly what I tried to tell my mom. I had the nosiest friends on the planet.

"I am not depressed!" I yelled, and I went under the water, making my body heavy so I could sink. My friends' voices were muted, and their legs wavered in the flickering sunlight. What a wonderful way to disappear. If only I could sink into a quiet place whenever people got on my nerves. After a moment, GumWad came underwater too and did all kinds of hand signals. Who knew what he was trying to say? The way his hair floated like a wild mane and his cheeks puffed out as he held his breath made me want to laugh, so I had to go up for air.

"What were you trying to say down there?" I asked GumWad when he surfaced a few seconds later.

He said, "I was trying to let you know that I'm going to Disney World next week."

"You go to Disney World every summer," I told him.

"No, I don't." He glanced at the other Robins, but they could only agree with me.

"*Every* summer," Iliana repeated. Then she turned to me. I knew she was about to question me again, but before she could, a bunch of boys from our Boyfriend Wish List walked in.

"It doesn't get better than this," Shawntae said, nodding toward the guys as they got ready for the water.

Iliana turned to us. "Quick. Do a face check. Do I look okay?" After we gave her a thumbs-up, she gasped. "They're taking off their shoes and their shirts!"

"Big surprise," Patty said, unimpressed. "We're at the pool, remember?"

"Yeah, that's why *my* shirt's off, too," GumWad said, sticking out his chest. He probably meant to look muscular, but he looked like a puffed-up rooster instead.

I turned away. After all, GumWad was like a cousin. I'd been meeting him at this pool for as long as I could remember. He has a dime-size birthmark behind his left shoulder and a scar on his belly from the time he ran into a barbed-wire fence at his uncle's ranch. So, of course, the other guys

were more interesting. I wondered if they had scars or birth-marks. I scanned their bodies, but instead of scars or birthmarks, I saw nice tans and athletic arms and legs. I hadn't worn my mood ring because I didn't want to lose it in the pool, but if I *had* been wearing it, it'd be all sorts of colors because I had emotions that weren't even described on the mood ring chart.

"Snapshot," Iliana said, pretending to take a picture of the boys.

"Tattoo that image on my heart," I added.

"I *dreamed* about this," Shawntae said. "I dreamed we'd see cute guys at the pool. That's why I wanted to come today."

Our eyes followed the boys wherever they went. And, of course, they went to the diving board. Cool guys didn't bother with the pool. They weren't going to bob around like the rest of us. They were fearless. They were going to climb up the high board and jump.

Chad went first. When he got to the top, he stood at the edge, his toes curling over. Then he lifted his hands over his head and dived, doing a beautiful somersault before hitting the water. Derek Smith went next. He did *two* somersaults. Alejandro did a twist in the air, and Forest, a graceful swan dive. Each time they jumped, they got back

in line to wait their turn again. And we just watched, speechless.

"Hey, girls," GumWad said, tapping our shoulders to get our attention, "check this out." He plunged and did an underwater flip, and when he came back up, his red gum was floating in the pool. How gross! GumWad coughed and snorted. "Water up my nose," he explained.

"Don't be disgusting," Patty scolded, pointing to the red blob.

GumWad obeyed. He picked up the gum and headed to the ladder so he could throw it away.

Meanwhile, we turned to the diving board. It was Chad's turn again. This time he hugged his knees and curled himself into a human bomb. The other guys copied him, bragging that they could make bigger splashes.

"I just love how they shake the water from their hair as they climb out of the pool." Iliana sighed.

"Yeah," Patty said, "like wet dogs shaking out their fur."

While we watched the guys, I decided to multitask by holding the edge of the pool and kicking my legs. That way, they could get ready for my *promesa*. Little by little, my legs felt heavier, which meant they were getting stronger, too. Soon I was on autopilot, hardly noticing that I was exercising while watching the diving board and visiting with my

friends. Ten minutes must have passed when Patty said, "Is that Roberto in line?"

It *was*! We had forgotten all about him after he left the pool to throw out his gum. Patty did the Robins' *cheerily cheer-up cheer-up* whistle to get his attention, and when he glanced our way, we waved. He waved back and pointed to the high dive.

"I thought he was scared of heights," Shawntae said.

"Maybe he's conquering his fears," I suggested.

Sure enough, when GumWad reached the ladder, he paused a long time before grabbing hold. The person behind him had to nudge him. Finally, he climbed a couple of steps, stopped, climbed a few more, glanced down, and climbed a few more. At one point, he put his arms around the ladder and hugged it. Some nearby kids started to laugh. "Check out that scaredy-cat," they said. Even though I knew it was true, I didn't like other people making fun of my friend.

"Hey, GumWad!" I called out. "You can do it!"

He nodded, then made his way to the top. When he got there, he stood at the back of the board for a while, shaking out his hands. Someone said, "Quit holding up the line!" And that's when GumWad jogged forward, the board bouncing beneath him. He didn't pause at all. He simply ran off, and while he was falling, his arms and legs went in

crazy directions. He looked like a rag doll, and he was screaming like someone on a roller coaster. Then he hit the water, one giant belly flop, with a splash more forceful than the stream that comes out of a fire hydrant. Everybody laughed, including me, because it was the most awkward dive I had ever seen. Poor guy. He must have felt embarrassed as he swam to the edge, where he gripped the side of the pool and coughed like someone who had swallowed the wrong way. Luckily, a lifeguard helped him out of the pool and sat beside him, patting GumWad's back till he caught his breath again.

When he returned to us, he said, "Did you see my dive?"

"Sure," Patty said, "you were as graceful as a...as a..." She snapped her fingers in front of my face.

"As a duck in ballet slippers," I said.

We all laughed.

"I wasn't trying to be graceful," GumWad explained, a bit defensively. "I was *trying* to be funny."

"If that's the case, then you scored a perfect ten," Shawntae said.

We laughed again, but then Iliana got serious. "You scared me. I thought you almost drowned when I saw you with that lifeguard."

"You were supposed to close your mouth before hitting

the water," Patty told him. "But you were too busy scream-ing." She couldn't contain her chuckles.

"It was all part of the act," GumWad insisted. "I *wanted* the lifeguard to help me. Not the guy lifeguard, but the one who's a pretty girl."

We glanced around. Sure enough, a pretty girl studied the pool from her perch.

"You're always staring at the guys," he went on, "but I *can't* because I'm a guy, too. I can't be talking about them. Sure, Chad has nice hair and Derek looks like he lifts weights, but I can't *say* that."

"You just did," I pointed out.

GumWad pretended not to hear. "So I search for the pretty girls instead, and there's a whole lot of them." He looked at me directly. "They're all around me."

"Then why are you hanging out with us?" Shawntae asked, her voice all offended.

GumWad thought about it, then said, "That's what *I'm* wondering." I could tell he was mad. He probably tried his best to do a fancy dive, and here we were, making fun of him. "See you later," he said. He climbed out of the pool and found a chaise lounge right between two high school girls. They were a lot more developed than us, and I had to admit, they looked great in their bikinis. One of them yawned as she adjusted her sunglasses. The other grabbed a

water bottle, took a sip, and poured a bit onto her head. They didn't have a care in the world as they sat under the sun—the *cancerous* sun. Didn't they know that ultraviolet rays could cause cancer? I looked at their chests. I couldn't help it, couldn't help comparing them to Mom, couldn't help wondering if someday they'd have to get mastectomies.

"Are you looking at those girls' boobs?" Patty asked me.

"No."

"Yes, you are. You are *totally* checking out their boobs." She laughed at me.

I decided to challenge her. "So what if I am?"

My harsh tone surprised her. She backed off, got quiet.

I glanced at Shawntae and Iliana. They wouldn't look at me. They probably guessed that I was thinking about my mom. So I took a deep breath, made my body a rock, and sank. I'd stay under as long as possible, as long as it took for my friends to find another topic to discuss. Anything was better than facing my problems when they were around.

O TEARDROPS

A few days later, Mom left Carmen and Jimmy with Grandma, so "You and I can go pick out my new boob," she told me, laughing because it sounded like a funny way to spend an afternoon. Up till now, she'd been wearing what she called her "boob pillow." It *did* look like a pillow, a round pad with the kind of stuffing that you find in teddy bears. But now that her wound had healed, she needed to get a silicone breast form that matched the size and weight of her remaining breast. "If I don't," Mom explained, "I'll start having back problems because I'm not balanced." I nodded, remembering how I ached when I wore my backpack over one shoulder, instead of two.

We went to a medical supply store that specializes in pros-

thetics. There were models of artificial hands and legs, some very lifelike. There were also different kinds of shoes, some attached to braces and others with very tall soles, like the platform shoes rock stars wore. When the assistant caught me staring, she said they were for people with one leg that was shorter than the other. I thought about those who were born this way and those born with a short arm or an extra toe and those born blind or deaf. Then I thought about people born with problems on the insides of their bodies—like lungs that couldn't breathe normally or hearts that had trouble pumping blood. Our bodies could fail in so many ways. Even if we were born normal, something, like cancer, could happen to us later. No wonder my parents told me to be grateful for my health.

"Follow me," the assistant said, leading Mom and me to the back of the store and into a private room with posters about "how to fit a bra" and "types of breast forms." When the assistant said, "Let's take some measurements first," Mom started to remove her blouse.

"Mom!" I didn't mean to shriek, but I couldn't believe she was undressing in front of a stranger.

"Quit acting so scandalized. We all have the same things." She sounded just like Mrs. Garcia, our coach, after we complained about having to change clothes for PE the first year of middle school.

"Shouldn't I wait outside?" I asked, not wanting to see my mom's bare chest.

"Absolutely not. I need your help. This is a big decision for me, so I need another woman's opinion." This was the first time she had called me a woman. I felt proud but also undeserving. After all, a true woman was a lot more mature. She had a job, a marriage, children, and a developed body. I was still in middle school! I was still waiting to have my first boyfriend.

Mom removed her shirt and the bra with the pillow boob. She turned toward a mirror, and I looked at her reflection, how one side was completely normal while the other had the line of her scar. Her mastectomy side wasn't completely flat like I'd imagined but a bit caved in. I must have frowned because Mom said, "Don't be scared."

"I'm not," I replied, glancing at my mood ring, which was between colors, black and brown—nervous but with a sense of anticipation, too. Did this mean I was between emotions? That I really *was* scared, but also fascinated?

"Time to measure," the assistant said, measuring tape in hand.

She told Mom to lift her arms. Mom winced, explaining that she was still struggling since the surgery and would be starting physical therapy the following week. The assistant

wrapped the tape around Mom's torso beneath her breast, then measured her cup size, and finally the length for the shoulder straps. As she wrote everything down, Mom put her shirt back on. Then the assistant took out a catalog of breast forms, along with some samples. She handed them to us. They felt like water balloons, only firmer. Some were smooth, while others had nipples. They came in different colors, too, one for every skin tone.

"Where's the Mexican one?" Mom asked, because the one she held was too peachy for her skin. When the assistant handed it to her, Mom laughed.

"What's so funny?" I wanted to know.

"Look at us," she said, "touching all these fake breasts. Imagine telling your friends that you and your mom went shopping for boobs."

"And talking about whether or not we should order one with a nipple." I giggled.

"And asking for the Mexican color even though no one's going to see it because it's going to be under my clothes."

"And discussing whether you should get the teardrop or the triangle shape," I added.

"Oh, you're definitely a triangle," the assistant told my mom, all serious.

"Did you hear that?" Mom asked me, laughing harder now. "I'm a triangle—like something you study in geometry."

We had the kind of giggles that wouldn't stop, that made our bellies ache, but eventually, we settled down and made our selections. Who knew buying a fake boob was so complicated? Not only did Mom have to choose a skin tone, but she had to decide whether to buy the adhesive kind or the kind you slipped into a pocket in the bra. When it came to the choice between the triangle or teardrop model, I said, "Yep. You're a triangle. The teardrop doesn't fit you at all."

Mom took my hand, squeezed it, and said, "That's right. No teardrops here."

The next week, Mom started going to physical therapy, so she left me in charge of Carmen and Jimmy for a few hours every afternoon. The first time, I was nervous. I kept thinking something bad would happen. When Jimmy crawled under the table, I worried that it would collapse and crush him. When Carmen went to the garage to get a hammer and nails for something called "string art," I worried that she'd lose a hand at the table saw even though she wasn't going anywhere near it. And when she started hammering the nails, I knew she was going to break a finger, so I told

her she couldn't work on her project till Mom or Dad came home.

And who knew there were so many breakable things in our house? Glasses, plates, windows, vases, Chia Pets. Who knew there were so many poisons? Bleach, Windex, hydrogen peroxide, every medicine in the cabinet. I didn't want Jimmy or Carmen to leave my sight. If something bad happened to them, I'd never forgive myself.

Once, I spent the whole afternoon in a near panic. When Mom returned, I gave her a giant hug and said, "I'm so glad you're here! Taking care of kids is hard work. Do you know how many things can go wrong?"

She just laughed and said, "Well, I'm glad everyone's still in one piece."

By the second week, babysitting my brother and sister felt a little more routine, but that didn't stop me from imagining all sorts of horrible accidents.

In the meantime, Carmen kept the bathrooms clean, and I took long walks to get ready for the 5K in October. I felt stronger every week and could walk the whole distance— twice! I was still a little suspicious about the power of *promesas*, but I was beginning to believe that they worked because Mom was getting better. So maybe a 5K was enough after all.

"We do stretches in therapy," she explained at dinner

one evening. "That way, my tissues will stay flexible. Otherwise, they'll get rigid and tight, making it hard for me to move my shoulder around." She cautiously rolled her shoulder.

"Soon you'll be able to carry Jimmy again," I said.

"And do your step aerobics tapes," Carmen added.

"Are you kidding? I'll be strong enough to go to the gym and lift weights with all those musclemen."

"Let's not get carried away," Dad said. "We can't have some muscleman falling in love with you."

"One already has," Mom replied, winking at him. And then she said something in Spanish, something romantic because Dad blushed.

3 GRADES

Soon it was time to return to school. Normally, I loved school—not the classes, but the chance to be with my friends and to see cute guys. Plus, I was going to be in eighth grade, the oldest group on campus, which meant extra privileges, like first choice in the computer lab, a junior high homecoming and prom, and end-of-year field trips. But instead of being excited, I felt bummed. After all, this year my sister was going to junior high too, not because she was old enough but because she was skipping a grade, and, to make matters worse, she was skipping *three* grades in math. That meant she was taking eighth grade math like me, only she got to take the advanced class.

Carmen bragged about it nonstop as we got dressed

for our first day. "When I met my teachers at registration," she said, "they didn't remember you."

"Gee," I replied, all sarcastic. "I wonder why. Wait. Maybe it's because I wasn't in their class."

"That's what I figured, since you take the classes for *normal* people."

"You're the only one who thinks 'normal' is an insult."

"Oh, there's nothing wrong with it," she said, "but there's nothing *memorable* about it, either."

"You mean as memorable as your outfit?" I pointed at her clothes. While I, and everybody else, wore regular T-shirts and jeans to school, Carmen was wearing a pleated skirt, a starched blouse, knee-high socks, and a blazer. The blazer had brass buttons and a patch with a fake coat of arms. She wanted to look like a student at a fancy boarding school, the kind with redbrick and ivy, because she thought she was better than the rest of us.

"No," she answered, "I mean memorable like someone with a high IQ, someone like me. But what am I saying? You probably don't know what 'IQ' stands for."

I knew it meant "intelligence quotient," but I said, "It means 'idiot quotient,' and you're right. It's a perfect description of you."

She stuck out her tongue and marched out. Good. Mission accomplished. Privacy at last. Still, I kept thinking

about the teachers who did not remember me, how I failed to make an impression. Well, how about *this* for an impression? For the first day of school, I put on a T-shirt that said, "I'm right 97% of the time. Who cares about the other 4%?"

Thirty minutes later, Dad dropped us off, and I walked Carmen to her first-period class.

"You're on your own from here," I said. "I'm sure you'll find your way around since you have such a high IQ."

"No problem," she replied, though she didn't sound as confident as she usually did.

I left her at the classroom door and made my way through the noisy hall of North Canyon Junior High. My campus was one of the newest on the north side of San Antonio, and like all the new buildings on this side of town, it was built in a hurry to make room for the growing population here. This meant no time for an architect to design interesting archways, windows, or courtyards. Everybody said we went to North Canyon Savings & Loan because our school, a three-story rectangle of bricks between two strip malls, looked like a bank.

"Hi, Erica."

I turned to find Derek beside me. I had seen him at the pool a few weeks ago, but he seemed taller and more

muscular now. I glanced at my mood ring. It was purple, the color for love.

"Where are you headed?" he asked.

I glanced at my schedule. "Math. Room 215. With Mr. Leyva."

"Hey, that's where I'm going, too." He seemed so happy to have a class with me. Was this the beginning of a serious romance? He'd never noticed me before, so I couldn't believe he was walking beside me. "Are you going to try out for the talent show this year?"

"I really want to," I answered, "but I sing worse than a cow with a sore throat."

He laughed. He said, "You crack me up!" and laughed some more. That *had* to be a good sign, right? Didn't guys think girls should have a sense of humor?

The warning bell rang just as we stepped into class. I scanned the room for Robins. No Patty, Shawntae, Gum-Wad, or Iliana. Bummer.

"Let's sit over here," Derek said, choosing a desk in the middle row.

Did I hear right? Derek wanted me to sit next to him? So far, this was a terrific first day of school.

All the students settled into their desks as Mr. Leyva started the class. He had a reputation for being a no-nonsense

teacher, but everyone said he was nice as long as you behaved and tried your best. He took roll, and when he got to my name, he said, "Montenegro. Are you related to *Carmen* Montenegro?"

"She's my sister," I grudgingly admitted.

"Well, it's nice to meet you. I'm sure you're going to breeze through this class."

I shrugged as if I didn't care, but I *did* care. Was I going to be compared to Carmen in every class? She just started coming to this school. How did he know her already? Was he her math teacher, too? I wanted to change my last name, so my teachers wouldn't make the connection. After all, having a smart sister didn't mean I was smart, too. Just ask my T-shirt.

My second class was social studies with Mrs. Gardner. I sighed with relief because everyone knew how nice she was. On my way to her room, I bumped into GumWad.

"Hi, Erica," he said, his mouth all blue from his gum. He studied my T-shirt. "Ha-ha." He laughed. "That's funny. You're really good at being sarcastic. You're the most sarcastic girl I know."

"Gee, thanks," I said. "I'll put 'sarcastic' on my résumé when I apply for a scholarship."

"Ha-ha." He laughed again. "You're such a natural."

Leave it to GumWad to think sarcasm was an admirable quality. I had to change the subject before he started pointing out other "admirable" qualities, like the big zit on my forehead.

"Do you have Mrs. Gardner for social studies, too?" I asked.

He showed me his schedule. Yep, we had the same class. And so did Patty. "Hi, guys," she said. She walked right between us and took a seat near the back of the room. GumWad and I followed, choosing the desks beside her.

Luckily, social studies is my favorite subject. I love learning about societies and cultures. Last year, for example, my teacher assigned each of us a country and asked us to create a menu featuring that country's food. I got Kenya, where they drink cow blood mixed with milk. The class was grossed out when I told them, but my teacher said that every culture has weird food, even ours. Like *menudo*. San Antonio people think it's delicious, but people from other parts of the country think it's gross because the main ingredient of *menudo* is the stomach lining from a cow.

"Let's spend today introducing ourselves," Mrs. Gardner suggested. "Tell us something interesting about your summer."

One by one, my classmates shared stories, mostly about

places they went for vacation. One girl went to Canada, a city called Banff "where the clouds are *below* you." Another girl went to a dude ranch in the Texas Hill Country. "I can ride a horse now," she exclaimed, "and start a fire with flint." One guy played on a summer baseball league and made the all-star team. GumWad, of course, went to Disney World. No surprise there, though everyone else seemed interested in his adventures.

What was *I* going to say when it was my turn? My family didn't see the Carlsbad Caverns after all, and for the first time since I could remember, we skipped going to the coast, to Malaquite Beach, our favorite spot. We didn't even have a Fourth of July picnic.

"And how about you?" Mrs. Gardner asked Patty. "Did anything interesting happen to you?"

"Oh, yeah," Patty said. "Lots of stuff." She looked at the ceiling as if to read her past there. "I startled a skunk. That was lots of fun. Then I got a bad sunburn and spent a whole week peeling off dead skin. And then"—she tapped her chin—"I threw up after getting eighth place in a hot dog eating contest."

"How many people were competing?" a guy asked.

"Including me?"

He nodded.

"Eight."

The whole class laughed—Mrs. Gardner too, even though I could tell she was trying to hold it in. Then she said, "And how about you, Erica?"

Suddenly all eyes were upon me. "I didn't go anywhere exciting," I said.

Patty punched me. "Yes, you did. Tell them about that miracle place where you saw those human scalps."

"They weren't scalps. They were braids of hair."

"And teeth and bones and little baby feet," Patty added.

Everyone leaned forward to hear more. "You're exaggerating," I said. "There was a jar with teeth but there weren't any bones. And the baby feet were made of this metal called pewter." I went on, sharing the story about the suicide pilot and how the church had burned except for the statue. I described the little doll in the Aztec sundial above hundreds of candles. "And after praying," I explained, "people leave gifts at El Cuarto de Milagros, the Miracle Room."

"Why did you go?" a girl asked.

I shrugged.

"Don't people go there when someone's sick?"

I looked down, not wanting to answer.

"Sometimes people go because it's an interesting place," GumWad said. "No one *has* to be sick. Anyone can go."

"I'm just asking," the girl said, all offended.

When the teacher turned her attention to someone else, Patty whispered to GumWad, "Good save."

"Yeah, thanks," I said, giving him a grateful smile. Once in a while, between the silly things he did or said, GumWad acted like the coolest friend.

6 QUIET RULES

After school, Carmen and I found Mom leaning back on the recliner with her legs outstretched on the footrest. This had been a first day for her, too. Her surgery had been about seven weeks ago, and now that she had healed, it was time to start radiation therapy. So I wasn't surprised to find her resting, a pillow on her lap and a glass of water on the side table. Meanwhile, Jimmy, who had spent the day with Grandma, was on the floor breaking up his train track.

"I feel sapped," Mom said.

Carmen and I kissed her. Then I sat on the floor with Jimmy while Carmen grabbed the laptop and surfed the Internet.

"According to this website," she explained, "fatigue is the most common side effect of radiation therapy."

"I believe it," Mom said sleepily.

Carmen surfed the Net a little longer. Then she asked, "So what's it like at the cancer center? How do they 'nuke' your cells?"

I wasn't sure Mom wanted to discuss this, so I said, "You don't have to tell us if you don't want."

"It's okay," Mom said. "I don't mind talking about it." She pointed at the afghan on the couch. I gave it to her, and she spread it over her lap. "The therapists take me to a room with a machine called a linear accelerator. They put me on a bed, only it's not soft and comfy like a *real* bed. It's more like a table. They position me, just so, making me lift my arm over my head, and they move the gantry, the part of the machine where the radiation beam comes out. They point it right where my breast used to be."

"Can you see the beam?" Carmen asked.

"No, it's invisible."

"But doesn't it scare you to know that something invisible is hitting your body?"

I wanted to tell Carmen to quit being nosy, but I was curious, too. I'd probably ask the same questions if my sister weren't around.

"Yes," Mom answered. "I was a bit scared because after they prepped me for treatment, they said, 'Don't move.' And then they walked out. They can't turn on the machine until they're in another room behind a thick wall that protects them from radiation. There isn't even a window. They've got cameras to see me, but I can't see them. I just hear their voices when they tell me they're turning on the beam now." She paused a minute, and I mind-traveled to a spaceship filled with mad scientists doing experiments on people because that's how I imagined the room Mom described. "When I sat up after my treatment," Mom continued, "I noticed all the 'caution' signs with the symbol for radiation. One even said, 'Danger! Radiation Treatment Area.' The therapists wear these things called dosimeter badges that change color if they're exposed. So I knew we were working with some very dangerous stuff, and I kept wondering if I was crazy for doing this. You may not realize, but I grew up during the Cold War."

"We had a cold war?" I asked, imagining battlefields in Alaska with weapons that hurled sharp, lethal icicles.

"We called it the Cold War," Mom explained, "because we fought with threats instead of weapons. The United States and the Soviet Union had made enough nuclear bombs to destroy the entire world, so we lived in fear of

bombs falling from the sky, especially here in San Antonio, with all its military bases. We constantly heard about radiation sickness, how it made you burn from the inside out."

Carmen and I squirmed. "That's awful," I said.

"You know what the funny thing is?" Mom said. "I grew up thinking that radiation *caused* cancer, not *cured* it. I mean, it does cause cancer, doesn't it? Isn't that why the therapists have to leave the room? I'm sure there's a joke here somewhere." She laughed to herself.

"So does it hurt?" Carmen wanted to know.

"A little," Mom said. "Let me show you." She lifted her shirt and her arm, showing us the side of her body. The skin there was red, like a bad sunburn.

"It itches," Mom said. "But don't worry. They tell me it's perfectly normal to get a rash like this."

She covered up again and placed the pillow behind her head.

Meanwhile Carmen returned to the laptop, probably looking for information about burned skin as a side effect. "It says you might get nausea, too," she said. "You might lose weight or damage healthy tissue."

Mom nodded, her eyes droopy now. "The doctors mentioned that." She lifted the afghan to her chin and

closed her eyes. I could tell Carmen wanted to say something else, so I lifted a finger to my lips and said, "Shhh." Jimmy mimicked me, putting *his* finger to *his* lips and saying, "shhh," too.

"It's only five o'clock," Carmen whispered, worriedly. "Are you sure Mom should sleep? She hasn't eaten dinner."

"It's okay," I assured her. "She might feel nauseated, remember?"

Carmen glanced at the computer again, clicked a few more times, then said, "Maybe I should go clean the bathroom."

She was still cleaning for her *promesa*, and each time she cleaned, she also counted something. So far, she had counted the tiles around the bathtub, the stripes on all our towels, and the number of ingredients in toothpaste, deodorant, hairspray, mouthwash, and soap. She even took a roll of toilet paper one day and counted out each square. She was acting weird. She *always* acted weird, but all this counting was even weirder.

I shouldn't complain, though. At least Carmen was doing her *promesa*. At least it was challenging, because no bathroom stayed clean forever. I was working on mine too, but it wasn't as challenging as Carmen's.

Soon, Jimmy wanted cartoons, so I switched the TV to Nickelodeon, and he and I danced when some funny-

looking aliens started to sing. That's when Dad came home. As soon as he saw Mom sleeping on the recliner while Jimmy and I jumped around, he grabbed the remote and turned off the TV. Immediately, Jimmy said, "Gimme cartoon! Gimme cartoon!"

Dad shook his head, so Jimmy started to cry.

"Take him to your room," Dad told me.

I wanted to say that we were having fun, that Jimmy was being good, but Dad didn't give me a chance.

"Take him before he wakes up Mom."

I obeyed and picked up Jimmy. He didn't want to go to my room, so he started to bawl.

"Gimme cartoon!" he cried.

"Be quiet!" I said as I shut the bedroom door.

Poor Jimmy. As soon as the door closed, he gave up bawling and started to sob, his cheeks all wet with tears. He looked like one of those sad-eyed puppies on the Adopt-a-Pet commercial.

"Want to pillow fight?" I asked, hoping to cheer him up.

He stomped. "No!"

"Want to jump on the bed?"

"No!"

"Want to color? Want to take pictures with my iPhone? Want to play hide-and-seek?"

"No, no, no!"

I made one last effort. "Want to try on my shoes?"

He hushed, glanced at the closet door, then at me, and then at the closet again.

"Gimme shoes!" he announced as if it were his idea in the first place.

"Sure thing," I said. "You can try on *all* my shoes if you want."

We went to the closet. First he put on my tennis shoes, then my sandals, then the dress shoes I wore for special occasions, and after that, my boots. Of course, all of my shoes were too big, but he didn't care. And when he tripped over himself, he laughed. After he got bored with matching pairs, he tried different combinations—one tennis shoe with a boot, one sandal with a dress shoe. He thought the oddball pairs were the funniest things he'd ever seen.

A while later, Carmen peeked in and said, "Dad wants to have a family meeting."

I told Jimmy to pick his favorite pair, but he shook off the shoes and decided to go barefoot for a while.

We found Dad at the kitchen table. "Have a seat," he said. "We need to talk."

He sounded as serious as a strict principal. I just knew we were in trouble. I scanned my brain, trying to figure out what we had done wrong. Had I gotten in trouble at school

already? Had Jimmy broken another Chia Pet? Had Carmen used Dad's PayPal account for something as useless as the motorized solar system model she bought last year without his permission? Wait a minute! Maybe one of the guys from my Boyfriend Wish List had called. Maybe Derek had called! After all, he did talk to me today. He even asked me to sit by him. Dad probably wanted to set some ground rules now that he knew I was interested in boys. He probably wanted Carmen and Jimmy to spy on me. I was about to protest when Carmen spoke up.

"Where's Mom?" she asked. "I thought this was a family meeting?"

"She's resting," Dad said. "And we *are* having a family meeting...but it's about Mom. So let's keep this between us, okay?"

Carmen and I nodded, but we glanced at each other, too. She looked as nervous as I felt. I wondered if something had gone wrong with the operation or with the radiation treatment.

"Is Mom okay?" I asked. "She seemed fine this afternoon. She was tired, but she was fine other than that."

"She's okay," Dad said. "But like you mentioned, she's tired. She needs to rest. And we need to let her rest."

I didn't know what he was talking about. Mom looked

very comfortable on the recliner earlier. She had her feet up. She had a pillow and a blanket. Sure, Jimmy and I were jumping around, but it didn't seem to bother her.

"I've come up with a few quiet rules," Dad said. "We need to make sure we follow them." He turned to Jimmy. "That means you too, little buddy."

"What do you mean by quiet rules?" Carmen asked. "You want us to whisper from now on?" She wasn't being sarcastic, only curious.

"That would help," Dad said. And then he stated the rules, counting them off with his fingers:

1. Do not turn the TV volume above level 10.
2. Use your earbuds, not the speakers, when listening to your iPods.
3. Put your cell phones on vibrate.
4. Do not vacuum or run the dishwasher or the washing machine while Mom is asleep.
5. When Jimmy cries, take him to your room and close the door till he settles down.
6. Take off your shoes when you come into the house and tiptoe when you walk around.

He paused, thought a minute, then said, "That should do for now, but if I think of any more, I'll let you know."

He pushed his chair away from the table so he could stand. It made a scraping sound against the floor. Dad thought a minute and said, "Instead of scooting your chair, lift it, so it doesn't make any noise."

Before leaving the room, he lifted the chair to set it back under the table. He was right. It didn't make a sound.

If only cooking were as quiet. Dad tried to make dinner without a sound, but he couldn't hush the vent over the stove or ask the meat to stop sizzling in the pan.

"Who knew tacos were so noisy?" he said. And when Mom woke up, he apologized over and over again.

"It's okay," she said. "I can't be sleeping all the time."

She didn't have a big appetite, so she heated up a can of soup instead. All in all, it was a normal dinner. Carmen bragged about how many times she knew the answers in class and how the teachers were excited to work with such a smart girl this year. Jimmy kept asking for things like my taco and Carmen's glass of water even though he had his own. Dad shared a story he'd heard on *All Things Considered*. And Mom didn't seem sick at all. She asked questions about our first day at school and laughed at the funny things we said. Maybe she was lucky. Maybe Mom's surgery was the worst part of her treatment. And it was over. She'd felt sick for a while, but besides being tired, she was okay. At least, that's what I thought, until Mom grabbed

her stomach and raced to the restroom. She stood up so fast, knocking over her chair. It startled Jimmy, so he began to cry. It startled Dad too, and he hurried after her.

"What happened?" Carmen asked, all scared.

"I don't know," I said. "Watch Jimmy. I'll be right back."

I found Mom in the bathroom, vomiting into the toilet. Dad stood beside her. He was gathering her long hair, holding it away from her face. He kept saying, "It's okay. It's okay," but it wasn't. Mom made awful heaving sounds, and she kept throwing up, even though all she'd eaten was a tiny bowl of soup.

I *knew* walking a 5K was too easy. After all, one guy ran a thousand miles. A 5K was only three miles. Should I be doing two 5Ks in a row? Three? How much is enough? How much to keep Mom from feeling sick?

I ran to my room, ignoring Carmen and Jimmy, who were still in the kitchen, both crying now. I shut the door, grabbed a notebook, and started to brainstorm. There must be something extra I could do. I jotted down ideas, my pen hard against the paper. "Extra prayers," I wrote, "running a thousand miles, giving up chocolate, being nice to my sister." These seemed impossible.

I wrote:

Dear Virgen de San Juan,

Ayúdame por favor. My mother has breast cancer and she is very ill. She already had surgery, but the doctors say she needs radiation therapy, too. The next couple of months will be very difficult, and she will need all the help she can get. I have been training for a 5K, but it's not enough. What else can I do? If only I had a sign.

4½ PROJECT IDEAS

The following week, Mr. Leyva gave us a math quiz. We had spent the first week reviewing last year's math, so he wanted to see how much we remembered.

The quiz wasn't too hard. It had addition, subtraction, multiplication, division, and some easy algebra like "$2x + 9 = 45$." I breezed through until I reached the word problems, which I absolutely hated, especially when it had "please show your work" in the instructions.

"A blue car and a red car are at location A," the first problem read. "They both want to go to location B, which is sixty miles away. The blue car leaves at 1:00 PM and drives 20 miles per hour, while the red car leaves at 3:00 PM and drives 30 miles per hour. Which car will arrive first? Please show your work." Of course, the blue car would get there

first because it had a two-hour head start. I didn't need an equation for that. It wasn't as if the test were asking about that fable with the turtle and the rabbit racing each other. If *that* were the problem, I'd have to figure out how much time the rabbit wasted as it took naps, ate snacks, and played Wii. But this was about two cars with full gas tanks driving along the same road. I could solve it with common sense. The bad news was that Mr. Leyva didn't give credit for common sense. He gave credit for showing work. What work? I just couldn't see it. This was a classic example of somebody making something harder than it really was. Besides, who cared what time the blue car got to "location B"? I mean, whose car was it anyway? And where was location B? *What* was it? A store, a park, a friend's house?

I felt so confused. Thank goodness, the bell rang. If I had to spend one more minute thinking about word problems, I'd lose all my hair.

"See you later," Derek said as he rushed out. He'd been talking to me every day and was now numero uno on my Boyfriend Wish List.

I grabbed my things and headed to the door, where Mr. Leyva stood to collect our papers. When he saw mine, he said, "You didn't finish."

"I got stuck on the word problems," I explained.

He seemed surprised. "But your sister..." he began.

"What about her?" I interrupted, not meaning to be rude but unable to stop myself. "I'm the dumb one, okay? She's the one who was born with all the brains."

"That's not what I meant," he started to say, but I didn't wait around. I left as fast as I could and hurried to the rest-room so I could calm down. The entire first week of school, teachers oohed and aahed about my sister. It made me so angry to hear about her in every class. I literally had to cool down, so I splashed some water on my face. As I dried off, I caught my reflection. Today, I wore my "Siamese Twins" T-shirt with two Siamese cats, instead of two people joined at the hip. Is that what people thought about Carmen and me, that we were twins—exactly the same like the cats or joined at the hip like best friends? And all because we shared a last name?

Luckily, Mrs. Gardner never compared me to my sister, which was another reason to enjoy her class. I stepped in and took my seat beside Patty. She said hello and so did GumWad. Today, his mouth was blue. I always checked the color of his gum just like I checked the color of my mood ring. I couldn't help myself.

After taking roll, Mrs. Gardner said, "Every year, my students do a service learning project."

"What's that?" GumWad asked. "Is it a paper or a speech? Are we working in groups or alone? When's it due?"

Mrs. Gardner raised her hand to silence him. "A service learning project," she explained, "is one that helps the community. Activities like cleaning up a park, reading to preschool kids, volunteering, or organizing a fund-raiser."

"Great," Patty whispered to me. "More chores, only no allowance."

"At least you'll get to help people," I offered.

"Why would I want to help strangers? I barely want to help my friends."

I turned my attention back to Mrs. Gardner.

"Anybody have ideas?" she asked.

"Can we look for dogs?" GumWad said. "That would be helping the community, right? Finding lost dogs so little kids won't cry."

"That's a good idea," Mrs. Gardner said. She wrote it on the board. Then she asked us if we had other suggestions. Lots of hands went up. Someone wanted to start a community garden. Someone else wanted to teach people about recycling. Another wanted to paint over graffiti.

While the class brainstormed, I wrote "service learning project" on a piece of paper. Normally, I got excited about projects like this, but I also had "study math," "read three poems for English," "fix the toy train Jimmy broke," and "remind Dad that we're almost out of toilet paper" on the list.

"Erica?" I heard.

I looked up. Mrs. Gardner was staring at me. I'd been too busy with my list to notice that she had called on me.

"Yes, ma'am?" I said.

"Do you have any ideas?" she asked.

I looked at my classmates' suggestions, but none of them interested me. Then I thought about my *promesa*, how perfectly it fit.

"Does walking a 5K for cancer research count?"

Mrs. Gardner nodded, but then she said, "Maybe you can do more than walk. Maybe you can get people to sponsor you. That way, you can raise more money and increase awareness."

I glanced at my mood ring. Bright blue for happy. Of course I was happy! Here was the answer I'd been looking for. I was going to ask for sponsors—lots of sponsors! It was the perfect service learning project and the perfect *promesa* for Mom.

Later, I met the Robins in the cafeteria for lunch. Only the second week of school, and we had already staked a claim on our table. As soon as GumWad joined us, Shawntae saw his tray and said, "You do *not* have blue Jell-O. Can you believe I had a dream about that last night? Seriously. I

dreamed that you got blue Jell-O, and I remember think-ing, 'GumWad doesn't like that flavor.'"

"You're right. I don't," he said. "But it was the only color left." He stuck his fingers in his mouth and pulled out his gum. "Guess it matches this," he said, showing us the slob-bery mass before sticking it beside his milk carton.

Patty was mashing her peas, but when she saw his gum, she said, "Really? You're going to make us stare at that while we eat?"

"You don't have to look at it," GumWad said.

"I look at everything that's gross. I can't help it. I see someone with a giant, oozing zit, and guess what—I *stare*. It's human nature."

"Hey, this isn't a zit," GumWad said, all offended.

"Maybe not," Iliana interjected, "but it *is* kinda gross."

"Amen to that," Shawntae added.

"Fine, then," GumWad said. He wrapped it in a paper towel and left to throw it away. "All better?" he asked when he returned, and the rest of us nodded.

"Guess what!" Iliana said, all excited. "I had a close encounter of the third kind with Alejandro. He asked me if I've seen any movies lately. Do you think he's trying to ask me out? I mean, why else would he mention the movies?" She reached in her purse, took out a compact, and checked

her mascara. "Do you think he likes my thick lashes or should I put on more mascara?"

"No!" Patty, Shawntae, and I said in unison, because Iliana had gobs of black around her eyes.

"Are you girls going to talk about boys again?" Gum-Wad asked. "That's all you ever talk about sometimes."

"If you don't like it," Shawntae said, "sit somewhere else. But before you do, consider this. If you pay attention, you'll get special insights about girls. You'll be the only guy in school with insider knowledge about the mysterious workings of a woman's mind."

GumWad thought a minute. "You make a good point."

"Of course I make a good point. I'm going to be captain of the debate team this year. It's my job to make a good point." She then turned to Iliana. "So what else did Alejandro say?"

We spent a while hearing about Iliana's close encounter, and then we moved on to other topics. That's when I said, "I figured out my service learning project *and* a new and improved *promesa*."

My friends leaned forward to hear more.

"I decided to get a lot of people to sponsor me for the 5K. All they have to do is sign their names and make a donation."

"That's a great idea," Iliana said. "I'll be your first sponsor."

"I'll sponsor you, too," Shawntae said, and GumWad also agreed.

"That makes three sponsors so far," I said. "I'm off to a good start."

We all stared at Patty, expecting her to donate too, but all she said was, "How many people is a lot?"

"I don't know," I admitted. "I guess I should be specific."

I glanced around the table. Five Robins, five hundred names.

"I hereby promise to get five hundred sponsors for the 5K."

"Five hundred people?" Patty said. "Are you crazy? It's easier to get five hundred people to pull off their toenails than to do something nice like help a real cause."

Iliana sighed. "Don't you believe in *anyone*?"

"Absolutely not," Patty answered, mashing a few more peas.

"If you ask me," Shawntae said, "getting sponsors is a great idea, and five hundred is even better." She took a sip of water. "So you want to know what *I'm* doing?" She and Iliana had Mrs. Gardner, too. "I'm going to educate everyone about the upcoming election. I plan to design brochures

listing this year's hot topics and what each candidate believes. Then, I want to do a YouTube video of random people to get their opinions. Finally, I'm going to collect links to articles and post them on my Facebook page, so everyone can keep up-to-date."

"Sounds like an awful lot of work," Patty said.

"Sounds like fun to me," Iliana countered.

"Especially the random people part," GumWad said. "I like helping random people. That's why I'm going to look for lost dogs."

Patty poured milk into her mashed peas. It looked totally gross. Then she turned to GumWad and said, "You're not looking for dogs because you want to help people. You want the reward money. Why don't you admit it?"

"I'm not doing it for reward money."

"Sure, you are."

GumWad plopped a fresh gumball in his mouth even though he hadn't finished his lunch. "I know what it's like to lose a pet," he said. "How you're always wondering what happened. Did he run away? Did he get hit by a car? Did someone steal him? And I see these poor dogs running around, probably trying to get back home. So I don't care about the reward money at all."

He seemed a little mad, so I said, "I wouldn't blame you

if you took it. After spending all day in the heat, you deserve a little reward."

"But that's not why I'm doing it," he insisted.

"I know," I said. "You're doing it because you're nice."

He smiled, and his dimples looked really cute, but then he blew a big orange bubble, and when it popped, gum got on his upper lip. He licked it off, which was really gross, in my opinion, especially since we were at the lunch table.

"Well, I came up with an idea, too," Iliana said. "I'm going to volunteer at the hospital by playing with the little kids. Some of them have to stay for a very long time, and they get bored. Besides, I want to marry a doctor someday, so this will be good experience."

"But these kids are in the hospital," Patty said, "which means they're sick. They have diseases, and diseases are contagious. Do you really want to get some awful disease? You might get sores on your body, or your arms and legs might swell up. You might have to eat through a tube for the rest of your life. The only doctor you'll have a relationship with is the one who's treating you."

"Quit being so negative," Shawntae scolded. "You're really getting on our nerves."

"Yeah," I said. "You have a criticism about everything.

So tell us about your great idea. It's obviously better than what we're doing."

"I don't have any ideas," Patty confessed.

We spent a moment thinking in silence.

"What about picking up garbage?" I suggested.

She shook her head. "I'm supposed to do a narrative. How can I write a narrative about throwing away trash?"

"Don't throw it away," I said.

"You want me to *keep* it? I thought *I* was the one with the dark sense of humor."

"I'm serious," I went on. "Use the trash for something else."

"That's a great idea," Iliana jumped in. "You take art every semester. Maybe you can do something artistic."

"Hmmm..." Patty tapped the table a few times. "I'll think about it," she said.

We eventually moved on to other topics, mostly glancing around to see who had changed the most. Some guys, for example, were cuter this year, or they walked around with more confidence. A few boyfriend-girlfriend couples had broken up over the summer, while others had gotten together. With so many changes, we definitely had to revise our Boyfriend Wish List.

A large group from a nearby table stood to return their trays. That's when Shawntae spotted my sister. Every table

in the cafeteria was rectangular except for the circular one Carmen picked. She *would* sit at the only oddball table in the room. After all, she was wearing that silly school uniform again and had already earned the nickname Miss Prep, as in "prep school."

"Your sister's so cute," Shawntae told me, "with that fancy uniform and her suitcase."

"But it's got to be hot under that jacket," Patty said. "She probably has big underarm stains from sweating a lot. And that suitcase must weigh a ton."

"It *is* hot in that blazer," I said. "I keep telling Carmen to wear normal clothes, but she won't listen. And that suitcase is full of books, too many books for a normal backpack. She likes to pretend she's in private school instead of with the rest of us dummies."

"I'm sure she doesn't think we're dumb," Iliana said.

I shook my head. "She doesn't think we're smart, that's for sure."

"She looks so focused," Shawntae noticed. "It's like she's working out problems while she eats."

"She's counting," I explained.

"Counting?"

"Yes. She counts how many times she chews. She won't swallow till she reaches a certain number."

"What a chore," Patty said.

143

"She can't help it. Ever since my mom's operation, she's been counting. It drives me *insane*." I knew I shouldn't tell everyone about Carmen's quirks, but I couldn't stop myself. "We can't take her to the grocery store anymore. Too much stuff to count. Once, she wouldn't leave till she counted all the bananas, the ones in the fruit section *and* the ones by the cereal."

"Maybe counting makes her feel better," Iliana said. "Instead of stressing out about your mom, she counts. It takes her mind off things."

I shrugged. "I guess."

"It must be tough," Iliana continued, "to be so smart."

"What's tough is being the *sister* of someone smart," I said.

Iliana ignored me. She started to wave Carmen over, but I grabbed her arm before Carmen noticed.

"What are you doing?" I asked.

"Trying to get her attention. She looks so lonely all by herself."

"Well, that's her fault," I said. "She can get her own friends. If she's smart enough to do advanced math, then she's smart enough to meet people on her own."

I must have sounded angry because all the Robins, even Patty, looked at their plates and stayed silent. They were not about to disagree with me.

5 CUL-DE-SACS

The next Saturday, Carmen had a practice meet for the University Interscholastic League A+ academic competition. She was competing in calculator applications, science, and number sense. "I could enter all the contests if I wanted," she bragged, "but there isn't enough time in one day."

I could only roll my eyes and be grateful she was limited to twenty-four hours. Our room already looked like a pirate's chest with all the fake gold of her trophies.

Dad planned to drop her off and take Jimmy to the zoo while she competed. Meanwhile, Mom's sisters were coming for a visit. That meant I finally had a free day. No Carmen, no Jimmy, no chores. So I went to Iliana's house to work on my social studies project. My mom had experienced

the worst week, throwing up several more times. I needed to fulfill my *promesa* as fast as possible. I had to show La Virgen how much Mom needed her help.

"Do you think Chad knows I exist?" Iliana asked, and "Have you noticed that Alejandro talked to me every day this week?"

Instead of answering, I grabbed my spiral notebook. "Mrs. Gardner wants us to write out the steps for our projects."

"I can't believe it!" she cried. "You really want to do homework. No wonder my parents like you so much."

"Don't get mad because I'm being responsible," I said as I wrote a title on the first blank page.

"Fine," Iliana said. "But if you get bored, my brothers are around."

I looked up. "Really?"

"And they've been exercising a lot because of football season, so they're all muscular right now."

"I can't imagine your brothers being *more* muscular."

"You should say hi to them. They're always asking about you."

"They *are*?"

She nodded, and I glanced at her bedroom door, imagining her brothers somewhere on the other side, the garage

probably, since that's where they kept all their weights. Normally, I'd pretend to get thirsty and, on my way to the kitchen, peek into the garage and catch them working out. I'd stay there for a while offering to get them water and answering their questions because they always asked me about school and family. It sure was tempting.

"Well?" Iliana said. "You want to spy on my brothers?"

My mood ring was yellow, the color for feeling creative but also for feeling distracted.

"I can't," I decided. "This isn't just for school, remember? It's for my mom."

She sighed. "Suit yourself."

I returned to my notebook. "Steps for completing my service learning project," I wrote. "Visit 'Race for the Cure' website and learn how to become an official participant. Print a sponsor form. Go to people's houses and ask for donations." I thought a moment. What happens after I get donations? "Continue training to get in shape for the event." I looked at the ceiling and scratched my head. Hmmm... this sounded like a complete plan to me. "All done," I said.

Iliana glanced up. "No way! You finished in two minutes?"

I shrugged. "It's not that complicated."

"Lucky for you," she said. "It's going to take me all day

to work out a plan. I don't know the first thing about playing with little kids or working at a hospital."

"Doesn't Santa Rosa have a volunteer department?" I asked. "All you have to do is make an appointment, right? And then you show up and play with the kids. What's so hard about that?"

"I wish it were that easy, but in my house, *I'm* the little kid, so I never have to babysit."

I nodded, thinking about Jimmy Gimme. "Yeah, it's tough. I babysit a lot, and my little brother can be a giant headache sometimes."

"But he's so cute."

"You're right," I admitted. "He's a really cute, giant headache."

She laughed and threw a pillow at me, and I remembered how Jimmy liked to throw things too, especially after he begged to hold them, and of all the things in the world, his favorite objects to hold were...

"Chia Pets!" I blurted.

"What about them?" Iliana asked.

"Jimmy loves to hold our Chia Pets, just like you would a real puppy or kitten. He likes other stuff too—crawling inside the closet, jumping on the bed, and climbing on the table—but the hospital kids are probably too sick for activities like that. Still, they're kids. And all kids are the

same in certain ways. So I thought, what does Jimmy like to do? We call him Jimmy Gimme for a reason. Every minute of every day, he's grabbing something, and one of his favorite things to grab is a Chia Pet. Something about them calms him down, but they make him laugh, too. He thinks green hair is hilarious. I'm sure the hospital kids would think so, too. You should find a way to get people to donate Chia Pets. Then the kids could keep them in their rooms, make sure they're watered, watch them grow. They could name them. They could have Chia Pet parties. They could—"

"Slow down!" Iliana said. "I can't write fast enough."

"They could set up a pretend farm or zoo in the play area and even sponsor Chia Pet adoption days if they want to trade or if someone new gets admitted."

Iliana scribbled frantically. "Pet parties," she mumbled, "farm or zoo." She wrote a few more lines, put down the pen, and shook the stiffness from her hand. "Wow," she said. "You really know how to brainstorm."

"If only brainstorming were useful for math." I sighed. "I'm so nervous about the test next week. I just know I'm going to fail. I already failed a practice quiz."

"But you do great in your other classes, so you can't be *that* bad in math."

"Yes, I can."

Iliana smiled at me, but instead of being happy, her smile seemed to say, "I'm sorry," even though it wasn't her fault I couldn't solve word problems.

Maybe I couldn't pass Mr. Leyva's class, but I *could* pass social studies. I took Iliana's laptop and began the first step for my project, "Visit the Race for the Cure website." On the home page was a slideshow from past races. Most of them featured groups behind company banners or runners crossing the finish line. Beneath the slideshow, a box offered fund-raising tips like "most people donate simply because they were asked" and "make the first donation and watch your family and friends follow." Another box listed the top fund-raisers. One lady raised more than $67,000. That was probably more than I could ever get, but lots of people had raised $5,000 or $6,000. Maybe I could, too. After all, how hard could it be? All that money must mean people really wanted to help.

Eager to get started, I clicked on "Register as an individual." The form asked for information, like my name, address, phone number, and T-shirt size. I cheered because I love cool T-shirts. After my contact information, the registration form had a questionnaire. "Please tell us the primary reason you are participating," it said, followed by a drop-down menu. My choices included "I care about finding a cure for breast cancer," "I enjoy walking or running," and

"My workplace organized a team." Nowhere did it say, "School project" or *"Promesa"* or "My mom's sick," so I selected the first option. After all, I *did* care about finding a cure even though it wasn't my *primary* reason for doing this. The next question asked, "How did you hear about this event?" and luckily "Newspaper article" appeared in the drop-down menu. Finally, I had to pay a fee. I didn't have $35, so I called Dad's cell and asked to use his PayPal account. He said, "Sure thing, *mija*. You have a great idea, so just let me know about whatever you need for your *promesa*." Now as an official participant, I printed a donation form that had the Race for the Cure logo on the top, a "please sponsor me" paragraph, and a grid where people wrote their names, addresses, and donation amounts.

The entire time I worked, Iliana talked to people at the hospital and set up an appointment. She hit her "End" button at the same moment I shut the laptop.

"Ready for the next step," I announced.

"Me too," Iliana said. "But I can't do anything until next weekend. I have to go to volunteer training before I can work with the kids."

"What a bummer."

"Actually, I'm glad. I *need* that training. I'll probably feel more confident after I go. And maybe I'll meet a cute guy there, too."

I laughed. Iliana could turn any event into a setting for romance.

"I guess I'm ready to bug people for donations," I told her. "I'm going to do it the old-fashioned way, by going door to door."

"Sounds like fun," she said. "Want to start right now?"

"Sure, but you don't have to go with me." I didn't mean to leave her out, but part of me wondered if a *promesa* counted when you didn't do it by yourself.

"I want to," she insisted. "It'll be fun."

"Well, okay," I said, not wanting to be rude.

I pinned the fund-raising forms to a clipboard, grabbed a pen and a manila envelope for the money, and we headed out the door.

Our neighborhood has several winding streets with cul-de-sacs. When I was in elementary school, I called the cul-de-sacs "mushrooms" because that's what they reminded me of, and now my family and friends called them mush-rooms, too. We live in a suburb, so the houses are still new. My dad said this area had nothing but rocks, shrubs, and creek beds when he was growing up, but I can't imagine it without houses, especially because we moved here when I was two. He must be telling the truth, though, because the

trees don't tower over the houses on my street like they do in the neighborhoods closer to downtown.

"Let's do your mushroom first," I told Iliana.

"Sure thing. We can start with my neighbor."

We knocked on the door, and an old woman answered. Her face was as wrinkled as a wadded burger wrapper, and she moved as if every muscle ached.

"Hello, Señora Alderete," Iliana said. "Is Carolina here?"

"*No, no está aquí.*"

Iliana turned to me. "Señora Alderete is my neighbor's mom. She doesn't speak English, but she can understand everything we say."

I glanced at Mrs. Alderete, and she nodded.

"Is it okay if my friend asks you something?" Iliana said.

"*Por supuesto,*" Mrs. Alderete answered.

"That means 'of course,' " Iliana explained.

"I know," I said. "I speak Spanish, remember?"

"Since when?"

"Since right now." I was totally lying. I wasn't bilingual. Not really. My last name is Montenegro, but that didn't matter when everyone spoke English at home. I could count to one hundred in Spanish and order at a restaurant, but beyond that, I got confused. Still, I hated to admit that I

wasn't bilingual because it made me feel dumb. I was already weak in math, and I didn't want to be weak in Spanish, too. So I turned to Mrs. Alderete and said, *"Buenos días."*

"Buenos días," she answered.

"Mi mamá está ... está ..." What was the word for "sick"? I looked up, trying to remember.

"Enferma," Iliana whispered. "And remember, she understands English."

I nodded. *"Mi mamá está enferma."*

Mrs. Alderete sighed. *"La pobrecita,"* she said. *"¿De qué está enferma?"*

I stared at her, trying to find the words, but I didn't know how to say "because she has cancer" in Spanish. So how could I explain my mom's situation to Mrs. Alderete? How could I say, "My mom had an operation to remove her breast and two weeks ago she started radiation treatments so the doctors could 'nuke' the extra cancer cells and it is making her feel worse on top of how frustrated she feels about not being able to wear bikinis anymore." How could I say something so complicated in Spanish? Sure, Mrs. Alderete understood English, but even so, how could I answer in English? In *any* language? It was too personal.

"Her mom has cancer," I heard Iliana say. "And my friend's raising money to help find a cure. There's a race

coming up, so she's asking people to sponsor her by making a donation."

Mrs. Alderete nodded the whole time Iliana spoke. After a moment, she said, *"Lo siento, pero no tengo mucho dinero."* She held out empty hands. Then she reached in the pocket of her housedress. *"Solamente tengo diez dólares."* She handed us a ten. *"¿Está bien?"*

"Oh, yes, Mrs. Alderete," I said. *"Es muy bien."* I took the bill and put it in the envelope. *"Muchas gracias."* I bowed as if Mrs. Alderete were the queen of the cul-de-sac.

"Vaya con Dios," she said, about to close the door.

"Just another minute," I pleaded. "Can you fill this out?" I handed her the sponsor form. She wrote her name, address, and donation amount, and we thanked her about twenty more times before we left.

"She's so nice," I said to Iliana as we walked along the sidewalk. "With people like her, I'll reach my goal in a couple of weeks."

"If not sooner," Iliana predicted.

We went to the next house and rang the doorbell. No one. Same for the second and third houses.

"That's strange," Iliana said. "Their cars are in the driveways."

When we rang the fourth doorbell, a lady peeked through a curtain, but she didn't answer. I knocked and

heard movement inside. I knocked again. Nothing. "We know you're in there," I called. "We just want to ask a question." But the lady didn't respond. I turned to Iliana. "She's ignoring us."

"That's so rude," Iliana said.

A few people answered their doors, but they weren't very nice. "Can't help you," they kept saying.

Now and then, we met someone who had an experience with illness. One person, for example, had a cousin with cerebral palsy, and another, a grandmother with leukemia. They were more than happy to donate. We went through several mushrooms, and after an hour, we had four yeses, eight nos, and countless unanswered doors.

Getting five hundred people to sponsor me was not going to be easy.

30 QUARTERS

We never missed church on Sundays. During mass, we made petitions, which meant thanking God or asking Him to help us. Last year, I mostly asked God to help me with my Boyfriend Wish List—no miracles like the cutest guy in school becoming my boyfriend, but small things like moving from a close encounter of the first kind to a close encounter of the second kind. This year, asking for help with boyfriends seemed so immature. Sure, I was still boy crazy. How could I *not* be? There were so many cute guys in the world. And Derek had been talking to me every day. We were definitely having close encounters of the third kind. But I couldn't waste my petitions on boyfriends anymore. Last night, Mom ate applesauce and toast with strawberry jelly. She didn't throw up, and we all cheered

like during a Super Bowl. But by seven thirty, she was completely exhausted. She tried to stay awake and watch videos with us, but she fell asleep sitting on the couch. Dad told us to turn down the volume, and then he helped her to the bedroom. We finished the movie, but then Jimmy still needed a bath. I couldn't let him go to sleep all dirty, so I got the tub ready for him. The whole time he fought me and cried, "Gimme Mommy! Gimme Mommy!" And when I tried to read him a bedtime story, he grabbed the book, threw it to the floor, and cried for her again. That's when Dad came in and told me to settle Jimmy down.

"I *am* settling him down," I said, all frustrated, "but he's not listening."

Eventually, Jimmy wore himself out. He wore me out too, but my night wasn't over. When I walked into the bedroom, Carmen had toppled over a big jar where we dumped spare coins. She was sorting them. "And then I'm going to count them," she explained.

"Tonight?"

She nodded. I didn't want the light on, and I didn't want to hear her mumbling numbers. But I was so tired, and since it took too much energy to fight, I just put on my earphones and listened to my iPod. Normally, good music calmed me down, but my mood ring was the amber color

that meant I felt unsettled, probably because I couldn't help thinking that even though only Mom had cancer, my entire family seemed sick.

On Sunday, I was still thinking this at church, so during petition time, I closed my eyes and asked—no, *begged*—for help. "And for my part," I prayed, "I'm going to work on my *promesa*."

Keeping my promise, I changed into some comfortable clothes as soon as I got home. I wore a T-shirt that had a picture of the Abominable Snowman with a caption that read, "Yeti or not, here I come." I grabbed my clipboard and headed out, approaching the cul-de-sac with more determination than Jimmy when he wanted an ice-cream cone. Most of these neighbors didn't answer yesterday. Maybe they weren't home at the time. Maybe I'd have better luck now, especially since it was Sunday. Weren't people nicer on Sundays after they came back from church?

I knocked on the first door. Nothing. I knocked on the second. Nothing again. The third person answered but quickly said, "I already give to charities," and the fourth one said, "I have diabetes. Are you going to raise money for my diabetes, too?"

What was wrong with these people? Any amount was acceptable. I'd take one dollar if that's all they could afford.

I looked at their houses. They had two-car garages, chimneys, and automated sprinkler systems. Many had signs that let everyone know about their security alarms. Security alarms meant expensive stuff inside. If they could buy expensive stuff, then surely they could donate five bucks to a good cause. So why were they being so selfish?

I was getting angry. I wanted to stand in the middle of the street and scream, "I hate this neighborhood!" But I didn't. Instead, I dragged my feet, dreading the next doorbell. At one point, a little dog joined me. He had white fur that was all muddy. He stayed with me for a whole cul-de-sac, and then he disappeared.

I decided to try one more set of houses. I walked up to the first door, pushed the button, and heard the ding-dong and then some footsteps. I knew someone was spying on me from the other side of the peephole, so I rang the doorbell again. A few seconds passed, and then a man answered.

"Weren't you here yesterday?" he asked. "You and another girl?"

"Yes," I said. "But you didn't answer."

"Because I don't like to be bothered."

How rude, I thought, wanting to walk away but remembered my mom and stood firm.

"I'm sorry. I didn't mean to bother you," I said.

"Then why did you? And why are you here today? You're not selling Girl Scout cookies, are you? Those things are overpriced, if you ask me."

"No, sir. I'm not a Girl Scout."

"Then why are you carrying that order form? You want money, don't you?"

I nodded.

"You kids," he said as if being a kid were the worst thing in the world. "I can't go one week without some kid bugging me for money. First, it's the school band. Then it's the church choir. And always those Girl Scouts. Haven't you kids heard of working for things?"

"I *am* working for it," I blurted. "If you'll only let me explain. I plan to walk in this year's Race for the Cure. It's for breast cancer, and the reason it matters so much is because my mom's sick. She had an operation this past summer, and now she's getting radiation treatments. They're making her sick, but it's all the doctors know how to do. So I'm out here, ringing doorbells, *working*, to raise some money. But if that isn't enough for you, I'll wash your car or mow your lawn or bathe your dog if you have one. I'm not asking for a lot. Just whatever you can spare." I had to catch my breath after all that.

He stared at me a moment. I thought for sure he'd slam the door in my face, but he didn't.

"I'm sorry to hear about your mom," he finally said. Then he pulled out his wallet and handed me a twenty-dollar bill. "You don't have to wash my car or anything."

"Thanks," I said, handing him the clipboard.

He signed my sponsor form, and as he returned it, he said, "You keep bothering people, okay?"

"I will," I said.

He smiled, and then he shut the door. This was going to be tough, but maybe it wouldn't be impossible.

I spent another hour bugging people. A few more offered to help, but most ignored me or gave an excuse. Maybe going door-to-door wasn't the best strategy, but I didn't know how else to reach people.

I was about to head home when I heard a familiar voice calling, "Rover! Hey, boy! Where are you?" Sure enough, GumWad turned the corner. He carried a stack of papers in one hand and a dog leash in the other. From a distance, he looked like a normal guy, even a little cute, though his arms and belly were a bit soft.

"Hey, GumWad!" I called. "Over here."

He spotted me and jogged over. "Didn't think I'd see you today. What are you doing out here?" He smacked a yellow piece of gum.

"I'm working on my social studies project," I explained.

"Me too." He blew a bubble, popped it, and licked the gum off his upper lip. "Look here," he said, handing me the stack of papers. They were "lost dog" signs. One had a caption that read, "Have you seen me?" over a picture of a sad-eyed dog that reminded me of Jimmy when he didn't get what he begged for. The others were like police descriptions with the color, size, and breed of dog. All of them had reward amounts.

"Are you sure you aren't going to keep the rewards?" I asked.

"No. I really want to find these dogs. I don't care about the money at all."

He seemed a little mad as if I'd accused him of something awful. Maybe I should have apologized, but I didn't do anything wrong. Honestly, if I found a lost dog, I'd keep the reward, and no one would think I was a bad person. We stood there without saying a word, the only sound his constant smacking. Being alone with GumWad was... awkward. Usually the other Robins were around so I hardly noticed him, but out here, away from school and alone, I *had* to notice him. But I didn't want to look at his face, so I looked at the dog posters instead. That's when I saw a picture of the muddy white dog.

"I just saw him!" I exclaimed.

"Really?" GumWad beamed. "Where?"

"Follow me. I'll show you."

I hurried to the last place I saw him. Now that I knew his name, I could call out. "Max! Come here, Max!" Gum-Wad called for him, too. It took a while, but eventually, the muddy white dog appeared. He ran to me, all happy. While I petted him, GumWad checked his dog tag. Sure enough, he was the one on the poster. We managed to get the leash on him, and then we walked him home.

"Did you see how happy those people were?" GumWad said after we returned Max.

"Max seemed happy, too. I bet he hadn't eaten in days."

"And he was probably drinking water from a ditch," GumWad added. Then, "Speaking of thirsty dogs, do you want to get a Slush from Sonic?"

"Are you calling me a dog?"

"No," he said. "I just thought you'd want a drink since you've been working so hard to get names for your mom."

Great. I didn't look like a dog; instead, I looked like someone who was about to pass out after working so hard.

I didn't *really* want to spend more time with GumWad, but how could I turn down an opportunity to go to Sonic, especially when the cute high school boys liked to go there,

too? Besides, it was close by, right at the end of the major street that branched into the cul-de-sacs.

"Sure," I said, "I'll go, but I don't have any money." I glanced at the manila envelope. "This is for my project," I explained.

"Don't worry. I got cash." He reached into his pocket and pulled out a handful of quarters. I'd never seen so many quarters in my life. He must have had thirty. "See?" he said. "I got enough here for a hamburger too, if you want."

"Okay, okay." I laughed. "Let's go, then."

I sent a text to my dad, telling him where I was going and when to pick me up. Then GumWad and I headed to Sonic. As we walked, he told me about his gumball machine, how his parents bought it one Christmas and how they gave him enough quarters to buy the gum. When he ran out, his mom bought a fresh supply. Then he took the quarters from the machine and started over. The same quarters have been going into that machine since he was eight.

We both ordered lime Slushes at Sonic, and GumWad surprised me by throwing out his gum instead of sticking it to the side of his cup. While we enjoyed our cool drinks, he told me about the dog he lost when he was in kindergarten, how he never got over it.

"That's the real-life story of why I'm looking for lost dogs," he explained.

"You're too sentimental."

He said, "Just because I care doesn't mean I'm sentimental." He was so serious when he said this, but then he started to laugh. "You can put that on one of your 'used-to' T-shirts." My face must have looked confused because he added, "I used to be sentimental but now I care too much. Get it?"

After a moment, I got the joke and laughed. "You're right," I said. "That's a perfect line for a T-shirt. I'm going to write that down." And I did, right on my manila envelope.

GumWad talked on about the cool rides at Disney World, where his family had spent vacation, but I hardly paid attention because I had already heard his Disney World story. Besides, a sporty black Volkswagen had parked at the ordering console right in front of me. When the tinted window rolled down and the driver leaned out to push the call button, I saw a god. Honestly, a god. Not like *the* God at church, but like the gods in mythology, the ones with long hair and bulging muscles, the ones who rescued helpless mortals like me from evil stepmothers or seven-headed monsters. I couldn't stop looking at him. He was a shiny new toy, and my eyes were Jimmy begging, "Gimme, gimme." And then he caught me staring. He rubbed his

eyes. To get a better look? Then he winked. I couldn't believe it. He winked!

"What are you looking at?" GumWad said, turning around and seeing the VW guy I was secretly calling Thor. "Are you staring at *him*?"

I could only sigh.

"Why are you staring at him?"

"Because he's super handsome and because he's winking at me. Can you believe a cute guy like that is flirting with me?"

"He's not winking," GumWad said. "He's got something in his eye. Either that or his contacts are bothering him."

I studied the guy's frantic winking. Okay, maybe Thor's contacts were bothering him. That's probably why he kept rubbing his eyes. But it didn't matter because he was handsome even with all those tears and blinks.

"When guys are flirting," GumWad went on, "they wink in a different way."

"Like how?"

He ran his hand across his face as if erasing a chalkboard. Then, he opened his eyes, looked at me, and winked, putting his whole cheek and forehead into it. Seriously, he squeezed half his face.

"That's not flirtatious at all," I said. "You look like Popeye."

"Let me try again," he insisted. "I got all nervous."

"Why would you be nervous? It's just me."

He didn't answer. He just looked away for a minute.

After a while, he said, "That guy's old enough to be in high school. He's probably old enough to be in college."

"Maybe," I said.

"You should be interested in guys your own age, not guys like him. He's too old for you."

"Says who?" I asked. "At most, he's six years older than me. I've got an aunt and uncle who are eight years apart, and they get along just fine. Besides, I'll be in high school next year." I glanced at my mood ring. "Look, it's purple!" I lifted my hand to GumWad's confused face. "The stone is purple!"

"So?"

"So that's the color of smoldering passion."

"How can you feel passion for someone you don't even know?"

"It's called 'love at first sight.' People have been writing poems about it since forever."

GumWad frowned. He probably hadn't discovered love poems yet.

Just then, Dad pulled into the parking lot and waved me over.

"Gotta go," I said. "Thanks for the Slush."

"Sure. You're welcome. Anytime. We should—"

I hopped into the car, and as Dad drove away, I glanced back to get another glimpse of Thor, but GumWad was blocking my view.

1 SILLY DREAM

On Monday, Mr. Leyva announced that we would have a math test later in the week. This wasn't a pretest. This would be a recorded grade. I panicked just thinking about it. Luckily, I was doing well in my other classes, especially social studies. Mrs. Gardner asked us to discuss our projects. Some of the students hadn't started yet, but I was right on schedule. I talked about asking for sponsors, and Gum-Wad talked about searching for dogs, running into me, and having Slushes at Sonic.

After everyone gave an update, Mrs. Gardner said, "Since a few of you are behind, let's take fifteen minutes to catch up. Write out a plan for accomplishing your goal, and for those who have already tried the first steps, write a narrative about your experience so far."

"How do I write out a plan for picking up trash?" Patty whispered. She was definitely resisting this assignment, but she opened her notebook anyway.

I took out my own paper and wrote, "My friend Patty said people would tear off their own toenails before helping me raise money for cancer research. I didn't believe her, but now I know she's right." I went on, describing in detail all the variations of "can't help" I'd heard as I knocked on door after door. Then, because I hated to be so negative, I described the people who *did* help, like Mrs. Alderete and the man who thought I was a Girl Scout.

"Finish your thoughts," Mrs. Gardner said when the class was about to end. I completed my sentence and then glanced at Patty's page. She had drawn a tattered cardboard box, a crushed soda can, and a banana peel.

"Trash," she said. Then she tore out the page and wadded it. "*Real* trash."

I had to take my science book to the cafeteria. I hadn't read the assigned chapter because I was so busy with my *promesa* over the weekend. I was frantically skimming the pages when Patty arrived.

"Why are you studying during lunch?" she asked.

"Because I have a quiz this afternoon, and I didn't have a chance to study." I quickly glanced over the bold print

words in the chapter and tried to memorize the definitions, but concentrating was difficult when my friends were nearby.

As soon as Shawntae took her seat at the lunch table, she said, "GumWad and Iliana told me about your weekend."

I glanced at them, and they nodded.

I couldn't believe my friends were talking about me again. When were they going to stop sharing my business with the whole world? Even if they weren't saying anything negative, it still bothered me. Shawntae must have noticed because she said, "I'm your friend, remember? I need to know these things. Besides, I *knew* you wouldn't get a lot of names. I *dreamed* it. You should have talked to me. I could have saved you some time."

"And when *exactly* did you have this dream?" I asked, feeling myself getting impatient. Honestly, I had a lot on my mind. The last thing I needed was to hear another one of Shawntae's fake predictions.

"Friday night, before you went looking for sponsors."

"And I'm supposed to believe you?"

Shawntae crossed her arms. "Yes, you're supposed to believe me. Just ask Patty. She knows all about my dream."

Patty was tearing her napkin in half, but she stopped in

the middle of the rip, looked at Shawntae, and said, "You told me you dreamed that Erica and GumWad were looking for candy in a dark, scary forest and that it must mean they were going to dress up as Hansel and Gretel for Halloween."

"That's so cute," Iliana said. "You think Alejandro and I could dress up as a fairy-tale couple, too? We could be Snow White and Prince Charming. That is, if he really likes me. I can't tell. What do you guys think?"

No one had a chance to answer because GumWad turned to me and said, "I don't mind being Hansel if you want to be Gretel. We can give gum to the little kids." He reached in his pocket and pulled out a handful of gumballs. I saw lint on one and wanted to gag.

"I don't believe in trick-or-treating anymore," I said. "No one in my neighborhood gives out candy. I live next to the most selfish people on the planet."

"Hello!" Shawntae interrupted. "Can we get back to the *real* subject? We're supposed to be talking about my dream."

"What else is there to say?" I asked. "You had some silly cartoon dream that, in my opinion, has nothing to do with what happened this weekend."

"You can't take dreams so literally, Erica. They're not

facts; they're symbols. Just think about it. The candy symbolizes the money you were trying to earn. The dark, scary forest symbolizes the rude people you met."

Patty was tearing her napkin into smaller and smaller pieces. "I liked it better when Erica and GumWad were going to dress up as Hansel and Gretel," she admitted. "It's such a cool story, especially the part when the witch throws the kids in a giant pot of boiling water."

"I don't know about symbols," Iliana said, "but I do see similarities between Shawntae's dream and what really happened."

"Thank you," Shawntae said.

"That's the problem with dreams," I explained. "People can interpret them however they want. They aren't predictions about anything. And even if they were, what's the point if they're always so symbolic, if you have to decode them all the time, and if they don't make sense until it's too late? For once and for all: No...more...predictions!"

"I'm going to make a believer out of you," Shawntae decided.

"It'll never happen."

She ignored me. "I'm going to tell you my dreams," she went on. "I'm going to tell you as soon as they occur. Then we can see what happens next. That way, we can test my abilities."

"That's a great idea," GumWad said. "Can you call when you have a dream about me? I'd love to get a preview of my life, especially if it involves something like me getting hit by lightning or chased by a tornado."

"Sure thing," Shawntae said, and she and GumWad shook on it.

"And can you let me know which guys like me in a romantic way and which ones only as a friend?" Iliana added.

"If I dream about it, I'll let you know."

"Are you serious?" I asked Shawntae. "You're going to call me every morning and report your dreams?"

"Well, not *every* morning, since I don't remember my dreams sometimes, and not *every* dream, since you're not the only person in my subconscious mind, but if I do dream about you, I'm going to call. You can count on it."

"She doesn't mind calling *me* every morning," Patty said, her napkin pieces as small as confetti now.

Shawntae lightly punched her. "That's because you need a wake-up call or both of us will be late for school." They often carpooled together, and at least once a week, they had to run to class so they wouldn't be late.

Iliana jumped in with her opinion. "I think you should try it, Erica. What can it hurt? We'll finally know whether or not Shawntae's a psychic."

I took a minute to consider the plan. Maybe Iliana was right. Maybe this *was* a good idea. Shawntae wanted to teach me a lesson, but *she* was the one who had a lesson to learn. When her predictions did not come true, I'd get to say "I told you so." And then I'd be free of Shawntae's dreams forever because she could *never* predict the future, just like I could never make a perfect score in math.

"It's a deal," I decided. I held out my hand, and Shawntae shook it, the whole time with one of her big, flashy smiles.

2 SPARE INVITATIONS

Dad took Thursday off so he could go with Mom to her radiation therapy appointment. He said he'd pick me and Carmen up after school, but he was running late because he had to get Jimmy from Grandma's house first. Carmen waited in the sixth grade area, while I waited in the eighth. Nobody had assigned waiting spots for different grades, and there weren't any signs. But somehow everyone knew that the sixth graders were supposed to wait on the hot cement around the flagpole, while the eighth graders waited beneath the shady trees. The seventh graders had their own spot, too. Luckily, Shawntae and Patty's ride hadn't arrived yet, so I waited with them. We barely had time to discuss the afternoon when Derek showed up.

"Hi," he said to me. "I wanted to talk to you after class, but you were still working on the test."

"Yeah," I admitted. "Math isn't my best subject. And the test really takes a long time when you have to show all your work."

"Tell me about it. I barely had time to finish."

"At least you worked through all the problems. I still had five to go."

Patty stomped on a line of ants crawling along the curb. "That means you failed it," she said.

My shoulders drooped. I felt as crushed as the ants beneath her shoe.

"I'm sure you passed," Derek said. "You probably got all the other questions right since you were taking your time."

"Yeah, probably," I said, though I wasn't convinced.

"So why did you want to talk to Erica?" Shawntae asked, all nosy.

Derek reached into his backpack, took out a stack of postcards, and handed me one. It was red with black letters that said, "Let's party!" In the middle was a black-and-white photo of Derek and on the back were the details.

"I'm having a birthday bash," he explained. "My cousin's a DJ, so there's going to be music, dancing, and food." He handed postcards to Patty and Shawntae, too. "You should *all* come. Your *presence* is the only *present* I need. Get it?"

"You are so corny!" Shawntae said, slapping his arm with the postcard.

"Maybe so, but I made you smile, right?"

Patty said, "She smiles for everything. She'd smile at a funeral." She glanced down at the dead ants and smiled at *their* funeral, looking away only when Shawntae elbowed her.

"Thanks for the invitation," I said to Derek. "It sounds like fun."

"Good," Derek said. "Then I'll see you there. And you girls, too," he added, pointing to Patty and Shawntae before walking off to join a group at the basketball court.

"Can you believe that?" Shawntae said to me. "He is totally into you."

I shook my head. "No, he isn't."

"Oh, yes, he is." She mimicked Derek's voice. "Here's an invitation for *you*, Erica. I was waiting for you after class, but since you took so long with the test, I had to hunt you down after school, so I could personally hand you this invitation because the only present I need is your presence. Oh, and by the way, I guess I can spare two invitations for your friends."

"It wasn't like that," I said, secretly believing it was. "He meant to invite all of us from the beginning."

"No," Patty said, "you were the main objective. We were total afterthoughts."

"Are you serious?"

They nodded.

My fingers and toes got all wiggly. Who knew fingers and toes could feel excitement? Finally! I was making "close encounter" progress with a guy from my Boyfriend Wish List. I fumbled in my backpack for my phone and texted Iliana. "OMG. On solid level 3 w/Derek. Details later." After a few seconds, she replied with the happy face icon.

Just then, I spotted Dad's car.

"See y'all tomorrow," I said to my friends.

"Your presence is the only present we need," they teased as my dad pulled up.

I jumped in the backseat with Jimmy because Carmen had grabbed the front since Dad reached the flagpole first. As soon as Jimmy saw the postcard in my hand, he wanted it. "Gimme paper. Gimme paper."

"No, Jimmy. It's important."

"What is it?" Dad asked.

"An invitation to a party."

"Let me see," Carmen said.

"No, it's not for you. It's for me."

Just then, Jimmy grabbed the postcard, and when I tried to snatch it back, it tore right across the picture of Derek's cute face.

"Ha-ha," Carmen said. "That's what you get for being selfish."

"Girls," Dad said with a tone that meant "you better behave."

We didn't want to upset him, so we stayed quiet and listened to *All Things Considered*, this time with a story about elephants and how they communicate across long distances using something called infrasonic rumbles.

"Isn't that amazing?" Dad said. "I wonder what they're saying to each other."

Secretly, I wondered, too. I'm sure the elephants gave boring announcements like "cool watering hole one mile to the east" or "three zebras grazing on our turf," but maybe they sent love letters, too. Maybe they had parties and used their infrasonic rumbles to invite their friends. Maybe they told stories about warrior elephants that trampled dangerous beasts of the night or brainy elephants that devised plans to outsmart poachers. If only I could be an elephant interpreter. Wouldn't that be a cool job?

"I wish humans could talk across the miles, too," I said.

"We *can*." Carmen held up her cell phone and pointed to it. "It's called using a phone." She exaggerated each word as if talking to an infant or a monkey. I hated the way she always made me feel like a dummy.

"Gimme phone. Gimme phone," Jimmy cried, reaching for Carmen's.

She pretended to hand it over, then snatched it away at the last minute. Poor Jimmy bawled.

"Look what you started," I complained. "He was fine a few minutes ago."

He cried even louder. "I wanna phone! I wanna phone!"

"Here," I said, taking mine out. I let him touch a few buttons, and he immediately settled down. Then I showed him pictures of my friends.

"Who that?" he asked, pointing at each one. When we got to a picture of GumWad sticking out a purple tongue, Jimmy laughed.

"He looks funny, right?" I said.

Jimmy laughed even louder. Then he got bored. He was always begging for things and getting bored two minutes later. I handed him his toy puppy, the one Mom bought in the valley. We kept it in the car so Jimmy could have something to play with. Jimmy and I growled like angry dogs and barked like happy ones. He was a pest most of the time, but sometimes I really liked playing with him.

When Jimmy settled down, I held up the torn postcard and said, "Can I go to the party? Lots of my friends will be there."

"Including boys?" Dad asked.

"Yes," I said, blushing because I hated discussing boys with him.

"Chia's totally boy crazy," Carmen squealed. "That's why she can't concentrate in school. If you let her go, you'll be feeding her boy-mania."

"You're just jealous," I said, "because the boys at school don't know you exist."

"They *do*."

"Oh, really? Then why do you sit by yourself during lunch? Why do you walk by yourself to class?"

"Is this true?" Dad asked Carmen. "Are you always by yourself at school?"

"Yes, but not because I'm pathetic or something. I *like* being by myself. The kids at school are total morons. They don't even care about calculating their carbon footprint."

I rolled my eyes. "That's because they wear regular tennis shoes, not carbons."

"Your carbon footprint has nothing to do with shoes," Carmen said. "It's about creating carbon dioxide and destroying the environment, but how would you know? You're a moron just like the boys at school."

"*Por favor*," Dad said. I was about to complain because she did it again, made me feel like a dummy, but Dad added, "Not another word from either of you."

We reached the stop sign a few blocks from our street.

Dad braked and let the car idle. "Let me see that invitation." I gave it to him, and he held the two parts together. "It says, 'Feel free to bring guests.'"

I nodded. "That's why I want Iliana to come. You see? It's not like I'm going to be alone with boys. A lot of girls are going to be there, too."

Dad returned the invitation and edged the car forward. "That's right," he said. "A lot of girls, including your sister."

"Really?" Carmen nearly hopped out of her seat. She hadn't been this excited since the Discovery Channel promised to air a new documentary about black holes.

"I thought we were morons," I told her.

"I was just kidding," Carmen said. "Besides, I'm sure I was going to be invited anyway."

Just then, Jimmy threw his toy puppy on the floor. "Gimme dog. Gimme dog," he said.

"She can't go," I insisted as I handed Jimmy the toy, which he immediately threw down again.

"Gimme! Gimme!" he cried.

My mood ring was brown, which meant I felt feisty, troubled, and mad.

"No!" I snapped, and I meant it. No to Jimmy and no to Carmen.

Dad pulled into our driveway and turned off the car. While we unbuckled our seat belts, he said, "Carmen, help

Jimmy out. Take him inside. I need to talk to Chia for a minute."

"You are in so much trouble," she gleefully whispered as she lifted Jimmy from his seat.

As soon as they entered the house, Dad said, "Listen, I want you to take Carmen to the party. It's not because I don't trust you, but because she never gets invited places. I don't like how she's by herself all the time."

"She's by herself because she's a brat."

"She's not a brat. She's"—he thought for a minute—"different. That's all. And sometimes people who are different have trouble fitting in."

"She doesn't *want* to fit in. You heard her. She thinks everyone is a moron."

Dad sighed. "Just take her to the party. Do it for me, okay? Do it for Mom."

I could not believe he would manipulate me this way, but I knew what would happen if I refused—an ultimatum: either take Carmen or don't go at all.

"Fine," I said, exiting the car and stomping toward the house.

20 MESSAGES

Saturday began with a phone call from Shawntae. At seven o'clock in the morning!

"Not another dream!" I complained. So far, she had called to tell me about dreams with sports cars, hot air balloons, and talking lockers. I was a character in each, but honestly, the only thing remotely connected to my real life was my school locker, and it had *never* uttered a word. Why couldn't Shawntae dream about me with a guy from my Boyfriend Wish List or about me getting a good grade in math or about my mom feeling better?

"In this one," she began, "you're roller-skating on a beach."

"You mean on a sidewalk or pier?"

"No, on the sand."

I wanted to pull out my hair. "Are you serious? Have you tried roller-skating on sand? It's next to impossible."

"But that's the point," Shawntae insisted. "In the dream, it *wasn't* impossible. Not only were you skating, but you were gliding. People were pointing at you and talking about how easy you made it seem. You should really buy a new pair of skates."

"But we don't have a beach in San Antonio," I reminded her.

"I had another dream, too."

I sighed. "And what was this one about?"

"You were with Iliana's brothers."

"Really?" Now this sounded like a dream I could relate to. "What were we doing?"

"Talking."

"That's it?" I couldn't help being disappointed. I was hoping for a close encounter of the fourth kind.

"Yes," Shawntae said. "And their words were very clear. They said, 'You can be two places at once if you ask your twin for help.'"

"What's *that* supposed to mean?"

"My subconscious is showing you how to cover more ground when you look for sponsors."

"But I don't have a twin," I said, all frustrated. Shawn-tae didn't seem to notice.

"Buy those skates," she commanded, "and ask your parents if you have a secret twin somewhere."

I sighed. So far, Shawntae wasn't scoring well on this test of her psychic abilities. The only thing she truly accomplished was waking me up with her phone calls.

"I wish I did have skates," I admitted. "I have to walk around the neighborhood again for my *promesa*."

"That's great. I'll go with you."

At first this seemed like a good idea, but last week, Iliana had joined me. I liked her company, but all she did was talk about boys. Shawntae didn't discuss boys so much, but she loved to give me advice and share her strategies for becoming the first black woman mayor of San Antonio. Plus, she'd probably make up more dreams. No, this was something I had to do by myself.

"That's okay," I said. "I better go alone."

"Are you sure? I have terrific persuasive skills. I'm on the debate team, remember? That means I know how to talk people into things."

"I know. You *are* great. But this is something I have to do on my own."

"Suit yourself," she said. And with that, she hung up.

After breakfast, I headed out, deciding to start on the other side of the neighborhood. The weather had cooled, so lots of people were out mowing grass and washing cars.

"Hello, sir!" I called to a man edging his lawn. He didn't hear me. "Hello!" I shouted.

He looked up and turned off the edger when he saw me. "Can I help you with something?"

As I told him about needing sponsors, a woman came from the side of the house. She had gardening gloves on and her clothes were full of dirt and leaves. "What do we have here?" she asked.

"This girl," the man explained, "is asking for donations." He turned to me. "Sorry, but we can't help today. Maybe another time."

"Now wait a minute," the woman said, pushing him aside. She took off her gloves, stuck them in her pocket, and held out her hand so I could shake it. "My name's Ann. What's yours?"

"Erica."

"Well, Erica, what are you raising money for?"

"Breast cancer research. It's for a service learning project I'm doing at school, but mostly it's for my mom."

"She has cancer?"

I nodded.

"You poor thing," she said. Then she looked at her husband. "Don't just stand there. Go inside and get some money." I wanted to laugh at the way she ordered him around, but I didn't want to ruin this chance at a sponsor. "How old's your mom?" the woman asked as we waited.

"Forty."

"That's young, which means she's strong. I bet she's going to be just fine."

"I hope so," I said.

Her husband returned and handed me thirty dollars. I gave him the clipboard, and he filled out the sponsor information.

"Can I get back to the yard?" he asked his wife, the way kids ask parents for permission to play.

She nodded, so he turned on the edger. As soon as he got back to work, Ann put on her gardening gloves and headed to the side of the house again. I tried to say good-bye, but I don't think they could hear me over the loud machine, so I moved on to the next house.

I really wanted to get more sponsors, but almost everyone waved me away. A lot of them said "not now" or "come another time." I knew they never wanted to see me again, that they were trying to get rid of me, but I wrote their addresses on a list called "Come Back Later," vowing that I

would return in a few days. After all, the 5K was one month away! So I kept walking, the day getting hotter and hotter, my nose feeling sunburned, sweat trickling into my eyes, and blisters forming on my feet. Once in a while, someone donated, but at this rate, it would take a year to get five hundred names. I didn't have a year! *Mom* didn't have a year! I glanced at my mood ring—amber again, a deeper shade, which meant I had moved from feeling unsettled to feeling despair. No wonder my shoulders drooped.

I noticed that I was near Patty's house, so I decided to stop for a break. She wasn't the best cure for despair, but maybe she could help me take my mind off my own problems for a while.

When I knocked on her door, her grandfather answered. He had moved into her house after his wife died two years ago. Patty was real close to her grandparents, so when her grandmother died, she felt awful. We Robins bought and signed a card for her, and then we got together and baked cookies. We must have given Patty four dozen. Normally, she loved cookies, so we thought they'd cheer her up, but when she bit into the first one, she didn't smile. She didn't frown, either. She had no expression at all. And when I watched her eat that cookie, I imagined it was as bland as pasta with no sauce or spices. We wanted to help Patty, but when you're sad, nothing, not even cookies, can make you feel better.

Is that how I would feel if Mom died? I hated to think about it, but I had to be prepared. What if radiation therapy didn't work? What if Mom got sicker and sicker till she couldn't take it anymore? Would I ever get over the sadness? A few weeks after her grandmother died, Patty returned to her old self, but I don't think I could ever get back to normal if something awful happened to Mom. My mood ring would probably stay black for months, maybe even years.

"Are you okay?" Patty's grandpa asked. "You look like you've seen a big, hairy watermelon."

I looked up at him. "I've never seen a *hairy* watermelon before." Then I tried to imagine a watermelon with hair. What a ridiculous image! I couldn't help laughing, and it was such a relief to smile after spending the whole morning with a frown.

"Grandpa!" I heard Patty's voice behind him. "Quit teasing her." He moved aside and Patty waved me in. "I'm so glad you're here," she said, leading me to the kitchen, where a bunch of papers had taken over the table. "Can you believe my English teacher called and told my parents I hadn't done a single thing this week?"

"You haven't," I said, remembering how Patty had complained about her homework.

"Sure, but did she have to call?"

"It's her job."

"So now I have a whole bunch of homework," Patty went on, "and if I don't finish, I'm going to be grounded."

"I'm going to be in trouble, too. I can barely keep up. Who knew eighth grade was going to be so hard?"

She nodded.

"How long will you be grounded if you don't catch up?" I asked, hoping she wouldn't be grounded during Derek's party.

"For forever," her grandpa said from the other room.

Patty just rolled her eyes. In a quieter voice, she said, "I have a serious case of writer's block. You have to help me. You *never* have writer's block."

"I don't?"

"No. Everybody knows you're the one to turn to when we can't think of ideas."

"Really?"

"Yes, really. So will you help?"

"Of course," I said, pointing at my T-shirt. It had two stick figures. One had a circle for a head, but no body. The other stick figure was complete. It held a straight line in one hand, and its speech bubble said, "I've got your back."

Patty studied it a minute. Then she laughed. "Oh, I get it. This one guy's holding the line that would make up the other guy's back."

I shrugged and nodded at the same time. Except for GumWad, my friends always took a while before getting my T-shirt jokes.

"So what's your homework?" I asked.

"I have to write similes, and I can't think of a single one."

I thought a moment. "How about as droopy as a thirsty sunflower or as panicked as a cat-chased mouse."

She wrote them down, and together we thought of a few others. Then she had to pick a popular story and write it from a different point of view.

"I don't even know what that means," Patty complained.

"It means to forget the main character and pretend the story belongs to someone else."

"So instead of Cinderella," she said, "pretend the story is about the fairy godmother?"

"Sure. You could do that, but how about pretending the story is about the glass slipper?"

"But that's an object, which means it doesn't have a brain. How can something without a brain tell a story?"

"That's the fun part," I said. "What's the slipper thinking as it dances around the ballroom? As it gets left behind when Cinderella runs off? And as the stepsisters stick their fat, smelly feet in it?"

She thought about it. "I guess I could write a story about

that." She sounded doubtful, but an intense brainstorming session convinced her that she could write the story.

Just then, her grandfather walked in. "All done?"

"Almost," Patty said. "At least I know what to do now, thanks to Erica."

"Sounds like you owe her one," her grandfather said.

"That's okay," I said. "I had fun helping with the homework." I stood, ready to leave.

"And where are you going?" Patty's grandfather asked.

"I need to walk around the neighborhood. I'm raising money for cancer research." I grabbed my clipboard. "Would you like to donate?"

Patty's grandpa reached into his pocket and pulled out a five. "I guess I should," he said, "since you helped my Patty with her homework."

"Thank you so much," I said, taking the money and handing him the form.

As he filled it out, he said to Patty, "You should return the favor and go with Erica."

"You want me to knock on a bunch of weird people's doors? Can't I pay her back by buying her lunch or something?"

"I don't need help," I said. "I can do this on my own."

Her grandfather thought a minute. "Make sure you knock on that red door two houses over."

"I already did."

"So Mrs. Cavazos signed your form?"

"No. She didn't even answer the door."

Patty's grandpa put his hands on his hips. "Well, I'll be." Then he said, "Just a minute." He took out his cell phone and dialed a number. "Hello?" I heard him say. "How are you doing, Mrs. Cavazos?" A woman spoke on the other end of the line but I couldn't understand her. "And how's that pipe I fixed last month?" He listened a bit. "I'm so glad to hear it isn't giving you any more trouble and that I was able to save you from hiring an expensive plumber." While he listened, he winked at me. "Actually, I do need a favor," he said to the phone. "I'm sending Patty over with a friend. She's raising money for a fund-raising event, and she's been going around the neighborhood looking for sponsors. I told her how nice you are and that you'd really like to donate." I don't know what the woman said, but when Patty's grandpa got off the phone, he said, "Mrs. Cavazos is going to help, so you two go over right now before she changes her mind. And, Patty, go to Johnny's, too. Tell him he can borrow my lawn mower any time, and tell Sally that I'll feed her dog when she goes out of town next week." He paused, looking up at the ceiling. "Oh, yeah, tell Jamal he can donate the ten dollars he owes me. Got all that?"

"Johnny, Sally, Jamal," Patty repeated, counting them off on her fingers. "Got it."

I didn't really want her help, didn't want her to see me get doors slammed in my face. That was the *last* thing I wanted my friends to talk about. They had already gossiped about my troubles last week when I wasn't *supposed* to have any trouble. And I worried that my *promesa* counted only if I did it on my own. But Patty's grandpa was forcing her to help me.

"Let's kill two birds with one stone," I suggested to Patty. "Grab a trash bag and we'll pick up garbage along the way."

"What a sensible girl," her grandpa said, all impressed. Patty just rolled her eyes, but she grabbed the trash bag anyway.

As we walked to the house with the red door, Patty said, "Before my grandpa moved in, I didn't know any of these people. But he went and made friends with everyone, which means they're always in our business. It's such a pain." The red door was open, so instead of knocking or ringing the doorbell, Patty called through the screen. "Mrs. Cavazos? Are you in there?"

A middle-aged woman approached. She said, "Patty, it's nice to see you."

"Nice to see you, too," Patty replied. "My grandpa's glad

to hear the plumbing's okay. Those leaky pipes can sure mess up your floor." Patty paused a minute before remembering why we were really here. "This is my friend Erica."

"*Mucho gusto,*" Mrs. Cavazos said.

"*Mucho gusto,*" I replied.

"Her mom has cancer," Patty said, "so she needs money for a cancer race next month. My grandpa said you'd help."

I couldn't believe how blunt Patty was, but Mrs. Cavazos didn't seem to mind. She said, "*La pobrecita.* What kind of cancer does your mother have?"

"Breast cancer," I said, and since she had a small statue of La Virgen de Guadalupe on her porch, I added, "I made a *promesa* at that shrine in the valley, so I have to get five hundred names."

Mrs. Cavazos nodded. I could tell she knew exactly what a *promesa* was. She had probably made one herself. She told us to wait a minute, and then she returned with a check for twenty-five dollars. As she filled out the sponsor form, she said, "Mrs. Martínez's car broke down last week. When you get to her house, tell her to call if she needs a ride to the grocery store. I'm going in a couple of hours."

Patty nodded, and when we got back to the street, she said, "See what I mean? Everybody knows what's going on with everybody else. No privacy at all."

How awful, I thought. After all, I hated my friends

talking about me even when they were just reporting what happened over the weekend. Iliana wasted no time telling the Robins about my mom's cancer or about my first attempt to get sponsors, and GumWad told our whole class about Sonic. Never mind Shawntae, who blabbed about every dream with me in the starring role.

As we walked, Patty found some bottle caps at the curb and a crushed aluminum can. When I pointed at a burned-out match, she shook her head.

"Are you being selective about the trash you collect?" I asked.

"Yep."

Who knew what that girl was up to?

We soon reached Mrs. Martínez's house and mentioned the grocery store. *"Gracias, gracias,"* she said, all grateful. For a minute, I thought *we* were giving her a ride. When Mrs. Martínez saw that her friend had already given money, she matched the donation.

When we got to Johnny's house, Patty said, "Your yard looks great. My grandpa said you could borrow his mower whenever you want."

When we got to Sally's house, she said, "So are you looking forward to your trip next week? My grandpa said not to worry about the dog. It's no trouble for him to come fill his bowl."

And when we got to Jamal's, she said, "My grandpa's in no hurry to get back his ten dollars, but if you have it on you, he said you could give it to my friend. She's raising money for cancer research." As we walked away, she said, "I'm really getting the hang of this." She sounded excited.

I didn't like the way she blabbed my whole story to everyone, but how could I complain when her blunt attitude resulted in sponsors and when Patty was having fun? It seemed as if everyone donated, and like Mrs. Cavazos, they gave us messages, too. We must have passed along twenty.

"Call us the pony express," Patty joked.

"Or the ponyless express," I said.

She giggled at that. "Ponyless but not penniless," she added, glancing at my manila envelope. Seeing Patty in a good mood was putting *me* in a good mood, too. Even my mood ring sensed it and turned to a sapphire blue.

One message led to another. A guy named Luke said he had extra tomatoes from his garden. Mrs. Johnson said she would donate them to the soup kitchen. Hector said he could drop them off when he picked up his daughter, who volunteered there and who agreed to babysit for a lady named Lindsay, who in turn said she had coupons for free car washes at the gas station and was giving them away on a "first come, first served" basis.

"Isn't it crazy?" Patty said about all the messages. "My grandpa doesn't mind, but it drives me nuts."

"Maybe," I said. "But look at us. You found some cool trash, and I got twenty-five new sponsors. This has been my most productive day yet!"

3 SIDE EFFECTS

After spending time with Patty, I made my way home. I felt exhausted but excited, too. Finally, I was having success with my *promesa*.

As I turned onto my street, I heard the familiar roar of a lawn mower. Mr. Landon, our neighbor, was working on his yard. I could tell he had just started because most of the grass was still long. When I got to my front yard, I waved at him, and then Dad stepped out.

"Hi, Dad," I said, eager to show him the names I had collected.

"In a minute," he answered. He seemed angry, and I wondered if Jimmy was acting up. Maybe I should have stayed home. With Mom ill, Jimmy was hard to control, and Carmen liked to pick on him, making things worse.

But Dad wasn't angry at the family. He was angry with Mr. Landon because he went straight to him and said, "Can you mow another time? My wife can't rest with all that noise."

Mr. Landon shrugged. "Sorry. Got to do it now."

"But she needs her sleep," Dad said.

"If it's too loud, tell her to wear earplugs. Why's she turning in so early anyhow? It's only four o'clock. Who goes to bed at four o'clock?"

"Do you want to know who goes to bed at four o'clock?" Dad said, his voice getting loud. "You really want to know? People who are sick, you hear? People who have cancer."

I could tell Mr. Landon felt bad because he got apologetic. "I'm sorry to hear that Lisa's sick. Really, I am. She's always been a kind lady."

Dad stood there a minute, took a deep breath. "Thanks," he said, calmer. "Thanks for understanding and for agreeing to do your yard another day."

"Now wait a minute," Mr. Landon quickly said. "I said I'm sorry, and I meant it, but I have to mow today. I work all week, so it's the only time I have. I'll do it quick, though, I promise."

For a minute, Dad looked like someone who had just lost a championship game. Then he looked like someone

who felt cheated by the referee. "How's this for a promise?" he said. "Next time you need something, don't bother to ask because I *promise* not to help."

"Oh, come on now, don't be that way," Mr. Landon said. "Don't be making a mountain out of a molehill."

Dad ignored him and stomped toward the house. He didn't even remember that I was standing right there. Somehow the anger had blinded him.

But Mr. Landon saw me and said, "Tell your folks I'll just be an hour, if that. Sorry about the noise, but I have to do my yard. Hope you understand."

"It's okay," I said, feeling embarrassed because Dad wanted quiet rules for the whole neighborhood now.

I went inside and found Jimmy on the floor with his toy cars, while Mom lay on her recliner all bundled up. Her lips looked chapped and her skin paler than usual because she hadn't been enjoying the sun. She was watching TV, but her eyes were nearly closed. When her head fell forward, she jolted, surprised. I could tell she was fighting to stay awake awhile longer.

"I got some more names for the cancer race." I held up the clipboard and my manila envelope.

"That's wonderful," Mom said.

I sat on the couch, got comfortable. "Are you doing okay?" What was I thinking? I just asked the dumbest

question in the world. Of course Mom wasn't doing okay. She was sick.

She answered anyway. "I'm fine."

Dad must have heard because he stepped in. I could tell he was still mad. "You are *not* fine."

"Maybe not," Mom said, "but why worry if I don't have to?"

"What do you mean?" I asked, sensing that something had happened.

Mom sighed. "Last night," she began, "my arm started to feel funny. It didn't hurt, but it felt tight, like something inside was pushing against my skin. And when I woke up this morning, it looked like this."

She pulled down the blanket and showed me.

"Fat arm! Fat arm!" Jimmy laughed as he pointed at Mom. Her right arm was totally bloated. I could see her skin stretched tight like a spandex gym suit. She had no wrist, so her arm looked like a preschool drawing, a puffy rectangle with five sticks for the fingers. "Fat arm! Fat arm!" Jimmy laughed again.

"One more time," Dad said through clenched teeth, "and I'll spank you."

He gave Jimmy the harshest stare-down, and Jimmy's eyes started to water. I couldn't blame him for wanting to cry. Dad *never* got this angry.

"What's the matter with you?" Mom said to him. "Jimmy's just making an observation."

"He's making *fun* of you."

"But he's only two," Mom said. "He doesn't know what he's saying."

Jimmy started to sob. I picked him up, and he wrapped his arms around me, putting all his strength into the hug.

"You're upsetting him," I scolded. Now *I* was angry, and I sounded like the parent instead of the kid.

"We're sorry, *mijo*," Mom said to Jimmy. He hid his face in my shoulder, but little by little, he calmed down. "Besides," Mom added, "I *do* have a fat arm." She lifted it and studied it as if it were a separate part of her body. "It looks like an elephant leg. And it's got these hard cable things under the skin. Come touch it."

"Lisa," Dad warned.

"It's *my* arm," she snapped back. "I can't hide it or pretend it's normal. Maybe I'm crazy, but I think the way the body reacts is fascinating, too."

Dad stared at her. Then he stared at her arm. He looked...afraid.

"Don't fight," I pleaded.

"We're not fighting," Mom assured me. "Sometimes your dad takes things too seriously."

"And sometimes your mother doesn't take things seri-

ously enough," Dad answered. "Like the neighbor. If he weren't mowing the lawn, you'd be able to rest, and your arm would feel better. I'm sure of it."

"He has every right to mow his lawn," Mom said. "I told you to leave him alone, but you talked to him anyway. Now you're all short-tempered."

Dad shook his head, too tired to argue. After a few seconds, he stepped out. When he left, Mom seemed sad. I could tell she wanted to fight the sadness just like she had tried to fight sleep a minute ago.

"Don't worry," she said. "These are tough times, and we're all a little anxious."

That part was definitely true. Lately, my mood ring's favorite color had been black, for "100 percent stressed out."

"Come touch my arm," Mom suggested again.

Jimmy and I poked it. There *were* hard cables under the skin but the areas between were squishy.

"Does this mean the cancer spread to your arm?" I asked, trying not to sound afraid but unable to keep my voice from trembling.

"No," Carmen said, walking in with the laptop. She must have been in the other room doing research. She set the computer on the coffee table and studied the screen. "This is a side effect from the treatment. It's called lymphedema. It happened because Mom's lymph nodes were

damaged, and one of the things they do is drain tissue fluid. It's like she has a clog in her armpit, so the fluid is all backed up."

"That's what it feels like," Mom said. "It's very uncomfortable. I already called the doctor, and he wants to see me tomorrow. He said I'll have to go to physical therapy again."

"They're going to massage you and put wraps on you," Carmen said. "Look." She showed us pictures of swollen arms and legs being wrapped. Most of them were a lot bigger than Mom's. "That's how they get the fluid to move along. But it'll take several days for the swelling to go down. If you don't do anything, your arm will just get fatter and fatter."

"I sure hope this is the last side effect," Mom said. "I'm already dealing with nausea and fatigue. The arm isn't so bad as long as something else doesn't happen. I want to do things again. I feel like I can't do *anything* anymore."

So why *was* she having these side effects? It made no sense, especially after I'd been working so hard on my *promesa*. Was it because I wasn't working fast enough? But what else could I do? I had gone to lots of doors, many of them twice. I had asked all my friends and called my aunts and uncles. Why did I promise five hundred names when I didn't even know five hundred people?

"Since I can't lift my arm," Mom continued, "I won't be able to go to radiation treatment for a while."

"Does that mean the cancer's going to spread?" I sounded more panicky than before.

"I don't think so," Mom said, though I could tell she wasn't exactly sure.

Carmen scrolled down the website and started to read. "It says that lymphedema can happen after surgery and that it occurs on the same side as the mastectomy. That's exactly what's happening to you." Mom nodded. "You'll have to wear compression bandages to 'assist with lymphatic flow.' How cool is that?" She was getting more and more excited, while I was getting more and more butterflies in my stomach. "Can I go to therapy with you?" Carmen asked. "Maybe they'll let me help. Maybe they'll teach me how to bandage the arm. That way, I can take care of you at home."

Mom nodded. "You should be a doctor," she told Carmen, and my sister smiled as if she had just received the biggest compliment. That's when I stopped listening to all her medical facts. After all, no one ever told *me* I could be a doctor. But why would they? You had to be smart for something like that, and I couldn't even come up with a *promesa* that was good enough to help Mom.

2,051 PAGES

Monday morning, my hair flipped up in every direction. That's what I got for going to bed right after taking a shower. I didn't want to go to school looking so awful, so I tried leave-in conditioner, the straightening iron, and even wetting my hair and blow-drying it, section by section, just like a professional stylist. But my hair was as uncooperative as Jimmy when he needed to go in his car seat. So I grabbed a rubber band, made a ponytail, and slipped on a T-shirt that said "Bad hare day" over a picture of bunnies in striped prison uniforms.

Then I went to school, excited about seeing Derek in math. He was still at the top of my Boyfriend Wish List, but before I had a chance to talk to him, Mr. Leyva called me to his desk. School hadn't officially started, so the room was

mostly empty. He said, "I'm glad you came early, so we could talk about your test."

My whole body slumped. "I failed, didn't I?"

"Now, now," he said, as if calming a baby. "If you knew you were struggling, why didn't you ask your sister for help? Sometimes students learn better from their peers, and you've got the best math student right there in your house. I'm sure she'd be happy to tutor you."

I looked up at him, wishing my stare could zap him like a stun gun.

He must have seen how angry I was because he said, "It's just an idea."

"A bad idea," I grumbled.

Mr. Leyva studied me a moment, to figure me out, I guess. After a while, he said, "Well, you didn't complete the test, so at this point, you haven't technically failed."

He showed me my paper. Some of the answers were wrong, but others were correct. Mr. Leyva explained how I was "on the bubble," and how, if I got the remaining questions right, I could pass. "Go to the library," he said, "and complete the test. Take the entire hour if necessary and remember to show all your work."

I felt so grateful for the chance to complete the missing questions. Maybe a bad hair day didn't have to mean a bad math day, too. I wanted to salute Mr. Leyva and say, "Sir,

yes, sir." After all, I felt like a soldier going to war against math. Maybe this time, I'd be victorious.

I gladly took the test and headed to the library, getting there just as the tardy bell rang. Since classes were scheduled for visits, the librarian let me use her office. "Make yourself comfortable," she said.

So I did. I pushed aside her papers to clear a spot. Then I readjusted the height and the armrests of her chair, took a pencil from a cup on her desk, and turned up her radio. To loosen up, I popped my knuckles and did a few neck stretches. Time for battle, I told myself. Math is your foe, but it can be conquered.

The first problem went like this: Mary went to the store to buy a dress. The price of the dress is $40, but a sign announces that the store is offering a 20 percent discount. How much will Mary pay?

How was I supposed to know the answer? This was the most ridiculous problem on the planet. First, what store was this? Because stores like Macy's had sales all the time with big red signs that said "20% off." But it was never that simple since the small print always began with "discount does not apply to..." How could I know if the discount applied to Mary's dress when the problem didn't list the exceptions? Second, *when* was Mary buying the dress and what kind of dress was it? What if the sale was happening

right now, in the fall? What if the dress was a sundress? Would Mary really buy something she couldn't wear for the next six months? Next, what condition was the dress in? Sometimes the clothes on sale were stained or missing a button, which meant Mary could argue for a bigger discount. That's what Mom did. She *always* got a few dollars taken off. Finally, how much money did Mary have? Did her parents expect her to pay for the whole thing or did they plan to pitch in? Did Mary even have parents, or was she an adult with a job?

I couldn't stop fretting over the question. How could the word problem ignore such important details? This *had* to be a trick. I tapped the pencil on the desk, wondering what to do. "Need more information," I wrote beside the word problem. Then I saw in bold print, "Show all your work." Suddenly, I understood. Mr. Leyva wanted me to explain what kind of information I needed. I grabbed a sheet of notebook paper since there wasn't enough room to explain on the test. I wrote down everything that might affect the price of the dress—the store, the small print on the ad, the style, the condition, the season, and even Mary's personal situation.

The remaining questions were similar, so I wrote "Need more information" again and again, explaining why each time. My hand got so stiff from all that writing, but

passing the test was worth the pain. After forty minutes, I was done.

I put the librarian's supplies back in order and headed to the circulation desk to say thanks, but then I spotted Carmen. I didn't want her to know about my math test, and I didn't want to talk to her, especially in front of a cute guy like Joe Leal, who was checking out the display of graphic novels. Sure, everyone knew Carmen and I were sisters, that she was a genius while I was *not* a genius. But if they didn't see us together, maybe they'd forget. So I hid behind the office door, and while I waited for a moment to escape, I spied.

As usual, Carmen had on her prep school uniform with its plaid skirt, knee-high socks, and blazer, and, as usual, she carried a stack of books that was as tall as Jimmy. The books were about to topple over, so as she walked, she swayed like a circus clown on a tightrope. Carmen approached a table, but the students there laughed and waved her away. She approached another table, but one of the girls threw a purse on the last empty chair and said, "We're saving this." When she approached a third table, a guy shook his head as if to say, "Don't even try it." So Carmen lugged her books to the counter. She wasn't far from me, but luckily, she faced the other way. I should have said hello because part of me felt sorry for her, but another part felt

like telling her, "That's what you get for being Little Miss Factoid all the time and making me feel like a dummy." Okay, so maybe I *was* a dummy because I needed extra time on my math test, but at least I had friends.

Carmen went directly to the last page of each book and wrote something on a piece of paper. She had just finished going through the stack when her teacher approached.

"What you got there?" she asked Carmen, who answered by reading out titles: *When a Parent Has Cancer*; *Is Pollution Making Us Sick?*; *Breast Cancer: What Every Teen Girl Should Know*; *The Disease Sourcebook*; *Cancer Treatments and Their Side Effects*; and *The Complete Medical Guide for Teens.*

"That's a lot of reading," the teacher said.

Carmen shrugged it off. Then she read out the numbers she'd written down. "It's 54 plus 212 plus 340 plus 298 plus 424 plus 723 for a total of 2,051 pages. If I get to keep these books for two weeks, that's 146.5 pages a day minus the pictures and glossaries and tables of contents and indexes." She glanced at the book spines again. "These books are okay," she said, "but they're written for teens. This"—she held up the thinnest book—"has pictures. Not photographs of tumors or blood cells, but illustrations like the kind in a kid book. What do the doctors read? That's what I want to know because I want to be a doctor when I grow up."

"You'll have to visit a university or hospital library for doctor books," the teacher said. "They're very technical."

"I know, but I don't mind reading technical stuff if it gives me the real answers."

"I don't think anyone has the real answer for cancer. But I'm sure the medical books are more detailed than these."

"That's what I want," Carmen said, "details."

The teacher patted her shoulder. "Why don't you start simple, okay, sweetie?"

Carmen nodded, then took the books to the checkout line. While she was busy with the librarian, I slipped out without letting her know I'd been there.

Later at home, Mom showed us her compression dressings. She was wrapped from armpit to hand. Carmen, Jimmy, and I couldn't help touching the bandages.

"You look like a mummy," I said.

She laughed. "Mummy, Mommy, not much difference."

"You should have taken me with you," Carmen said. "I really wanted to learn."

"You learn more in school, *mija*."

"No, I don't. I have to draw pictures." She reached in her backpack and pulled out pages of lines looping over themselves, forming odd shapes that she had colored in. "I

finish my work before everyone else, so this is what I do. I try reading, but..."

"But what?" Mom wanted to know.

Carmen glanced at me. She probably didn't want to admit how nerdy she was. "Nothing," she said.

"She doesn't read because she's too embarrassed," I guessed aloud. "She doesn't have any friends."

"I have friends," Carmen said, all offended.

"Name one."

She crossed her arms. "No, because you don't know them."

"I don't know them because they don't exist."

She stared at me. If her eyes were boxing gloves, I'd be knocked out by now. That's how angry she looked.

"That's enough," Mom said. "Carmen, go outside and water the plants for me. I'm not supposed to get my wraps wet. And Chia, get the towels from the dryer and fold them."

"You're giving us chores?" Carmen whined.

"About time you helped out," I said as I headed to the laundry room.

After I folded towels, I noticed that the furniture in the living room needed dusting, and the Chia Pets needed watering, and Jimmy's toys needed to be put away. When Dad came home, I helped him with dinner, *migas* again,

even though it was my night to clean the kitchen. Then I bathed Jimmy and read him a bedtime story so he could go to sleep. Finally, at about eight thirty, I had time for homework. By then, my feet throbbed and my back ached as if I'd been standing all day. I had trouble concentrating, not because I felt distracted but because I had a headache, probably from stress. I shouldn't be doing homework this late. I should be watching TV or chatting with my friends on Skype. I should be sleeping!

My cell phone rang. Shawntae. When I answered, she was all panicky.

"Erica, you have to help me. I'm in so much trouble."

My mind raced. Were her parents in an accident? Did her house burn down? Did she humiliate herself in front of one of the guys on our Boyfriend Wish List?

"What happened?" I asked, fearing the worst.

"I ran out of ink!" she cried.

I sighed, and even though she couldn't see me, I rolled my eyes. That girl had more drama than a reality show.

"Can you help me, *pleeeaase*?"

"Sure," I said. "What do you need?"

"I'm forwarding a file for my social studies class. Can you make fifty copies? It's an invitation to a presentation about the election. I'll buy you a new ink cartridge if you do this giant favor."

"Of course, I'll do it. No problem."

"I *knew* I could count on you," she said.

A few minutes later, she e-mailed the file. I made sure my printer had enough paper and asked it to print. Maybe now I could do my own homework and finally get some sleep. But when I pulled Shawntae's invitations from the printer, I noticed that they weren't flyers, but cards, which meant they had to be folded. More work! But what could I do? I already told Shawntae I'd take them to school tomorrow.

So I started folding, trying my best to get the lines straight because if Shawntae were doing this, *she'd* get them straight. She was a perfectionist. Never a hair out of place or a shoe that didn't exactly match her outfit.

When I was about halfway through, Carmen walked in. "Still doing homework?" she said as if I were too dumb to get it done in time. I ignored her, kept on folding, and realized that I was getting tired. There was no way I'd be able to concentrate on my own assignments.

Carmen got into bed. After a minute, she sat up. "Do you think Mom's going to be okay?" she asked.

I shrugged. "I don't know."

"But do you think—"

"I don't know," I said, impatient. I had so much on my mind and didn't want to deal with Carmen right now.

"But can't you guess?"

"No, because I can't see the future. Do you want me to lie? Do you want me to pretend everything's going to be fine?"

"Never mind," she said, turning away and hiding under the covers. A moment later, I heard, "One, two...three..."

"What are you counting now?" I wanted to know.

"The fan's on," she said. I glanced at our little fan, the one that turned back and forth. Every time it pivoted, it made a little sound. It made that sound twenty-three times before I finished folding cards. My homework would have to wait. If I woke up extra early, maybe I'd have time to do it then.

532 DOLLARS

The next morning, Mr. Leyva returned my test. I failed even after the second chance. I just wanted to hide. From everyone. I let my hair fall over my face as I stooped over my backpack to put away my test. I didn't notice Derek until he knocked on my desk and said, "That's funny."

How could he joke about my low grade?

"Your T-shirt," he explained, probably noticing that I had no idea what he was talking about.

I glanced at it. Today I wore a shirt with a dog dressed as a cowboy walking into a saloon and saying, "Who shot my paw?" His arm was bandaged. I guess it reminded me of my mom's lymphedema, but I couldn't explain that to Derek. He'd think I was weird for having a mother with a bloated arm.

"Was that your test?" he asked, staring at my backpack.

"Yeah," I sighed. "My grade's lower than the aquifer level."

He frowned. Each night the weatherman told us about the aquifer, our underground water supply. San Antonio was in the middle of a drought, so we had water restrictions.

"Cheer up," Derek said. "It's just one test. Everybody has a bad day. I bet you'll ace the next one."

Easy for him to say. He didn't live with a genius sister. But I acted as if it didn't bother me because I liked Derek and no guy wants to be with a girl who feels sorry for herself.

Who was I kidding? I *did* feel sorry for myself. At least I had social studies next, my favorite class. On my way there, I ran into Shawntae.

"Do you have the invitations?" she asked, her hands ready to take them.

"Sure," I said, reaching into my backpack. I pulled them out and gave them to her.

"I can't believe you folded them," she said, surprised but happy, too. "That was so nice of you. You saved me a lot of time."

"You didn't want me to fold them?" I asked.

"You didn't *have* to, but I'm glad you did. Now I don't have to skip lunch. Thanks a million!" With that, she took off, her zebra-striped pumps clacking on the floor.

I replayed our conversation last night. She *didn't* ask me to fold. I did all that work for nothing!

When I stepped into my social studies class, I mumbled hello as I took a seat by my friends. Patty didn't seem to notice my gloomy mood, but GumWad sent a note. "Are you okay?" it said.

I wrote, "I guess."

He looked at it and frowned. "Are you okay?" he wrote again. "Circle yes or no."

I circled no.

"What's wrong?" he wrote back.

"I don't want to talk about it."

He glanced at my note, and then he took out a clean sheet of paper and started to draw. After a while, he sent me a picture of a cat hanging from a limb, two hands reaching up to save it, and he wrote, "Remember the card I gave you when your mom had her operation?"

So that's why it looked familiar. But why was he sending me a picture of a card he gave to my mom? My life was hard enough without GumWad confusing me with mysterious riddles. Luckily, Patty got tired of passing the notes

between us. She said, "Will you two stop writing notes to each other and just talk when class ends?"

And then, an eternity later, class ended.

"See you guys during lunch," Patty said as she grabbed her things to leave.

"Wait for me," I said, but GumWad interrupted.

"Hold on a second," he told me.

Soon everyone was gone, including Mrs. Gardner, who had stepped into her storage closet while the class emptied out, and since she had a conference period next, the classroom stayed empty.

"Are you okay?" GumWad asked. "You were all fidgety during class. Do you have to go to the restroom? Why didn't you ask Mrs. Gardner? She's real nice about the hall pass."

"No," I said. "I don't have to go to the restroom. I'm stressed!" I held out my mood ring to prove it.

"Why?"

"You really want to know?"

He nodded.

So I told him, my words as fast as a caged hamster sprinting in its little wheel. In two or three minutes, I blabbed the whole story about math, my mom's fatigue and fat arm, my dad's quiet rules, my sister's nonstop counting and medical facts and how everyone bragged about her

extremely intelligent brain, and my little brother, who was starting to think that *I* was his parent. I told him about the chores I had to do and how I was such a long way from getting five hundred names. "It's too much," I said, "and there's no one I can talk to at home. And all Iliana talks about are boys and Shawntae about running for mayor. And Patty's an awful listener because she always complains."

"You can talk to me," GumWad offered.

He was the *last* person I wanted to speak to, especially with all that gum-smacking. But how could I say that without hurting his feelings? Plus, I didn't want him to feel sorry for me. I hated when people felt sorry for me. So I said, "Maybe, but it's easier to talk to girls."

GumWad sat there and thought quietly for a few minutes. He didn't even chew the gum that was in his mouth. Finally, he said, "Don't worry. I'll figure something out. I promise."

Just then, Mrs. Gardner came out from her storage closet. "What are you still doing here? You better hurry to your next class."

So we left, GumWad running through the hall so he wouldn't be late and me dragging my feet. I walked in a daze, as unaware of my surroundings as Jimmy when he got a new toy.

During third period, Iliana sent a text, "Where were

U?" because I didn't stop by her locker as usual. Between classes, I bumped into a guy, not realizing it was Chad until five seconds too late, but then not caring about the brief close encounter. And when I heard Shawntae's pumps clicking behind me, I didn't turn till she tapped my shoulder. She said, "Remind me to tell you about last night's dream," before rushing to her next class. Usually, I had some sassy comment about her silly dreams, but I couldn't think of one sassy thing to say.

I felt totally lost. I couldn't stop worrying about math. I really thought I did well on the test. I had put so much effort into those questions. I showed all my work, every detail. So where did I go wrong? How could I have failed? It just didn't make sense. Unless, of course, I was dumb. That *had* to be it. Whatever math intelligence was supposed to go into my brain went into Carmen's instead. That's why she was the genius, while I was the moron.

Honestly, I was too confused to tell the difference between a letter of the alphabet and a number. I took my science book to English, forgot my locker combination, and walked into the bathroom instead of my fourth-period class. The only thing I knew for sure was that I had issues. Lots of issues. No wonder my mood ring kept changing! It went from black for tense to pink for uncertain to white for frustrated. I kept waiting to see blue, the color for calmness

and peace, but no such luck. With all the craziness in my life, I couldn't see blue if I looked at the sky.

When lunchtime arrived, Iliana said, "Where have you been?" as soon as I got to the table.

"Nowhere. Hiding. Bad day."

"Why?"

"I don't want to talk about it."

Her face was full of worry, but she didn't press the issue. Patty said, "What day *isn't* bad?" and Shawntae said, "Here's something to cheer you up."

"Another dream?" I guessed.

"This one's about your mom," she said.

I leaned forward. "Good news?"

"Yes."

"Will she be cured?" Iliana asked.

"I don't know, but she *is* going to win the lottery. Pretty cool, right?"

Iliana and Patty cheered, but I felt a little disappointed. Winning money *was* cool but only if it could buy a cure for Mom.

"In my dream," Shawntae went on, "your mom's at a convenience store, all decorated with pink streamers, like when my aunt had a shower for her baby girl."

"That's weird," I commented.

"I know, right?" She paused before returning to the dream. "So your mom gives the cashier a Snickers bar."

"Wait a minute," I said. "She never eats chocolate."

"Well, she should. Apparently, chocolate brings her good luck because when the cashier scanned it, confetti fell from the sky and a big band started playing."

"At the convenience store?" Patty asked, all skeptical.

"Of course. That's where the dream took place."

"Since when do convenience stores have live music?"

"Since *I* started having my dreams," Shawntae said. "Can I continue now?"

Patty nodded.

"Next thing you know, the cash register drawer shot out and a number flashed on its screen. The anchorman from Channel Five said, 'Congratulations, Mrs. Montenegro! You are the winner of five hundred thirty-two dollars!' He handed her a check while a dozen photographers took her picture."

"Wait a minute," Patty said again. "When did the news guy and photographers come in?"

"Who knows?" Shawntae answered, getting impatient. "It's a dream. They just appeared. Let me finish, okay?"

Iliana laughed. "You mean there's more?"

Shawntae ignored her and turned back to me. "Mean-

while, your mom kept saying 'I can't take this check. You have the wrong Mrs. Montenegro. I never bought a lottery ticket, so how could I win?' But no one listened. They just wanted to party. Suddenly all the shelves of chips and candy bars disappeared and the store became a dance hall."

"Are you sure you weren't dreaming about Derek's party instead?" I asked.

"I wondered that, too. The streamers, confetti, and dance floor don't really fit. But the clearest image was the five hundred thirty-two dollars that flashed on the cash register, so this dream was definitely about your mom. My subconscious mind is probably merging two realities, your Mom's big win and Derek's party."

"I guess," I said, doubtfully.

"So you know what she needs to do, right?" Before I could say anything, Shawntae answered her own question. "She needs to go to the convenience store *today*. Tickets are only a dollar, and the jackpot is up to twelve million."

"I thought you said she was going to win five hundred thirty-two dollars," Patty said.

"I did, but my predictions aren't completely accurate, remember? There's always one detail that's off. That's why we have to interpret them."

"Are you sure it's the prize amount that's off?"

"No, Patty, I am *not* sure," Shawntae said, punching out her words because she was getting impatient again. "Why do you think I've been telling you my predictions after the fact? My dream interpretation skills are still in the development stages."

"Okay," Patty said. "I didn't mean to get you mad."

"Well, stop being such a critic."

The conversation moved toward things we could do with twelve million dollars. Iliana wanted to get a makeover so she could attract the cutest guys, Shawntae wanted to finance her political campaign, and Patty wanted to buy her own island so no one would get on her nerves. Nobody asked what I would do, probably because they knew I'd donate it to cancer research.

All of a sudden, GumWad arrived. "Hi, y'all," he said.

"Why are you late?" Patty asked.

"I went to the library."

"Since when do you skip lunch to go to the library?"

He shrugged.

"So where are your books?" Shawntae said, all suspicious.

"I didn't get any. I was looking for quotes—the kind that cheer people up." He reached into his backpack and

pulled out a spiral notebook. It was almost new, although I could tell a few pages had been torn out. He handed it to me. "Here you go," he said.

"What's this?"

"A journal. So you can write down your feelings."

I opened it. The first page had a collage of phrases like "U is for unique," "the inner me," "one of a kind"—and sayings like "Dare to be remarkable" by Jane Gentry, "For a long time she flew, only when she thought no one else was watching" by Brian Andreas, and "It is not given us to live lives of undisrupted calm, boredom, and mediocrity. It is given us to be edge-dwellers" by Jay Deacon.

"This way," GumWad said, "you can have someone to talk to. Well, it isn't technically a person since it's just a bunch of paper, and it isn't technically talking since you'll be writing instead. But you know what I mean. The next time you get mad, you can write down your thoughts."

"Thanks," I said.

"So where's *my* special journal?" Shawntae asked, all jealous. "I want a spiral notebook with motivational quotes, too."

"And I want one with beauty tips," Iliana said.

GumWad reached in his backpack. "Well...um...I only had one extra, but I'll go to the store after school if you want."

"Will you? That's so sweet," Iliana said.

"Really? You guys think I'm sweet?"

"Sure," I said. "And thanks again for the notebook. It's exactly what I needed."

He smiled, and for the first time, he didn't have any gum in his mouth.

9 CHIA PETS

Another Saturday rolled around. I had promised to help Iliana with her service learning project. She rang the doorbell at exactly nine o'clock, but I wasn't quite ready.

"Give me a minute to grab my stuff," I told her.

I ran to my room, slipped on some shoes, and put the manila envelope and the clipboard with the sponsor forms in my backpack. Then I put my Chia Pets in a laundry basket, leaving SpongeBob for Jimmy since that was his favorite. When I returned to the living room, Mom was talking to Iliana. I felt a little embarrassed because Mom was in her robe and her hair was all messy.

"Have fun today," she told me.

I noticed how she leaned against the doorway as if to hold herself up.

"Should I stay?" I asked. "I don't have to go. I can lend Iliana my Chia Pets."

"That's right," Iliana said. "If you need Erica to stay..."

"Don't be ridiculous," Mom interrupted. "Go have some fun."

I nodded, even though part of me felt guilty for thinking about fun when she was still sick.

"Miguel!" Mom called out. "Chia's leaving. Come say good-bye."

Dad rushed over, but instead of saying bye to me, he took one look at Mom and said, "What are you doing out of bed? I thought you were sleeping."

"I was," she answered. "But I heard the doorbell and wanted to say hello."

"The doorbell woke you up?" He sounded upset, and I couldn't help thinking that if the doorbell were a kid, it would be grounded.

For her service learning project, Iliana was going to play with the children at Santa Rosa Hospital, which is across from a popular tourist spot called El Mercado, where visitors could eat Mexican food, watch ballet folklórico dances, and buy souvenirs. Her father drove us, and the hospital soon came into view. Its most impressive feature was an eight-story mural on its outer wall, a mosaic of tiles featuring a guardian

angel in shades of purple and blue. She hovered over a Mexican boy with a dove in his hand. When I saw it, I glanced over my shoulder. I couldn't help wondering if I had a protective spirit, too. After all, I almost got hurt so many times—like when I ran into the street and a car screeched to a stop right before hitting me, and when I slipped and nearly fell off a cliff at Lost Maples State Park, and when a library bookcase tipped over as I climbed it, spilling its books but failing to crush me because a column kept it from crashing to the floor. Surely, I had a guardian angel, and if I had one, then my friends had one too, and my mom. But what about the times we *did* get hurt…or sick? Where were the angels then? Weren't they watching all the time? I was beginning to doubt because I'd been working so hard on my *promesa*, yet Mom was still sick…sicker, in fact, with her swollen arm and with dark circles under her eyes. I knew I shouldn't think this, but sometimes those angels did a terrible job.

Iliana's father dropped us off, and we carried the basket of Chia Pets to the children's ward. Every time we saw a cute guy in scrubs or a lab coat, Iliana said, "Do you think he's a doctor?" And every time we passed a glass door, she checked her makeup and said, "Do I have enough mascara?" or "Is my lip gloss shiny enough?"

"Are you here to help kids or find a boyfriend?" I finally asked.

She shrugged, but I knew what the answer was.

"Don't you think doctors are too old for you?" I said, remembering how GumWad had said the same thing to me at Sonic.

"It doesn't hurt to *imagine*. I *might* marry a doctor someday. You never know."

I could only shake my head.

We made our way to the nurse's station on the pediatric ward. I got a visitor pass, while Iliana got a special "I'm a volunteer" button. The nurse said, "They're waiting for you," as she led us to the patients.

"That's great," I said, and I asked how old the children were and what they normally did when volunteers came. Meanwhile, Iliana didn't say a word. She kept slowing down, and because we both carried the basket, I had to slow down, too.

Finally, we reached the play area. It had a giant floor mat with brightly colored squares, each featuring a letter of the alphabet or a number. Against the wall, goldfish swam in a tank with multicolored gravel, fake plants, a scuba diver bobbing up and down as he released bubbles, and a sunken ship with windows big enough for the fish to swim through. Buckets of crayons and colored pencils were on the tables, and toy boxes filled with stuffed animals, puz-

zles, and board games lined the walls. A few parents stood around, too.

"Have fun," the nurse said before returning to her station.

"What do I do now?" Iliana whispered. She sounded panicky.

"Talk to the kids," I suggested.

But she didn't say anything. She just stared at them. A few kids were in wheelchairs. Others had IVs or oxygen masks. One boy didn't have a leg, and one girl was bald with a long scar on her head. There were also kids who didn't seem sick at first. Except for the hospital gowns and ID bracelets, they looked like students on a field trip. But then, you noticed that they were tired or pale or extra thin. You noticed something else, too. All of them had added a personal touch to their hospital clothes—slippers shaped like fire trucks or teddy bears, crazy socks with stripes or polka dots, robes with cartoon characters, or baseball caps with the logos of their favorite teams. Sure, the children weren't feeling 100 percent, but that didn't stop them from having a sense of humor and a sense of style. They had a special kind of bravery, the kind I saw in my mom whenever she laughed at her own situation. She wasn't in denial, like my dad thought. She was trying to make the best of things.

I nudged Iliana. She didn't move. The kids stared at us, full of expectation, so I nudged Iliana again. Nothing. This was going to be a disaster if I didn't act fast.

"Good morning, everyone," I said.

They stayed silent.

"Good *morning*," I said again, this time with a big smile and my arms moving like a drum major's urging the band to play.

This time they said, "Good morning."

I glanced at Iliana. She was looking at me. Very quietly, she said, "Go on."

So I said, "My name's Erica, and this is my friend Iliana. You can call me Erica the elephant, and you can call her Iliana the iguana."

The children laughed at that.

"So who are you?" I asked, pointing to a girl who wore a jangly bracelet.

"Susan the swan."

"Hello, Susan. You have beautiful feathers."

She brushed her arm as if smoothing a wing.

"And you?" I pointed to a boy.

"I'm Hugo the..."—he looked up—"Hugo the hyena."

"And I'm Clarisa the camel," another girl said.

After that, everyone jumped in, all of them giving us

their names and laughing at the animals they chose. Soon, Iliana the iguana was laughing, too.

"Why don't we make name tags?" she said, finally warming up to her job.

She pulled some blank stickers from her purse, and the children wrote their names and drew their animals. Then they pressed the stickers onto their gowns. Now everyone knew everyone else.

"What's in the basket?" a boy named Juan asked.

"More animals for our zoo," I announced. I reached in and pulled out Mickey Mouse, his big ears peeking through the green hair.

The kids giggled.

Juan laughed, "Mickey doesn't have hair!"

"Well, this isn't Mickey," I explained. "This is Mitch, his green-haired cousin."

The giggles turned to laughter. The children wanted to see the other Chia Pets, so Iliana and I took them out, telling a story for each one. Then we handed them to the children.

Some were too weak to hold the Chia Pets, so we put them on their laps or nearby tables. They smiled and petted the funny green hair. Soon, Iliana and I heard animal noises even from Chia Pets based on historical figures. Abe Lincoln barked, and Einstein mooed. One girl had a kitten,

but instead of meowing, it quacked. Why not? If a kitten could have green fur, then it could quack, too. We were acting so silly, all of us, and I caught myself laughing till my belly hurt. When I glanced at my mood ring, it was red, which meant I was feeling energized and adventurous.

Now that Iliana knew what to do, I decided to work on my own project. Since I was at a hospital, I figured lots of people would know how I felt about my mom. After all, if they were here, then they knew someone who was sick. Surely they wanted to cure diseases, so I went to the lobby to ask for sponsors.

"Hello, can I speak to you?" I said to the first group who walked in. When they saw my clipboard, they hurried away. I asked the next group. They shook their heads and said, "Not now." This was turning into a repeat of going door to door. But eventually, people stopped to listen, and they were very understanding. Some even admitted knowing someone with cancer, too. So I was able to collect more sponsors. After a while, I was on a roll. Maybe this had been the answer all along. Instead of ringing doorbells, I should go to hospital lobbies. San Antonio had lots of hospitals. Maybe I could visit them all. What a great strategy! I finally had a genius idea. At least, that's what I thought until a security guard approached and said, "I'm sorry, miss, but you are not allowed to solicit here."

"I'm not soliciting," I explained. "I'm just trying to get donations."

He put his hands on his hips as if to scold me. "That's what 'soliciting' means," he said.

I felt so stupid. If I were Carmen, I would have known the definition and wouldn't have made a fool of myself. But I *wasn't* Carmen. I wasn't a child genius. I was Erica, dumb Erica, a failure at math, at vocabulary, and at finding five hundred names.

"I'm afraid I have to ask you to stop," the security guard said.

So I left, returning to the pediatric ward, all down in the dumps. When I got there, most of the kids were gone, and those who remained had moved to other activities, which meant my Chia Pets were scattered about, completely ignored. One was on the floor, not broken but on its side, the leaves getting squished. And over by the giant window, Iliana was giggling with some guy. Okay, he was amazingly cute, but he wasn't wearing a hospital gown, so he wasn't a patient, which meant she had no business talking to him. She was here to work with the kids.

"What are you doing?" I said to her.

She didn't catch my anger at all. "Oh, Erica. Back already?" She glanced at her watch. "I guess time flies when you're having fun," she said, smiling at the boy, who smiled

back. He was even cuter when he smiled, which just made me angrier.

"Aren't you supposed to be playing with the kids?" I said.

"I was. We had a great time, but then I met Alan, Clarisa's older brother. You remember Clarisa, right? Clarisa the camel?" She told Alan about the name game we played, taking all the credit. He said she was clever, and she giggled again.

Normally, Iliana's flirting wouldn't bother me. In fact, I'd be flirting, too. But not today, when we were supposed to be working on our projects! How could she play around like this in a hospital where people were sick or dying— even little children, the very children she came to meet? There I was, in the lobby, begging for sponsors and then being humiliated by the security guard, while she was up here playing around. This was a game to her, but for me it was life and death, my *mom's* life and death.

I knew I was about to cry. That's how angry I felt. So I decided to calm myself by collecting my Chia Pets. That's when I noticed some were missing. I counted. Yes, nine Chia Pets were gone!

"Where's Tweety?" I asked Iliana. "Where's the president?" I held out the basket to show her how empty it was.

She shrugged. "A couple of kids asked if they could have them, and I said yes. I guess the other kids thought they could take them, too."

"You gave away my Chia Pets?" I couldn't help it. I shouted.

That's when Iliana finally realized I was angry. She got apologetic. "I'm sorry, Erica. I thought you *wanted* to give them away. I thought that's why you brought them."

"I've been collecting them since I was a baby, so why would I give them away?"

"I don't know," she admitted. "I thought you were tired of them."

"But I *love* my Chia Pets. They make me laugh. They're like my friends! And my whole family calls me Chia. It's like my identity. What are they going to call me if I don't have the pets anymore?"

I wasn't making any sense. Even as I spoke, I could tell how ridiculous I sounded.

"My mom's the one who started the tradition," I said.

Iliana's eyes got watery. "I'm sorry."

I wasn't in the mood to forgive, but I didn't want her to cry, either. I glanced at my mood ring to figure out how I felt. It was orange, a firebrick shade, which meant I was feeling vexed. Breathe in, breathe out, I told myself. I did

this three times, trying my best to change the color of my mood ring.

"My sister took one," Alan confessed. "I'll go get it for you."

He turned toward the rooms and was almost out of the play area when I called him back. "Wait!" He stopped and looked at me. "She can have it," I said.

"Are you sure?" he asked.

I nodded. After all, how could I take a Chia Pet away from a sick child, especially one as cute as Clarisa the camel? If she was anything like Jimmy, she'd start to cry. All the kids would cry. I didn't want to cause so much sadness, especially when I came here to make them laugh.

"Are you sure?" Iliana repeated, and I nodded again. Sometimes, it was too late to get things back even if they were still close by.

I made another pass through the play area in case I had overlooked a Chia Pet, but, no, they were definitely gone. Meanwhile, Iliana and Alan exchanged cell phone numbers and said good-bye. Then Iliana asked a nurse to sign her timesheet, and we headed to the elevators. When we got there, I spotted a directory of the hospital departments. I pointed at the word "oncology" and said, "That's where the cancer patients go."

And that's when the tears finally came. I couldn't push them down anymore.

"Oh, Erica," Iliana said. She hugged me. She probably knew I wasn't crying about Chia Pets, but about my mom.

A moment later, the elevator doors opened. Some people came out. They saw my tears, but they didn't say anything. Why would they? We were in a hospital, where tears were more normal than smiles.

28 CARS PASSING BY

Because of the lymphedema, Grandma had been driving for Mom, and while I was in school, she watched Jimmy. But by the end of the day, she was ready to go home. "Your grandpa gets cranky," she explained, though I knew she got cranky, too.

When she dropped us off on Thursday, Carmen and I found Mom at the kitchen table, sound asleep, her cheek on top of a place mat. The swelling in her arm had finally gone down, so she had returned to radiation therapy. The treatment knocked her out, but Jimmy thought she was playing night-night, a bedtime game.

When he tugged at Mom's robe, Carmen pulled him away. "Mom's not playing," she said, but he didn't believe

her. He curled up on the floor, closed his eyes, and said, "I go night-night, too."

She was about to stand him up, but I stopped her. "Let him pretend," I said. Then I gently shook Mom. She lifted her head, confusion all over her face. "Come on," I said, helping her stand and letting her lean on me as I walked her to the bedroom. Once we got there, I pushed aside the blanket, and when she crawled into bed, I tucked her in and kissed her cheek.

She smiled. "Who would have thought?" she said sleepily. "You acting like the parent and me acting like the child?"

"You're still my mom."

"And you're still my baby."

She patted the bed like she used to when I was Jimmy's age. I shook off my shoes and curled up beside her. I knew I was leaning near her sore side, but she didn't complain. I was almost as tall as she, and I'd been washing clothes, vacuuming, and giving Jimmy a bath every night. I'd been trying my best to keep peace with Carmen even though she got on my nerves. But right now, I wanted to be a child again, Jimmy's age because he was too young to understand what was happening.

Mom stroked my hair and hummed my favorite lullaby

about little chicks who cried when they were hungry and cold. *"Los pollitos dicen, pío, pío, pío, cuando tienen hambre, cuando tienen frío."*

That's how I felt, like a *pollito* crying—not like Jimmy, whose shoulders shook, but like Dad, who got still as a wall.

As I lay there, I thought about the Race for the Cure and my project, both only a week away. Little by little, I'd been gathering names, but I still didn't have five hundred. Last Sunday, I had asked Dad to take me to the Medical Center area because lots of hospitals were on the same street. I went to the lobbies, asking for sponsors, and leaving only when the security guards explained the "no soliciting" rule. I knew it was lying to pretend I didn't know the rule, but each time, I managed to get several sponsors before getting caught. And I never really got in trouble. I just apologized and went to the next hospital. What else could I do? I had already knocked on every door in my neighborhood and called all my relatives. I had even bugged people after church. But it still wasn't enough, and I was starting to panic because it seemed impossible to get five hundred names in time for the walk—in time for Mom.

After a while, Mom's voice faded out, and her hand slipped away. She was asleep again. I wanted to stay and dream that things were back to normal, back to the time

before Mom brought those nine bikinis home, but something fell in the kitchen and the loud crash made Jimmy cry. So I crawled out of bed, took a deep breath, and went to investigate.

When I got to the kitchen, I discovered the trash flipped on its side. Last night's chicken bones were scattered on the floor, along with dirty paper towels and broken eggshells.

Jimmy was holding up a jar and saying, "Throw away!" It was a half-empty peanut butter jar. We'd made a few sandwiches from it, but the rest of the peanut butter was on his face, shirt, and hands. He even had peanut butter in his hair.

"How did you get this in your hair?" I asked.

He just held up the jar and said, "No more!" even though there was enough for several sandwiches.

"Why weren't you watching him?" I complained to Carmen.

She didn't answer because she was counting, her eyes staring at some invisible point. She said, "Twenty-three," and a few seconds later, "twenty-four," and a whole minute later, after I had time to dampen a towel and wipe Jimmy's face, she said, "twenty-five." That's when I realized she was listening for cars passing by. We didn't live on a busy street, and you could barely hear the cars from within the house, so counting them took a lot of concentration, something

Carmen had gobs of right now. She looked obsessed, in my opinion.

"If you're counting cars, you'll never get to the end," I said. "There will *always* be cars driving down the street."

She just said, "Twenty-six, twenty seven"—long pause—"twenty-eight."

I could only shake my head. My sister was going nuts.

I looked at Jimmy again. If I wanted to wash off the peanut butter, I'd have to give him a bath. Lots of kids probably cried about taking a bath but not Jimmy. He loved it. I filled the tub with bubbles and threw a bunch of toys in there. I helped him into the water, and then I sat on a stool beside the tub to make sure he didn't drown. While he invented adventures with his pirate ships and toy shark, I invented a story in the journal GumWad had given me. I'd been writing in it every day. And GumWad was right. Having a place to express myself helped. Maybe it didn't solve my problems, but it made me feel calmer. Often, I didn't even mention my worries. I wanted to forget them, so I wrote whatever came to mind—stories, lists, conversations I'd overheard, or letters to famous people.

Today, I wrote a story about a girl who liked to count. First, she counted the cans of soup in the cupboard. "It took her twenty-two seconds," I wrote. Then, she counted the lightbulbs in the house, which took five minutes and

forty seconds. She went outside and counted the trees on her street. Since the street was long, it took over an hour. She then made her way to the grocery store to count the cars in the parking lot. Cars weren't like trees. They kept leaving and arriving. The girl had to start over numerous times. Finally, around midnight, when the last person left, she finished counting. One car. "The girl wondered who it belonged to," I wrote, "since all the customers and employees had gone home. Finally, she looked at the sky and started to count the stars. She's still counting because you could never figure out how many stars there are. It would take a lot more than one lifetime to get that number."

All my stories were short and simple. When I had time, I went back and drew pictures. Sometimes, I read my stories to Jimmy, very quietly—not because of Dad's rules but because I didn't want Carmen to overhear.

I was just about to read him this one when Dad walked in. He sat on the edge of the tub, scooped up some bubbles, and threw them at Jimmy, who was too preoccupied with his toys to notice.

Then Dad said, "The counselor from your school called today."

"Is Carmen getting another award?" I asked, already dreading the news.

"No," Dad said. "She called about you."

"Me?"

I thought for a moment. The counselor called only when it concerned Carmen, usually to invite my parents to some type of recognition ceremony. No way was I getting an award. I hadn't done anything special. That could mean only one thing. The counselor called because I was in trouble. Of course I was in trouble. I'd been falling behind. My grades were okay, but I'd missed some assignments and my quiz scores were low Cs.

"She wanted to schedule a conference with some of your teachers next Monday," Dad said. "She mentioned Mr. Leyva. Isn't that your math teacher?"

Of course, I thought, dropping my head. "Yes," I said, my voice small because I felt like such a loser.

When the school called about Carmen, it was because she'd done something spectacular, like gotten a perfect score on a national test that's for seniors in high school. But when the school called about me, it was because I was... well...I was *not* spectacular. And because I was not spectacular, I was failing math. Sure, I could count, just like everybody else, but the most interesting thing I did with numbers was remember my locker combination.

"Any idea why he'd want a conference?" Dad asked.

"I think I'm failing his class," I admitted.

"Really? What's your average?"

"If I were good with numbers, I'd tell you." I couldn't help being sassy. After all, who cared about my average? I was failing, plain and simple. It didn't matter if my average was a sixty-two or a twelve because it was still an F in the grade book.

"I don't understand," Dad said. "Your sister..."

I stood up. "Don't even go there," I warned. "I'm so sick and tired of hearing how smart Carmen is and how dumb I am."

"I didn't say you were dumb."

"You were going to tell me to ask Carmen for help. To ask her for *tutoring*. That's what *everybody* tells me. They think Carmen has all the answers, and guess what...*she* thinks she has all the answers. And I'm the one who has to hear it all the time, who gets *corrected*. So excuse me if the last thing I want is to give her another reason to wave her superior intelligence in my face!"

With that, I stomped out. I knew Jimmy was still in the tub, but I thought to myself, *Let Dad deal with it!*

43 PHONE CALLS

About an hour later, Dad told us to start dinner without him. He wasn't hungry yet, so he was going to take a shower and watch the news first. I served our food on paper plates and handed out plastic forks so the clinking of *real* forks and plates wouldn't wake Mom. But she woke up anyway, and when she saw us at the table, she said, "There you are. I thought I was all by myself. I thought you guys went for pizza and left me behind."

Carmen and I glanced at each other. Somehow, this felt like getting busted for doing something wrong.

"Well?" Mom said. "Where's the cat?"

"What cat?" Carmen asked.

"The one that bit your tongues," Mom joked. When we

didn't say anything, she got suspicious. "Why are you being so quiet?"

That's when Jimmy blurted, "Rules!"

"What's that, Jimmy?"

This time he whispered, "Quiet rules."

"What's he talking about?" Mom asked Carmen and me.

"Just something Dad made up," I said. "It's not important."

"Yeah," Carmen added. "Just a few quiet rules."

Mom raised her eyebrows, curious. "And what are these rules exactly?"

We knew we had to tell her, so we described putting a towel against the crack beneath her bedroom door to drown out noise, and lifting the dining room chairs instead of scooting them, and not blow-drying our hair or hooking up our iPods to the speakers.

"And last weekend, Dad disconnected the doorbell," Carmen said, "because Erica's friends were waking you up."

"They're not the only ones who ring the doorbell," I snapped, because she was trying to make things my fault again. "Anyway," I continued, "Dad went a little overboard with that rule."

"With *all* of them." Carmen laughed.

I laughed, too. Dad's rules seemed ridiculous when you really thought about them.

Somehow, I expected Mom to join the laughter. After all, she made fun of her lymphedema and her replacement breast. She joked that she glowed in the dark after so much radiation. But when she heard about the quiet rules, she slumped in a chair, her shoulders drooping. Then, when Dad came into the room, she stood up, mad.

"No more quiet rules, understand?" she said.

Dad took a step back. "What? Who? What...do you mean?"

"The girls told me all about it."

I didn't want Dad to get in trouble, so I said, "Mom, we *like* being quiet. Right, Carmen?"

Before she could answer, Mom made the "stop" gesture with her hand, so we didn't say another word.

"I want to hear my children," she told Dad. "I want to hear their voices and footsteps. I want to hear toilets flushing and vacuums running. I want to hear Jimmy crying and laughing, and the girls fighting. And I want to hear you, too—tapping on the computer, shaving, brushing your teeth. Why aren't you brushing your teeth anymore?"

"I am," Dad admitted. "But I'm using the kids' bathroom now."

"Why?"

"So I won't bother you. So you can rest."

"But I can rest just fine with noise!"

She startled me because she rarely raised her voice. She startled Jimmy, too. He didn't cry, but he ran to me and lifted his arms so I could carry him.

Mom came toward us. She kissed the top of Jimmy's head, patted my back, and tousled Carmen's hair. "I'm sorry, kids," she said. And then her voice got shaky. "I feel tired all the time. That part's true. The radiation just zaps me, but I'm still alive." She turned to Dad. "Can't you see I'm still alive? Don't make this place like a tomb. I don't need to feel buried already. You understand? Noise is life, that's what I'm saying. Noise is life."

Dad approached her, hugged her, and said, "I thought I was helping you. I didn't mean to..."

I don't know what he said next because I carried Jimmy out and Carmen followed. We could be the nosiest kids on the planet, but we knew when it was best to leave our parents alone. But we were worried. As soon as we got to our room, Carmen said, "Mom and Dad never fight."

"You're right," I said. "I guess it's the cancer."

We just stared at each other for a minute, the way hikers in a blizzard might stare at each other, not because they're angry but because they're scared that if they look away, they'll be lost and all alone.

"I'm going to clean the bathroom," Carmen said, and she stepped out. A few minutes later, I could hear water running in the tub.

I grabbed a few toys from Jimmy's room. "You play with these, okay?" I said. He grabbed them, and soon was making crashing sounds as he rolled toy cars into the wall.

While he played, I made a list of everyone in Mrs. Gardner's class. They had to do a service learning project too, so maybe they'd help. Then I listed students from my other classes. After brainstorming two whole pages of names, I took out my school directory and made phone calls. I called forty-three students. Of course, some people didn't answer the phone, and other calls went to voice mail. But I did reach a lot of people. A good number were more than happy to sponsor me, so when my classmates said, "I'll think about it" or "I don't have any money" or "Let me talk to my parents first," I didn't feel so bad. I was still a long way from my goal, but every bit helped.

144 OUTFITS

My phone rang at six o'clock in the morning on the day of Derek's party—when I couldn't afford to lose a single minute of beauty sleep!

"Not another dream," I answered, because only Shawntae called so early.

"I'm calling about your mom's lottery ticket. I had that dream a week ago, and you still haven't told her."

"Because it's not going to happen."

"I haven't had any more dreams about you," she said. "You know what that means, right?"

I shrugged, but then remembered she couldn't see me because we were on the phone. "No, I don't know what that means."

"It means that the last dream is the *real* one. Your mom's going to win the lottery. I can feel it in my bones."

I sighed, unconvinced. "And we'll all live happily ever after. We'll have lots of money, and you'll put 'psychic' on your campaign posters when you run for mayor."

"Don't be sassy with me," she scolded.

"I'm sorry," I said. "It just sounds a little far-fetched."

She was quiet for a moment, but then she said, "Just make sure she goes to the store, okay? It only costs a dollar to buy a ticket, so even if my psychic abilities aren't one hundred percent accurate, she won't lose much."

"Okay," I promised. "Can I go back to sleep now?"

She said yes, but we talked a bit longer about Derek's party before hanging up. I couldn't fall asleep after the conversation, so I hid under the blankets and made my own prediction. Tonight, I was going to have a close encounter of the fourth kind—physical contact—maybe even a kiss! I just *knew* it, and I didn't need to dream about it first.

Iliana and GumWad planned to carpool with Carmen and me. After leaving us at Derek's house, my parents were going to take Jimmy to Chuck E. Cheese. He *loved* that restaurant. Three or four times a week, he said, "Gimme pizza. Gimme pizza," while pointing to a flyer with the

Chuck E. Cheese mouse on it. As for me, I hated the place. All those bells, whistles, and kiddie songs gave me a headache, but if Mom needed noise to feel alive, Chuck E. Cheese was the best noise factory in the city. She admitted, though, that she had no appetite for pizza and that she'd probably just sit at the table while Dad and Jimmy played games. Still, she was going out, which was a good sign, in my opinion.

Iliana arrived an hour and a half before the party. She brought a suitcase of clothes and a gym bag of shoes so I could help her find the perfect outfit. I'd been trying on clothes since midafternoon, so when she came, she stepped into a room with skirts covering the beds, blouses spilling out of drawers, and shoes littering the floor.

"What a mess!" she exclaimed.

She pushed some clothes aside to make room for her suitcase, and as she matched up different combinations, I finally settled on a black, ruffled miniskirt with an under layer of tulle peeking out below the hem. I also wore a pair of strappy, silver sandals, and a silver ankle bracelet with cute charms—an "E" for "Erica," the Pisces zodiac sign, a puffy heart, an angel, a tiny T-shirt, a laptop computer, a cell phone, and my newest charm, the pink ribbon for breast cancer awareness.

"What do you think?" I asked as I slowly turned to model.

"Thumbs-up for the skirt and shoes, but that T-shirt has to go."

I was wearing my faded brown T-shirt, a total yawn on the fashion meter. "I'm still trying to pick a top," I explained.

Just then, Carmen burst in. She had dressed in the laundry room because she wanted to iron her clothes first.

"I'm ready!" she announced. "At least, I think I'm ready." She had on black Mary Jane pumps, a black skirt, and a white, long-sleeved blouse buttoned all the way up.

"You look like a nun," I said.

Carmen glanced at Iliana to see if this was true. Iliana hates to hurt people's feelings, but she had to agree.

"I'll never figure out what to wear!" Carmen moaned as she threw herself on the bed. "Not counting my school uniforms, because you can't wear them to a party, I have five skirts, three pairs of jeans, four other types of pants, and twelve blouses. That's 144 potential outfits. I can't possibly try on *all* of them."

"I guess you can't go then," I teased.

Iliana threw a blouse at me. "Be nice," she warned. Then, turning to Carmen, she said, "I'll help you out. Besides, I've always wanted a little sister to play dress-up with."

"You can have my sister for free," I said. "In fact, I'll *pay* you to take her."

They just ignored me.

While they picked through clothes, I asked Iliana for her opinions. First, about a T-shirt featuring a gigantic ring with a glittery diamond and the words "You rock my world!"

"You'll scare the guys with that one," she said. "They'll think you want them to propose."

"What about this one?" I asked, pointing at a shirt with a picture of bowling pins and the caption "You're out of my league."

"Too intimidating," she said.

When I held up a shirt that said "Luv my badittude," she said, "Too sassy." For the one with butterflies, "Too cutesy." And for a shirt that said "Sacred Heart Church. Come in for a faith lift," Iliana could only roll her eyes.

Finally, I discovered the perfect T-shirt—a hot pink V-neck that said "dress shirt" over outlines of a wedding dress, a flapper dress, a ball gown, a sundress, and a muumuu.

"I'm ready!" I said, turning around to discover that Carmen was ready, too. As much as I hated to compliment my sister, I had to admit she looked great. The white blouse was now a loose jacket over a turquoise camisole, and a scarf with swirls of turquoise and gold acted like a belt for her jeans.

"That looks a lot better than the nun outfit you had on earlier," I said.

"Really?" Carmen ran to the mirror to see for herself. She flipped back her hair and put her hands on her hips. I think she meant to pose like a runway model, but she looked like Supergirl instead. And that's when I noticed…

"You have nubs," I said.

"What?"

I pointed at her chest. "You have nubs."

Iliana leaned forward for a closer look. "That's right," she said to Carmen. "You're developing."

I thought my sister would be excited, but instead she covered up and said, "Quit looking at me! It's embarrassing."

Iliana put an arm around her. "No, it's not. It's just nature. You should feel excited."

"Well, I'm *not*. How can I go to the party with nubs?"

"It's no big deal," I said. "Just put on a bra."

"I can't. I don't have one."

"Why not? All you have to do is ask Mom. You should have seen how happy she got when it was time to buy *me* a bra."

"I don't want to ask because…because…"

For once, I knew what my sister was thinking. "Because of the surgery?"

She nodded.

Poor Carmen. She didn't want to remind Mom about losing a breast, so she'd kept quiet about needing a bra. Luckily, she had me for an older sister. I reached into my underwear drawer and searched for my training bras, finding three in the back corner beneath the bikini tops Mom had given me. The bras seemed tiny—just a bit of padding and some straps. I couldn't believe they fit me two years ago. I tossed them to Carmen and said, "They're yours." She thanked me as she turned away to try one on. The straps were too big so she asked Iliana for help, and while they made adjustments, I glanced at the C cups of my mom's bikinis. I took one and put it against my chest, but I was a long way from fitting into it. I could *never* fill that bikini, I decided. Funny, how I could seem so big next to Carmen yet so small next to Mom.

Just then, my cell phone beeped with a text from Gum-Wad: "Want something from the store?"

I remembered Shawntae's dream. Before winning the lottery, my mom was buying candy at the convenience store. I decided to give Shawntae's prediction a try, so I wrote, "Snickers. Thx."

"OK. BRT," which means, "Be right there."

"GumWad's on his way," I announced. "We've got to hurry!"

Because she'd spent so much time helping Carmen and

me, Iliana had to rush her own outfit, but she didn't complain. She picked a short denim skirt with rhinestone-studded flip-flops and a shimmery white blouse. Simple but classy. We applied lip gloss and combed our hair once more. We were finally ready for the party, and just in time, because we heard knocking at the front door.

When we answered, GumWad said, "I think your doorbell's broken. I've been standing here for five minutes."

"My dad broke it on purpose," Carmen tattled.

"It's a long story," I said, not wanting to explain.

After a few awkward moments, he handed me the Snickers bar. "I got you a king-size."

"Thanks," I said. "Double chocolate, double luck."

Everyone looked at me. I could tell they were wondering if I'd lost my mind.

Just then, my parents and Jimmy showed up.

"Everyone ready?" Dad asked.

We all nodded.

"But first," I said, handing Mom the chocolate. "You have to eat this."

"But…" GumWad tried. Before he could finish his thought, Jimmy started crying. "Gimme candy. Gimme candy."

"Also," I explained to Mom, "you have to go to the con-

venience store, preferably one decorated with pink streamers and a mirror ball, and you have to buy a lottery ticket because tonight's the big night. You are going to win the jackpot."

"Oh, please," Carmen said. "Statistically speaking, a lottery with six numbers from one to fifty gives you only…"—she stared at the sky where, I imagined, a gigantic calculator flashed the answer—"only a one-in-thirteen million chance of winning."

If Iliana and GumWad weren't around, I would have stuck out my tongue and said something really immature like "nanny-nanny boo-boo." As it was, I could only stare at her and wish that I were Medusa so I could turn her to stone because, as far as I knew, stones were awful at math and they never, ever acted like Little Miss Factoid.

"Gimme!" Jimmy begged as he reached for the candy.

Mom peeled back the wrapper and handed him a piece. "What makes you think I'm going to win?" she asked.

"Shawntae."

"Really?" GumWad said, all excited. "Did she have another dream?"

I nodded. "You were in the library when she told us about it last week, and ever since, she's been bugging me." I turned to Mom. "She wants you to buy a ticket *tonight*."

"You really should," GumWad said to my parents. "Shawntae has psychic abilities. Last week, she told me I was going to eat enchiladas on Wednesday, and I did. Then she told me I was going to find a dog for my social studies project, and I did. I actually found four. Then she told me a pink gumball was going to come out of my gumball machine, and it did, right after the yellow and blue gumballs came out. And she also told me I was going to have a test in one of my classes, and I *did*. I had a test in science. So you see? She's been predicting all kinds of stuff for me, and they've been happening right before my very eyes."

"Well," Iliana said, "those predictions are kind of... well... those predictions are *predictable*. I mean, you always eat enchiladas on Wednesday, and you've been searching for dogs so it was likely you'd find one, and there's always a test in some class."

GumWad stared at her. He opened his mouth. I think he wanted to blow a bubble, but he hadn't chewed gum in over a week. After a minute, he spoke again. "I believe, Iliana. That's all I'm saying." Then he turned to Mom. "And if I were you, Mrs. Montenegro, I would buy that ticket."

Mom tore off another piece for Jimmy. "What could it hurt?" she decided. She glanced at Dad to see if he agreed.

He nodded. "I have to stop at the gas station anyway," he said. "We can buy the ticket while we're there."

I still doubted, but it was fun to hope. Winning would be great, but if none of her numbers matched, at least I'd get to say "I told you so" to Shawntae and finally put an end to her silly predictions and early-morning phone calls.

2 INTERRUPTED SLOW DANCES

When we got to Derek's house, he was out front, ready to greet his guests.

"Make yourself at home," he said, pointing toward the backyard. "There's lots to do and plenty of food."

A few more kids showed up, so he said, "Catch you later," before running off to greet them.

He had a great setup. As we entered the backyard, we walked beneath a giant banner that said, "Happy Birthday, Derek!" The detached garage meant a long driveway for the dance floor, and the DJ's huge speakers meant we could hear the music over the talking and laughing. A soft glow came from tiki torches and strings of white Christmas lights on the trees, garage, and patio. Also on the patio was a Ping-Pong table, so a bunch of kids stood around waiting

their turn to play. A glass sliding door led to the dining room with a table full of chips, dips, a veggie plate, a fruit bowl, hot dogs with all the fixings, and a giant chocolate birthday cake. In the next room was a TV with a Wii console.

A few adults stood around here and there, but they mostly left us alone. They were probably Derek's relatives, making sure we didn't break or steal anything.

As soon as we finished our "tour" of the party, Gum-Wad headed to the Ping-Pong table, while Iliana searched the crowd for Patty and Shawntae.

Before joining her, I told Carmen, "I hope you don't plan on being a tagalong. I'm not here to babysit, you know."

"I don't need a babysitter."

"Finally, we agree on something. The last thing I want is to hang out with you all night."

"Don't worry," she snapped back. "I've got my own friends to hang out with."

"Good. I'm glad to hear it," I said as I left to join Iliana.

I found her at a picnic table with Shawntae and Patty. We talked for a while, then Shawntae pointed at me and said, "Come on. Let's go liven up this party."

I followed as she clopped away in tiger-striped pumps.

"Nice shoes," I said.

"Tonight, I'm a wildcat," she explained. Then she held up her hand, made a claw, and growled.

I couldn't help laughing. "You're crazy, that's what you are."

"Boy crazy," she admitted.

She grabbed my elbow and walked me toward a group of kids.

"How come y'all aren't dancing?" she asked, all accusing. No one answered. "We've got good music and plenty of space, so quit standing here doing nothing like...like..." She glanced at me.

"Like lint on a sweater?" I offered.

"Like lint on a sweater," she said. Then she snapped her fingers and pointed to the dance floor. And the group went there and started to move, just a little at first, until a girl decided to go wild. That's all it took. Once she let go, everyone started laughing, clapping, and hopping around.

"How'd you do that?" I asked Shawntae. "How'd you get them out there?"

"I'm a natural-born leader," she explained. "Now, come on, let's dance, too. After all, your mom's going to win the jackpot tonight, so you have a lot to celebrate."

We joined the crowd. Shawntae found the beat in no time, but I felt so awkward. Except for the square dances we did in elementary school and a couple of dances with my dad at somebody's wedding, I had no experience. So I

just snapped my fingers, tapped my feet a bit, and hoped I wasn't embarrassing myself—especially in front of the guys from my Boyfriend Wish List, because all of them were here. In fact, at one point, Forest appeared, gave me a high five, and moved on before I could say anything to him. At another point, Iliana was in front of me. She said, "This is so much fun!" And later Patty tapped my shoulder. She danced too, if swinging your head without moving your feet counts as a dance. That's how it was. No one danced with a partner, but no one danced alone either. Soon I warmed up and let myself move a bit more, especially after seeing how silly some of my friends looked, how they didn't care if they were as stiff as zombies or as clumsy as clowns. There was no right or wrong way to dance, I decided. You just let your body find the rhythm, and if it *never* found the rhythm, that was okay, too.

After several fast songs, the DJ played a slow one. Most of the kids left the floor, but a few paired up, including Lou with his girlfriend, Paula; Forest with Shawntae; and Alejandro with Iliana. I stood on the sidelines feeling a bit lonely until Derek grabbed my hand and walked me to the floor. Next thing I knew, I was in the official dance position, holding one of his hands while my other hand rested on his shoulder. Was this really happening? Was I really in the middle of the closest encounter of the fourth kind I had

ever experienced? No wonder my palms felt sweaty and the beat of my heart was stronger than the beat of the music.

"Are you having fun?" Derek asked.

I couldn't speak, so I just nodded.

After a few seconds, he said, "Did you get something to eat?"

I nodded again even though it wasn't true.

"You're being really quiet tonight," he said.

This time, I *did* speak. A whole two words! "I know."

He squeezed my hand. He *actually* squeezed my hand, like some private code letting me know it was okay to be quiet. I could enjoy this moment without having to say interesting stuff. I could just be me, Erica, the girl who wears funny T-shirts and hates math.

This was the first slow song of the evening, and Derek was dancing with me. That meant he liked me. He *had* to. After all, lots of girls were here, and since he was the birthday boy, he could probably dance with anyone he wanted. Yet he picked me. I suddenly remembered the afternoon he gave me the invitation, when he told me, "Your presence is the only present I need," and when Patty said that I was definitely the main idea of that conversation while everyone else was the afterthought. Is that why he had this party? For me? So he and I could spend time together, dancing like this? He probably wanted to ask me out a long time

ago, but didn't know how I'd react. Then he had the perfect excuse—his birthday. He could invite me *and* everyone else, so it wouldn't seem as if he liked me, at least not until he knew exactly how I felt. And that's why I had to tell him. I had to admit my true feelings.

"Derek?" I began, but before I could say another word, someone tapped my shoulder.

"Hi, Auntie," Derek said to the woman standing beside us. I guess he was embarrassed because he let me go.

"I don't mean to interrupt," she apologized, "but are you Erica Montenegro?"

"Yes. Why?"

"Well, it seems your sister has locked herself in the bathroom."

I couldn't believe it. Of all the moments for my sister to be a brat!

"People are waiting," Derek's aunt continued, "but she won't come out. Do you think you could talk to her?"

Just then, the slow song ended, the couples split apart, and the dance floor filled up with a clapping, hopping crowd again.

"Sounds like your sister really needs you," Derek said. "You should go talk to her. I'll catch you later, okay?"

"Okay," I said as his aunt led me to the bathroom. I couldn't help feeling disappointed. I wanted to spend time

with Derek, not with my sister. I *knew* she should have stayed home.

We reached the hallway, and outside the bathroom door was a line of edgy girls. I wondered how long they'd been waiting.

"Your freak sister is having a meltdown," one said.

And another said, "Who invited her, anyway?"

Okay, I often called Carmen a freak and said mean things about her, but that's because I was her sister, which meant I had *permission* to pick on her. After all, we shared a room, so I had personal experience with her weirdness. It interfered with my peace of mind sometimes, my very sanity. But sharing a room also meant that no matter how mad Carmen and I got, we had to apologize and forgive because we couldn't avoid each other, at least not for longer than a few hours. So, yes, I could be mean to my sister, but I did *not* appreciate when other people acted mean.

"I invited her," I said. "And she isn't a freak, understand? She's a genius."

Usually, these girls liked to have the last word, but they didn't argue because they really needed to pee. Each one of them was about to have an emergency right there in the hallway. I could tell by the way they stood with their legs crossed tight.

"Carmen?" I called through the door. "You have to

come out now, okay? You can't hog up the bathroom when there's a long line waiting."

She opened the door, just a crack. I could smell Pine-Sol and bleach. My crazy sister had been cleaning again.

"Move," the first girl in line said as she pushed through.

Carmen stumbled out and the girl slammed the door behind her.

"Would you like a place to talk?" Derek's aunt asked us. We nodded.

She led us to the living room. It was dark, so she turned on a lamp. She said we could stay as long as we liked.

When she left, I said to Carmen, "Your eyes look red. Were you crying?"

Instead of answering, she said, "They have eighteen towels in the linen closet. Eight bath towels, four hand towels, and six washcloths. There are two hand towels on a rack by the sink, so actually they have *twenty* towels in there."

"Will you stop?" I asked.

"There's an arrangement on the counter with five flowers and a jar with thirty-six cotton balls."

"Carmen!" I said, shaking her a bit. "Stop counting. What's wrong with you? Why are you locking yourself in the bathroom?"

She sniffled. "Because no one likes me."

"That's not true," I said, at the same time remembering how her classmates had acted in the library earlier in the week.

"Yes, it is. Every time I open my mouth, people roll their eyes and turn away. They ignore me. Sometimes, they actually walk away. It's like I have a disease, and maybe I do. Maybe I *do* have a disease."

"That's ridiculous," I said. "You don't have a disease."

"Then why do people run away from me?"

I thought a minute. "When you talk to them, what do you say?"

"All kinds of interesting stuff," she answered. "Like those things I told Grandma the other day about the bees, and how the United States has more tornadoes than any other country in the world. And when this girl complained about the heat and how she was sweating, I told her that she should be grateful because that's how humans cool themselves. Sweat is a great evolutionary advantage. I mean, dogs and deer don't sweat. That's why they get heat strokes a lot faster than we do. And on top of that, our sweat glands carry pheromones."

"What's a pheromone?"

"That's what *they* wanted to know," she said, pointing in the general direction of the party. "So I explained how pheromones emit this smell that helps attract mates. And

they started laughing at me, *everyone*, just like you are right now. Stop laughing, Chia!"

"I'm sorry," I said. "I can't believe you were lecturing about sweat. So what happened next?"

"That girl, the one who was sweating and who started the whole thing, said, 'Hey, everybody, Carmen thinks BO is like perfume.' A couple of kids said I was totally gross. And they laughed at me. Then everyone walked off. They just left me there. It was the third time a group left me standing all alone. And I don't even know what BO is!"

"It stands for body odor," I explained, surprised to be the one giving her a definition.

She sniffled again. Luckily, a box of Kleenex was beside the lamp, so I handed her a tissue.

"Look," I said. "You can't go around talking about people's sweat."

"But I wanted to join the conversation. She *did* say she felt hot."

"I know, but instead of a lecture, just fan yourself and say something like, 'You're right. It sure is hot in here.'"

"But where do you go from there?" Carmen asked. "What do you talk about next?"

"Nothing. You let the other person talk. That's what a conversation is. You're supposed to go back and forth. Sometimes, most of the time, when *you* talk, you start to

act like a professor. You make us feel like we're in school, like we're going to have a test on all the information you tell us. That's why people walk away. No one wants to talk to a textbook."

She dabbed her eyes with the Kleenex. After a minute, she said, "You always look like you're having fun when you're with your friends, like it's easy to be with them."

"It is."

"But—and don't be offended, okay?—but if you don't know any interesting facts, then what on earth do you talk about?"

I thought a minute. "We mostly tell stories about stuff that happened to us or about things that we saw."

She sat silently as she considered what I'd said. "Are you going to tell *this* story?" she asked. "About me locking myself in the bathroom?"

I laughed a bit. "Probably."

And instead of getting mad and begging me not to say anything, Carmen laughed, too. "I guess it *is* funny, even if it's really embarrassing."

"People *love* embarrassing stories," I said, "especially when they're about someone *else* being embarrassed." After a minute, I added, "You don't have to be perfect, sis. It's okay to laugh at yourself."

She nodded as she crumpled the tissue in her hand.

"Forget about those other girls," I suggested. "Come hang out with the Robins. Iliana wants to adopt you as her little sister, so she'll be thrilled."

"But I thought you didn't want me to tag along."

"I didn't," I said. "But we can make a deal. You can hang out with my friends as long as you don't act like a professor. Every time I catch you starting a lecture, I'm going to tap your leg so you can stop, okay?"

She considered it. "Okay," she agreed. "I'll try my best."

So Carmen followed me to the picnic table where the Robins were stuffing their faces with hot dogs. When she started to list the ingredients of "processed meat products," including "preservatives like sodium nitrite," I tapped her leg, and when she mentioned that Patty's freckles came from something called melanin, I tapped her leg again. But when we heard an owl and Carmen explained how one of its ears was slightly lower to help it pinpoint sounds, I didn't tap her leg. Some of her facts were actually interesting, especially when she wasn't trying to show off. After a while, Carmen started to understand the give-and-take rules of conversation, and she started to enjoy herself. Maybe my sister wasn't so weird after all.

For the most part, I was having fun, but one thing bothered me—Derek. He came by a few times to check on us, but every time the DJ played something slow, Derek

asked a different girl to dance, including Shawntae and Iliana, who were nice enough to make an excuse because they knew I liked him so much. So what was going on? Was Derek trying to make me jealous? If so, his plan was working because every time I saw him with another girl, my mood ring turned amber, which meant I felt insecure. Then again, how could Derek know I liked him? I hadn't told him yet. I was about to confess my true feelings when we got interrupted. So maybe he thought I just cared for him as a friend. But didn't he notice that I wasn't dancing with anyone else? Every time another guy asked, I said, "Thanks, but not right now." This whole situation was more confusing than a word problem in math.

"I need your honest opinion," I said to the Robins. "Does Derek like me or not?"

They glanced at one another, afraid to answer. Finally, Iliana said, "I don't think he likes *anybody*, at least not for a steady girlfriend."

"That's not it at all," Shawntae said. "Derek is a player. He wants to be the center of every girl's universe. I've been watching him flirt with *all* the girls tonight. Including each one of us."

"Yeah," Patty said. "Even me."

"No way!" We gasped because no one flirted with Patty.

I'm sure a lot of guys thought she was cute, but she could be intimidating, too.

"He tried to be poetic," Patty went on. "Instead of the roses-are-red poem, he said, 'Your freckles are red, your eyes are blue, that's why there's no one as special as you.'"

"Gag me!" Shawntae screeched, sticking a finger in her mouth.

"Yeah, gag me, too." Carmen laughed.

"So how did you respond?" Iliana wanted to know.

"I answered with my own poem," Patty said. "I told him, 'Your pimples are red, your teeth are yellow, that's why you're such a lonely fellow.'"

"You did not!" Iliana said.

"Did too. And to think, I've been struggling in English. Apparently, the only time I can come up with poems is when I'm insulting someone."

We cracked up. Only Patty could invent an on-the-spot comeback like that.

After our laughter died down, I said, "That settles it. I'm not ruining my chance for love because Derek wants to flirt around. I'm saying yes to the next guy who asks me to dance."

"Looks like I have perfect timing, then." I turned to see GumWad standing behind me. He'd been at the Ping-Pong

table all night. I actually forgot he was at this party. The DJ had just put on a slow song, so GumWad bowed and said, "May I have this dance?"

I didn't answer right away because GumWad, in my opinion, didn't count as a guy, at least not one worthy of the Boyfriend Wish List. He was one of us, a Robin. This wasn't the type of close encounter I was looking for, but since no one else was asking me, I said, "Sure. Whatever. Okay."

So I found myself in the official slow dance position again, only this time I made sure there was at least a foot between GumWad and me. We danced for a little bit. Then GumWad said I looked pretty tonight, so I said thanks. And when he said I had a great sense of humor because no one in the whole school wore T-shirts as witty as mine, I said thanks again. And I said thanks when he told me that I was a real special person to keep asking for sponsors after so many people refused, and an even *more* special person to look out for my brother and sister and help my folks around the house. Then he said my mood ring was purple, and I just nodded because I wasn't paying attention to him. I was in auto-response mode, like when a friend is talking about something boring and you say "really" or "uh-huh" or "wow" but you don't mean it. You're just pretending. That's what I was doing. I was *pretending* to listen to GumWad, but

I was *really* watching the couples around me. Derek, of course, was dancing with yet another girl. Alejandro and Iliana were dancing for the third time tonight. But the couple who really had my attention was Lou and Paula. They were so in love. I couldn't help staring because that's what I wanted—a boyfriend, a *real* boyfriend, one who was as athletic, handsome, and popular as Lou.

"So which one would you like better?" GumWad asked.

For a second, I thought he was asking me which *guy* I liked better, but that made no sense. So I said, "What are you talking about?"

"Which charm? I noticed you wear that bracelet—"

"Anklet," I corrected.

"Oh, yeah, I get it. Because it goes around your ankle. Well, I noticed you wear it sometimes, and the other day, I saw some charms in this James Avery catalog my mom gets. Would you like the little angel with your birthstone or the little bird?"

"Why are you asking me about charms?"

"So I can buy one for you," he said.

"Why do you want to buy me one?"

GumWad looked at the space between our feet and blushed, all embarrassed or ashamed, I couldn't tell, but since he was avoiding eye contact, he had to be feeling

something awful. And then, all these details flooded in—the card he sent on the day my mom had surgery, the Slush, the journal, the way he defended me on the first day in social studies class.

"The presents," I said, "the compliments, the way you've been super nice. It's all because of pity, isn't it?"

"What do you mean?"

"You feel sorry for me. Admit it. My mom is seriously sick, and here you are rubbing it in my face by treating me like a person who's about to fall apart."

"I don't think you're about—"

I wouldn't let him finish. "I'm not some orphan girl," I said, "so don't give me any handouts."

"I don't think you're an orphan girl," he rushed to say, and he stepped forward like he wanted to hug me the way I hug Jimmy when he's acting like a baby.

I waved him off. "I'm not helpless. Don't you get it?"

And I marched to the picnic table, leaving GumWad alone on the dance floor. When I got there, I crossed my arms, refusing to talk. All night, the Robins asked what was wrong, but I said, "Nothing." When they kept pestering me, I said, "I don't want to talk about it."

GumWad had returned to the Ping-Pong table. Every time I glanced over, he was looking at me like I was the saddest *pobrecita* in the world.

When my parents finally picked us up, GumWad sat at one end of the SUV, while I sat at the other. My parents asked about the party. Carmen and Iliana filled them in, but GumWad and I stayed silent.

Finally, we dropped off my friends and made our way home. As soon as we walked in, we turned on the laptop to check the lottery numbers, but Mom didn't win the jackpot, or even $532. I didn't expect her to, but I still felt disappointed, so I sent Shawntae a text. "No jackpot for us," I wrote. "Once and for all, you do not have psychic powers!"

4 TEACHERS, 2 PARENTS, 1 COUNSELOR

Monday, my parents took us to school thirty minutes early. Carmen made her way to the library, while my parents and I headed to the office for the teacher conference.

"Don't worry," Mom said. "I'll tell them how hard you've been working on your service learning project." I dropped my head. She meant well, but that didn't stop me from feeling humiliated. How I hated being the dumb kid. For the past month, I had tried my hardest to juggle school with my new responsibilities. I was doing my best, yet here we were, walking through the counselor's door.

I thought wearing my TGIF T-shirt would make me feel better. It didn't stand for "Thank God it's Friday" like most people thought. Instead, TGIF stood for "Thank God I'm fabulous." At least, that's what the back of my T-shirt

said. But I didn't feel fabulous. Once again, my mood ring was black for stressed.

We entered the office, the counselor's desk buried beneath folders, papers, and writing supplies. Luckily, she had a large, round table in the middle of the room. Mr. Leyva waited there, as well as Mrs. Gardner; Mr. Watson, who taught science; and Mrs. Silva, who taught English.

The counselor introduced everyone as we took our seats at the table. Then she began. "We don't want to alarm you unnecessarily, but since it's still early in the year, we wanted to touch base before Erica's situation gets too serious."

"And what is her situation exactly?" Dad asked.

That's when my teachers chimed in. Mr. Leyva said I was failing. Mrs. Gardner said I was doing okay in her class but that I was often distracted. Sometimes, she had to call my name twice before she got my attention. And Mr. Watson and Mrs. Silva said that even though I wasn't failing their classes yet, I was about to because I hadn't turned in all of my homework assignments.

"Is this true?" Dad asked. "You haven't done your homework?"

I felt too ashamed to look at him, so I kept my head down and nodded.

"Why aren't you doing your homework?" he asked.

"I don't have time," I said, my voice small.

"What do you mean you don't have time? As soon as you come home, you should sit at the table and do your work. That's what Carmen does."

I looked at him. I could feel the anger like hot laser beams shooting out of my eyes. I could not believe Dad compared me to Carmen in front of all my teachers when every day I worked so hard to escape her shadow. Why was she the perfect one? Why did she get all the credit? At first, I was asking myself these questions, but then I started to ask them aloud.

"Do you really want to know why I'm not like Carmen? Do you really want to know why I can't find time to do my homework? Do you think it's because I'm lazy or something?"

"Erica, settle down," Dad warned, but I couldn't. I wasn't about to listen to these people talk about how dumb I was.

"When am I supposed to do my homework? That's all I'm asking. After I clean up the mess Jimmy makes? After I give him a bath or make him a snack? After I wash the clothes? After I go through the medicine cabinet and pantry and fridge to make a list of things we need from the grocery store? After I put away all those groceries? Or spend all my energy working on my *promesa* and trying to

keep Carmen and Jimmy quiet so they won't break your precious rules?"

Dad just sighed, but Mom blurted, "This is all my fault!" Her eyes were teary, and I felt horrible because the last thing I wanted was to make her cry.

The counselor and teachers stared at us. They probably thought we were the most messed-up family in the world.

"I have cancer," Mom admitted, but she couldn't go on because she was crying. And now, I was crying, my shoulders trembling, too. That's how upset I felt. Mrs. Silva placed a box of Kleenex before us, so Mom and I could grab tissues.

"Why didn't you tell us?" Mr. Leyva asked once we settled down, and I shrugged because I truly didn't know. Maybe I thought Mom's illness didn't matter to my teachers. Maybe I thought I was strong enough to handle it on my own.

"Erica's very independent," Dad said. "She's like an adult in a kid's body."

"And sometimes," Mom said, "we forget she's still a teen. She's so *responsible* at home."

"We don't have to ask her to do anything," Dad added.

Mom put her arm around me. "We're sorry, *mija*. We had no idea you were dealing with so much."

"We don't want you to fail school because of us," Dad said.

"That's why we're here," the counselor explained. "Now that we know what's going on, we'll be able to help."

"I can see how pressure at home is affecting your work," Mr. Leyva said, "but in math, at least, another factor is interfering with your success."

"What factor?" I asked, already thinking of "factor" as a math term.

"I've discussed your work with your other teachers," Mr. Leyva went on, "and we all agree that you're a divergent thinker."

"Oh, no," I moaned. I didn't know what "divergent thinking" meant, but it had to be some kind of learning problem. The last thing I wanted was for Carmen to find out I had a problem with learning.

"It's not bad," Mr. Watson said. "In fact, being a divergent thinker is a benefit in many classes."

He went on, and I listened patiently as my teachers explained how I saw lots of possibilities when faced with a problem or task. Mr. Leyva discussed how I wrote six pages to explain elements that might affect the solution to a word problem, and Mrs. Gardner and Mrs. Silva shared how my in-class writing assignments often went beyond the prompts, sometimes going in "new and startling directions." They said that divergent thinkers didn't do well on tests that had

one answer, "like IQ tests," the counselor explained. "And multiple choice tests in science," Mr. Watson added. Divergent thinkers were far more comfortable with essay tests that asked open-ended questions, which, I learned, was a question with no right answer. That part was true. I hated multiple choice tests. I could figure out a way to make every choice correct, so I never finished on time.

"Divergent thinkers have lots of imagination," Mrs. Silva said.

"The problem with math," Mr. Leyva explained, "is that it makes more sense to people who are sequential thinkers." He turned to me. "But that doesn't mean you can't do well. You just have to recognize what is and isn't important when you work through the problems. I know you don't want to hear this, but working with a good tutor will really help."

"I don't mind working with a tutor," I said, "as long as it's not Carmen. I am the older sister, and I wouldn't want to upset the natural order of things." Everyone laughed at that. Maybe they were starting to understand how hard it was to live with a genius sister.

Together, we made an intervention plan. Mr. Watson and Mrs. Silva were going to let me complete the missing homework assignments. Mrs. Gardner wanted me to move

to the front of the class, so I could pay more attention to her lectures. Mr. Leyva was going to tutor me himself, Mondays and Wednesdays, before school started. And my parents were going to make sure I didn't work too hard at home.

We had just finished our discussion when the nurse peeked in. "I'm sorry to interrupt," she said, "but Carmen told me you were here. She isn't feeling well and would like to go home."

"What's the matter?" Mom asked. "Does she have a fever?"

"No, but she says her body aches."

Dad said, "She was fine this morning."

"Maybe it's just nerves," the nurse said. "In any case, she's insisting that she's too sick for school."

I shook my head. Carmen wasn't sick. She probably wanted to skip school because she was embarrassed about the party. Someone probably teased her this morning. They must have said something really mean because Carmen *never* missed school. One year, my parents made her stay home because she had the flu. Instead of being grateful for having people who cared for her, she blamed them for ruining her perfect attendance record. Another time, we got a "bad weather" day due to an ice storm. This meant we got to stay home. All the students celebrated the extra day

off. Meanwhile, Carmen wrote a letter to the school superintendent *and* to the editor of the *Express-News*. She used a lot of big words, but her message was very simple—bad weather days are a dumb idea. "If you can get the TV stations to announce the day off," she wrote, "then you can get them to present our lessons. That way, we won't have time away from school." If you asked me, Carmen wasn't sick at all. She probably just wanted attention.

Even though the intervention plan sounded like a good idea, I still felt bummed. How was I going to finish my *promesa* when I had to catch up on my classes? Even if I didn't do any chores, I would still need every night this week to catch up.

I was going to try my best to focus on class, so as soon as I stepped into Mrs. Gardner's room, I took a seat at the front, telling Patty that I needed to concentrate when she asked why I was moving. GumWad came in late, so I didn't have a chance to explain. Then again, I didn't want to talk to him because I was still mad about the way he felt sorry for me.

Today, some students were scheduled to show their projects. Luckily, I had an extension till next week because the race was on Saturday. A few of my classmates had poster boards with pictures showing what they did, and others, like GumWad, went high-tech with PowerPoints.

He had a few slides about animal shelters, including one with a graph showing how many pets were euthanized each year. Then he had pics of the dogs he found and the happy reunions with their families.

Finally, it was Patty's turn. She walked up to the front of the class.

"I picked up trash," she said. "Trust me, it's not hard to find garbage. It's everywhere."

She stared at us as if waiting for us to ask a few questions, but no one's hand went up. Was that it? Her whole presentation? This was the worst presentation so far. I thought for sure Patty would fail, but then she turned to Mrs. Gardner, who nodded and went into the storage closet. When she came back out, she handed Patty some mobiles.

"So this is what I did with the trash," she explained. "I used wire hangers to hang stuff from them."

One had origami birds made from scraps of newspaper and magazines. "It's called *Birds*," Patty said. Another had strings of bottle caps. She held it up. "This one's *Bottle Caps*." A third had aluminum cans that were squished flat. Patty said, "*Cans*," as she shook it, making them clink against one another like chimes. The last had three clear plastic bottles. Inside one were small blue things she found—buttons, string, a plastic petal, but mostly candy

wrappers. In the other two were red and yellow things. I expected her to say "Plastic bottles," but instead she said, "I call this *Primary Colors*." Then she said, "The whole point is that trash doesn't have to be ugly. You can find a way to make it nice." She paused a moment, stared at us again. "And I guess there's a recycling message here, too."

This was definitely a new side to Patty. I was so impressed that I beamed, making my mood ring blue for joyful. But the blue didn't last long because when I went to my next class, I remembered how far behind I was and how I had only a few days before the race. Sure, Mrs. Gardner would be pleased by how many sponsors I'd found, but my personal goal was five hundred. I *had* to reach it.

So I felt a little preoccupied at lunch. I just stared at my plate while the Robins went on and on about the weekend.

"I think I have two boyfriends now," Iliana said. "Alejandro and Alan, the boy I met at the hospital. Do you think it's bad to talk to two boys on the phone if they haven't officially asked me to be their girlfriend?"

"Apparently not," Patty said. "Derek talks to a bunch of girls at the same time."

"Tell me about it," Shawntae said. "I scratched him off my Boyfriend Wish List as soon as I got home."

"Join the club," Patty said.

"We're all deleting him," Iliana added. "Right, Erica?"

"Sure, yeah. Derek's off my Wish List."

"So what's up with Roberto?" Patty said. "He moped all during social studies. And instead of eating lunch with us, he's hanging out with the Ping-Pong crowd from the other night."

"I guess they're his new friends," Shawntae said. "I should have predicted he'd leave the Robins. But I guess I'm not a psychic after all. I'm just like everybody else. Normal."

"Oh, brother," Patty said. "It's not the end of the world. I'm in that 'everybody else' category, too, but you don't see me down in the dumps."

Iliana said, "Shawntae, you couldn't be normal if you tried. Who else wears pumps every day? Who else can get a bunch of kids on the dance floor? You're a natural-born leader. Isn't she?" She nudged me, but I didn't say a word. "You're going to be the first black woman mayor of San Antonio, remember?"

"I guess," Shawntae said with a bummed-out voice, but then she brightened up. "At least my service learning project went well."

"It was awesome," Iliana admitted. "A whole other class came to listen."

"Thanks to the invitations, the other social studies

teacher decided to join us," Shawntae said. "So I presented in front of two classes!"

"Weren't you nervous?" Patty asked.

"Are you kidding? I was *so* nervous, but I kept it under control."

They talked a bit more and then ate silently for a while. Finally, Patty said, "Check out Roberto. He keeps glancing over. He keeps looking at Erica. He did that during class, too." She turned to me. "You hurt his feelings when you changed seats. He probably thinks you're avoiding him."

I shrugged.

"That's right," Iliana said. "You two were acting weird Saturday night. One minute you were dancing, and the next, you were stomping off the floor."

I still didn't speak.

"Erica!" Iliana said. "Wake up. Tell us what happened. Did you and Roberto get in a fight?"

"Oh, please," Shawntae said. "He's too nice to fight with anyone."

"Then what's wrong with Erica?" Iliana wanted to know.

"She thought she was going to be rich," Shawntae replied, "but her mom didn't win the lottery after all."

"That's not it," I said.

"Well, why else would you be in a bad mood?" Before I could answer, Shawntae went on, "I don't blame you. You probably hate me right now for putting those ideas in your head. I shouldn't have told you about my stupid dream."

"Are you really worried about the lottery?" Iliana asked me.

"No. I never thought we were going to win."

"I knew it!" Iliana said. "So you *did* get in a fight with Roberto. That's why you guys are acting so weird."

"They didn't get in a fight," Patty said, all impatient. "Erica's upset about Derek being a flirt."

"Come on," Shawntae said. "You don't need psychic powers to see that she wanted to win the lottery."

"Or that she had a fight with Roberto," Iliana insisted.

I couldn't believe they were talking about me when I was right in front of them.

"Stop it," I said, but they kept making guesses. I couldn't believe it. My mood ring—my inanimate mood ring!—knew how I felt better than my friends did. "Stop it!" I shouted.

And they did—they completely froze. All three of them looked at me like I was some stranger wearing an Erica mask.

"How can my friends be so clueless about what's going

on in my life?" They didn't dare answer. "Sure, if my life were normal, I'd be upset about boys and lotteries, but I can't think about that right now because my life is *not* normal. My mom's sick, remember? I made a *promesa* to help her, and it isn't working out. I still need a hundred names to reach my goal, but now I have all this homework because I'm about to fail school. Yes, my grades are awful! And I can't help thinking that if I don't keep my promise, my mother will die. Do you hear me? She'll *die!*"

With that, I ran out. They tried to stop me, saying they didn't know and they're sorry, but I kept moving, straight to the counselor's office. She'd told me I could go there whenever I needed to, and I desperately needed to right now.

When I got home, I went to the bedroom to check on Carmen. She was sitting on the bed with a box of paper clips, a stack of envelopes, and a ball of rubber bands, which she was slowly taking apart. "Fourteen, fifteen, sixteen," she counted.

"What are you doing?" I asked.

"Seventeen, eighteen," she went on like a mindless robot.

"Carmen!"

I startled her. She stopped counting and looked up at

me. "Don't interrupt," she scolded. "I lost my place. Now I have to start over."

"Why are you counting those rubber bands?"

"Because I've already counted the paper clips and envelopes."

She was about to start again, but I snatched the rubber bands away.

"This has to stop," I said. "You can't go through life counting things. At first, I thought you were just acting weird, but now I think you've got a real problem. No one counts all the time, not even geniuses."

That's when I noticed two book-shaped rectangles beneath her blouse.

"What's that?" I said, pointing.

She tried to cover up with a pillow.

"Let me see," I insisted.

She shook her head, so I grabbed the pillow. We played tug-of-war for a while, but since I was stronger, she gave up.

"Okay!" she said. "But don't laugh."

She lifted her shirt, and sure enough, she had used athletic wraps to tie two books to her chest.

"What on earth are you doing?" I asked, trying my best not to laugh.

She covered up again. "I was in the library this morning doing more research on breast cancer. Did you know

that if your mother has it, you have a greater chance of getting it, too? Some women even have preventive mastectomies, which means they get their breasts removed before they ever have a chance to get sick. But I figure that if I stop developing, I won't have to worry about it. That's why I wanted to come home. I'm going to stop my boobs from growing."

I started laughing. I couldn't help it. I know I promised, but this was too funny. My poor sister thought she was going to die, and all I could do was laugh. I couldn't stop long enough to tell her that she was wasting her time because you can't stop Mother Nature.

"Quit laughing!" she said, but I couldn't. Carmen might be smart and she might be developing, but she was still a little kid, especially when it came to the facts of life.

She threw the box of paper clips at me. It hit the wall and the clips rained down. Then she threw the pillow at me. It hit a figurine on my dresser, making it crash to the floor. I couldn't even get mad.

"Please!" she begged. "Stop laughing!"

I took a deep breath to calm myself. A few chuckles slipped out, but I quickly got them under control. "You're not going to get cancer," I finally managed.

"How can you be so sure?"

She was right. I couldn't make that promise. "Okay, I'm

not sure. If there's one thing I've learned," I said, thinking about Shawntae, "it's that no one can predict the future. But if you start worrying about it now, you're never going to enjoy life. Plus, don't you want boobs? *Every* girl wants to have nice boobs."

I went to my dresser, pulled out one of Mom's bikini tops, and put it against my chest.

"It's way too big for you," Carmen said.

"I know, but someday, I'll be able to wear a bikini like this." I tossed the top to her. "And so will you."

She examined it, and then she removed the books from her chest.

"So why do you count?" I asked.

She shrugged.

"I'm not going to make fun of you. I'm just curious. You're the only person on the planet who counts everything she sees."

She looked at me. I could tell she was trying to decide whether or not to trust me.

"Counting makes me feel better," she said. "I ask myself, how many of this? How many of that? And when I count, I get the answer. I like getting answers, especially when..."

"When what?"

"When I'm confused about things."

"You're *never* confused," I said.

"That's not true. I'm *always* confused."

"About what?"

She gave me a long list, things like friendships and emotions and Mom, mostly Mom. She had the same questions that bothered me, like why was Mom sick and would she get better?

"What do *you* do when you feel like life is out of control?" she asked me.

I glanced at the notebook GumWad had given me. "I started a diary," I said, "and it really helps."

She smiled. Finally, we had something in common.

We picked up the paper clips that had fallen on the floor. It was the first time we had ever cleaned the room together. After a while, Carmen said, "I know we fight a lot, but I'm really glad you're my sister. I owe you, especially for helping me at Derek's party."

I thought about my parent-teacher conference, how I refused to let Carmen help me. But if she owed me one, then maybe tutoring wasn't really helping. Maybe it was a way to pay me back.

I glanced at the mountain of books I'd brought for homework. "Can I show you something?" I asked.

"Sure."

I reached into my backpack and pulled out the math test. She looked it over, and when she got to the word

problems and my six pages of reasons why each needed more information, *she* started laughing. My paragraphs really cracked her up. Normally, I'd be offended, but I had to admit that my "divergent thinking" *did* lead me in new, startling, and just plain wrong directions.

When Carmen finally settled down, she said, "Okay, let's start with number one."

4 EXTRA ENVELOPES

Thursday afternoon, I sat on the front porch, waiting for my friends and watching Jimmy scribble on the sidewalk with chalk. The Race for the Cure forms were due, and as soon as Dad came home, I was going to turn them in. But my friends made me promise to wait. They said they had a surprise for me.

I pulled the list of sponsors from my manila envelope and tallied up the names—412. In a way, I felt proud. I had talked to every person I knew and a lot of strangers. So I didn't meet my goal, but hopefully, I'd get credit for trying my best, and in that way, fulfill my *promesa*.

"Gimme car!" Jimmy said, pointing to a toy truck at my feet. I kicked it to him. He rolled it across the curvy line he'd drawn on the sidewalk. The line looped over itself and

sometimes trailed off into the grass, but Jimmy kept following it, making zooming sounds as he pushed his truck. And I thought, if I were to draw a line of my life, it wouldn't be straight like the timelines in my history book but tangled like the squiggle Jimmy drew on the sidewalk because you had to change directions sometimes, trail off the normal path—like the way Carmen did eighth-grade math even though she was supposed to be in elementary school, or the way I took care of Mom when she was supposed to take care of me. Maybe there was no such thing as a normal path. Maybe we all traveled through confused squiggles instead.

A sedan pulled into the driveway, and after turning off the engine, Shawntae's mother got out.

"The gang's all here," she announced, and when the other car doors opened, all the Robins, even GumWad, stepped out.

"Hi, everyone," I said. "I didn't know *all* of you were coming."

"Are you ready for the surprise?" Shawntae asked.

"Sure, what is it?"

She laughed. "Not so fast. It's for your mom, too."

I told Jimmy to go get her, so he ran in, calling, "Mommy! Mommy!" A few moments later, Mom and Carmen came outside.

"Close your eyes," Iliana told us.

Mom, Carmen, Jimmy, and I closed our eyes. When the Robins told us to open them, we saw a white banner with bright pink letters that said, "Race for Lisa."

"I love it!" Mom said, clapping her hands like a kid who had just opened a birthday present. She gave Shawntae's mother a hug, and then she hugged each of the Robins.

"Look on the other side," GumWad said as they turned the banner around.

Dozens had signed their names. I didn't recognize every signature, but many were familiar. My teachers, classmates, even guys on my Boyfriend Wish List. I scanned the names, finally finding Iliana, Shawntae, Patty, and Roberto.

"There's more," Patty said. She reached into the car and pulled out four manila envelopes.

"We felt really bad the other day when you got mad at us," Iliana explained. "There we were talking about silly things when the whole time, you've been dealing with some big problems."

"Then we thought about the times you helped us," Shawntae said. "Like when you made those invitations for me."

"And when you helped with my English homework," Patty said.

"And when you found my first dog," GumWad added.

"And when you went to the hospital to help me with the kids," Iliana said.

"But you never asked *us* for help," Shawntae went on. "So when you said you were short one hundred names, we decided to pitch in."

"We didn't think it'd be hard," GumWad said, "if we each got twenty-five people to sign up."

"I got all my relatives to sponsor you," Patty said.

"I set up a fund-raising campaign on my Facebook page," Shawntae said. "Lots of people responded."

"I asked my brothers," Iliana told me. "They think you're cute, like another little sister, and when they heard about your *promesa*, they asked their whole football team to help."

"I went back to the people who had lost their dogs," GumWad said. "They were more than happy to donate the reward money."

I took the envelopes and peeked inside. Each had extra sponsor forms, checks, and real money. With the extra names from the Robins, I knew I had reached my goal.

"Thank you," Carmen and Mom said.

And I said it, too. "Thanks. This means so much to me. I know you helped because you care about me and not for other reasons"—I looked at GumWad—"like feeling sorry for me."

His smile told me that he knew I was apologizing for the night of Derek's party.

"Why don't we take the banner inside," Mom suggested, "so we can sign it, too."

"Good idea," Shawntae's mom said.

We headed toward the house. Everyone went in, but before GumWad and I entered, I grabbed his sleeve to hold him back.

"I'm sorry you wasted all your quarters on me," I said when we were alone.

"They weren't wasted," he answered. "I like helping out. Besides, I really needed to get rid of my gumball machine."

"You got rid of it?"

"Yep."

"What a coincidence," I said. "I just got rid of all my Chia Pets. I didn't throw them away. I just passed them along to children at the hospital."

"Even Scooby?" GumWad wondered. "He was my favorite."

"Sorry. Even Scooby."

"Do you miss them?" he asked.

"I thought I would, but no, I don't miss them at all. Do you miss your gumball machine?"

"Sometimes." He got this faraway look on his face as if

he were remembering special moments with gumballs. I couldn't help laughing a bit.

"Erica! Roberto!" Shawntae called. "You're missing all the fun!"

"Coming!" we called back.

And then GumWad said, "You should call me Roberto from now on too, since I'm not chewing gum anymore."

I held out my hand, so he could shake it. "It's a deal," I said.

He smiled. I had to admit he had cute dimples, cuter since he didn't have an annoying gumball in his mouth. And, like Iliana often said, he could be really sweet sometimes. I could never add GumWad to my Boyfriend Wish List, but maybe, someday, I could add Roberto.

500 NAMES IN PINK

The big day arrived! Dad dropped Carmen, Mom, and me near the Race for the Cure festivities, while he and Jimmy searched for a parking spot. The "Race for Lisa" group planned to meet by the flagpole fifteen minutes before the starting gun went off. We had arrived an hour early, so we had time to look around. Mom wanted to see the sights too, but she quickly got out of breath.

"And to think I wanted to do the whole walk," she said. She lifted a foot to show off her tennis shoes. "Next year," she vowed.

I gave her a hug. "Next year, you and I will *run* the 5K."

"We sure will," she agreed. "But for now, I'm going to sit over there." She pointed toward a row of chairs in front of a stage where an emcee introduced a speaker from the

city council. I was glad Mom had come, even though she didn't feel well enough to walk the 5K. She planned to sit near the finish line and cheer for us. "You girls look around, okay?"

"Okay," we said.

Carmen and I walked through the parking lot of the Alamodome, San Antonio's big stadium. The newspaper article I had seen in the valley said that last year, thirty thousand people came.

"I wonder how many people are here today," I said to Carmen.

"I don't know," she answered, "but I don't plan to count them." I smiled, glad that she was getting closer to normal.

Nearly everyone wore the official T-shirt, including Carmen and me. Some people went beyond the shirt by dyeing their hair or wearing pink wigs. One lady had wrapped a pink boa around her neck. She kept sneaking up to people and tickling them with its feathers. Other ladies wore pink bracelets or earrings. And the dogs had pink collars or leashes. One man had dyed his poodle so it looked like a ball of cotton candy on legs. There were so many shades—the pinks you find on roses, lipstick, bubble gum, pencil erasers, and pigs. Even the guys wore pink.

Carmen and I made our way to a tent called the Pink Hat Café. It served strawberry yogurt, apples, bananas,

bagels, Gatorade, water, and pink lemonade. Then we peeked through the windows of a giant inflatable castle filled with kids jumping around, and we visited a booth where a woman painted the breast cancer awareness ribbon on our cheeks. At another booth, we got autographs from Spurs and Silver Stars players, and farther down the aisle, we laughed at people singing out of tune with a karaoke machine.

Then, we found the Tribute Tent. When we went inside, Carmen said, "It's just like *el cuarto de milagros*."

I had to agree. I felt as if we had traveled back in time to the day we visited the valley and left our special items at the shrine. Lining each side of the tent were walls. One was called the Wall of Hope, and the other was called the Memory Wall. They had bulletin boards so people could tack up pictures and letters. I saw photos of smiling women, and some of women who were bald from chemotherapy or had arms swollen like my mom's. The letters on the Wall of Hope were mostly prayers, and some were *promesas*. One woman promised to work at a soup kitchen every day for a year. One husband promised to stop watching TV. And a child promised to do his homework "forever and ever." Other letters were thank-you notes or narratives from women who had survived cancer. On the Memory Wall, people who had lost someone wrote letters, many addressed

to the women who had died. "We miss you," some said, or "We wish you were here," or "Can you believe that Señora Chavez is dating a younger man?" And, just like in *el cuarto de milagros*, tables were filled with roses, hundreds of pink roses; and teddy bears, candles, balloons, greeting cards, and small statues of saints; and souvenirs like thimbles, refrigerator magnets, baseball caps; and T-shirts from all over the world.

"I thought I'd find you here," Dad said. He was holding Jimmy's hand, trying to keep him from grabbing the items. Jimmy kept saying, "Gimme! Gimme!"

"Do you want to jump in a castle?" Carmen asked him.

"Gimme castle!" he said.

Carmen took his hand. "Let *me* take care of Jimmy for a change." We nodded as she led him out. She'd been taking care of him all week. Maybe Mom and Dad told her to, or maybe she was being nice. After all, she *had* been helping me with math, and little by little, I was starting to understand.

When they were gone, Dad said, "Here's your backpack." He handed it to me. It stored my camera, a bottle of water, and the rest of Mom's bikini tops. I had brought them for good luck. I pulled out the hot pink one, remembering how Mom had left a bikini top at *el cuarto de milagros*. That seemed like years ago. Since then, she'd had

surgery and several weeks of radiation therapy. She had a couple of more weeks to go. Then we'd have to wait six months before the doctor ran tests to see if the cancer had disappeared. I knew those were going to be the toughest six months, and that every day, we'd silently ask ourselves, "Is Mom going to be okay?" So here I stood between the Wall of Hope and the Memory Wall, glad that Mom was still with us but also afraid that next year, things might be different.

"Do you really believe in *promesas*?" I asked Dad. "Do you think miracles happen if we keep our promises?"

He put his arm around me and took a deep breath. After a long moment, he said, "I don't know, *mija*. Sometimes, I think *promesas* aren't for the sick person. We do them for ourselves, so we can feel like we're helping in some way. But in the end, it's not in our hands."

That wasn't the answer I wanted to hear. I wanted Dad to be as confident about *promesas* as he was when we visited the valley. I wanted certainty, an answer as straightforward as the answers Carmen got when she counted things.

Dad reached into his pocket, pulled out a slip of paper, and tacked it onto the Wall of Hope.

"What's that?" I asked.

"The receipt from last week's visit to Chuck E. Cheese."

He laughed to himself. "I could hardly hear a word your mother said, and I spent most of the time chasing Jimmy. The pizza was cold, and the soda was warm. It wasn't like our first date at all, but we had fun. As much fun as we had the first time we went to the movies."

Dad didn't know Mom's future, but he knew her present and her past. He was going to celebrate and hope and be grateful, and so was I. So I placed the bikini top on a table and left it in the Tribute Tent.

When we stepped back outside, we saw Jimmy and Carmen. "Look who I found," she said.

The Robins were beside her. Roberto carried the banner, rolled up for now. Patty was kneeling as she put hot pink shoelaces in her tennis shoes. She must have found them at one of the booths. Shawntae had pink tennis shoes instead of pumps, and when she caught me staring at her feet, she shook a charm bracelet in my face. *All* the charms were pumps, each a different color. Iliana was there too, arm in arm with her brothers. They wore their football jerseys with pink bandanas tied over the sleeves.

I could only sigh. They were so cute. Maybe someday they'd see me as more than "another little sister."

"We decided to register so we can run," they said. "See you guys later. We're going to warm up."

I watched them disappear into the crowd. Was it

acceptable to put your friend's older brothers on your Boyfriend Wish List?

"Where's your mom?" Patty asked.

"Near the stage," I said. "Let's go find her."

We headed to the stage and found her talking to a few other women.

"Meet my new friends," she said as she introduced us to fellow cancer patients who planned to cheer for the people walking in their honor. We talked to them for a while. They were going through a hard time too, and it was nice to know that Mom wasn't alone.

"Time to make your way to the starting line," the emcee said.

"We better hurry," I told the Robins. "The race starts in fifteen minutes."

Before I left, Mom grabbed my hand. "I wish I could walk with you, *mija*, but I get so weak."

"I understand," I said.

She pulled me toward her and kissed my cheek. "I'm very proud of you. I'll be thinking about you the whole time you're out there."

"And I'll be thinking of you," I said as I gave her a hug.

At the flagpoles, an army color guard hoisted the Texas and United States flags. Then the soldiers did a short routine, twirling their rifles in unison before marching out.

Roberto and Patty rolled open the banner, each holding an end, and we gathered behind it.

"Let's race for Lisa!" I yelled, and everyone cheered.

All of a sudden, thousands of people packed themselves behind the starting line. The starter stood on a platform and spoke into a microphone, his voice booming through huge speakers.

"Are you ready?!"

The crowd roared with excitement.

"Then get set!" The runners positioned themselves. "Go!" We heard the loud pop of the starting gun and the crowd lurched forward, some running, some walking, but all going in the same direction.

The race was amazing. Music bands were positioned at different points along the route. We heard Scottish bagpipes, a drumming circle, a children's choir, jazz and rock bands, mariachis, and country and western groups. There were dancers too—cloggers, tap dancers, belly dancers, and young men doing something called capoeira, which looked like a combination of martial arts and break dancing. We saw air force recruits marching in full dress uniform, and the Spurs Silver Dancers doing routines with their pom-poms. A whole group of health professionals from the Cancer Therapy and Research Center walked in

pink scrubs, followed by groups of firemen and police officers. And others had banners, too. Some were from companies—Saks Fifth Avenue, Teachers Federal Credit Union, Trinity Baptist Church, and my dad's company, USAA—and others from private groups like mine.

At one point, we had to cross a bridge that went over the railroad tracks. I stopped a moment to take a few pictures and found myself in the middle of a huge river flowing with pink, each person like a drop of water. I looked at all the faces passing by, and even though they were strangers, I saw traces of my mother, my sister, and my friends because I felt related to *everyone*. After all, we were like a team, an *army*, fighting for those we loved.

It took us an hour to walk the 5K. When we crossed the finish line, Mom, Dad, and Jimmy cheered.

"Come on," Mom and Dad told us. "We want to show you something."

The Robins and I followed them to a huge sign shaped like the graduated cylinders we used in science class, only instead of milliliters, the sign measured the number of sponsors who had donated to this year's Race for the Cure. It was called "The Top Ten Fund-Raising Teams."

"Erica, look!" Iliana said, all excited as she pointed to

our team, Race for Lisa, which was number eight on the list. I had collected 526 names!

"I told you! I told you!" Shawntae said. She started jumping like a jackpot winner. "I'm a psychic! I'm a psychic!" she kept saying.

"What are you talking about?" Patty said. "Did you dream about this sign last night?"

"No," Shawntae replied. "But don't you get it? Don't you get it?"

We all looked at one another. "Get what?" Roberto finally asked.

"The dream I had about Erica's mother winning the lottery. It wasn't about the lottery at all, at least not *literally*." Shawntae put her hands on my shoulders and faced me. "My dream was telling me that you'd collect five hundred names. The lottery was a symbol. It wasn't about money. It was about sponsors. Don't you see? I am a psychic after all!"

The old me would have pointed out all the details that did not quite match and insisted that Shawntae was over-interpreting things, but the new me looked at my family, my friends, and all the people still crossing the finish line, many smiling even though they wore shirts that said, "In loving memory of," and others, so many others, with shirts that said, "I'm a survivor." And then I looked at my mom

and dad. I had always thought they were the strongest people in the world. I thought Dad could toss cars as easily as footballs. I thought everyone did what Mom said, not just me, Carmen, and Jimmy, but the neighbors, the teachers, the president of the United States. I thought my parents had the answers to everything, like the meaning of every word, the solution to every problem, and how to answer the big questions like why is there good and evil or why do some people, good people, get sick. I could never imagine my parents being babies once or toddlers or teenagers, going through everything I was going through. In my mind, they had always been adults, and they would always be there to help me. But then I saw Mom sick and Dad all nervous. Suddenly, they needed me. They weren't weak, exactly, but they weren't as strong as I thought. So *I* had to be strong. Even though I was still a kid, I had to do grown-up things like help around the house and keep everybody calm. But I couldn't do it alone.

I glanced at my ring, expecting it to be pink even though it wasn't a color on the mood ring color chart. Then I looked away from it. I didn't need my mood ring to tell me how I felt. I could see my feelings in the faces around me. When I was sad, they were too, and when I was happy, so were they. I still didn't believe that Shawntae was a psychic and even though I had fulfilled my *promesa*, I

couldn't be 100 percent sure that Mom would be cured, but after today, I most definitely believed in the people who loved me and that the real miracles happened when we worked together.

Roberto and Patty lifted the banner. "Race for Lisa!" they cheered. Carmen and I joined in: "Race for Lisa!" Then Iliana and her brothers shouted, and finally my parents. Soon, lots of people, including some we'd never met, were chanting, "Race for Lisa! Race for Lisa!" as we celebrated our five hundred names in pink.

AUTHOR'S NOTE

Dear Readers,

I have known about *promesas* and the story of the pilot who crashed his plane for as long as I can remember. My family has visited the church with the Virgen de San Juan many times, and though I don't make formal *promesas*, I like to leave candles and prayers in honor of whoever is struggling at the time.

Several years ago, my aunt was diagnosed with breast cancer. Luckily, the doctors discovered it in its early stages, and my aunt has been in remission for over a decade. To celebrate her recovery, my cousin invited all her relatives and friends to participate in the Komen Race for the Cure, and I signed up, happy to support my aunt in any way I could.

The first time I participated, I was amazed by the thousands of people who had gathered at the Alamodome, and when I saw them singing, praying, and celebrating their loved ones, I remembered the valley and the *cuarto de milagros*. How I loved reading the letters that people left at the shrine, just as I enjoyed hearing their stories at the Alamodome. This is what inspired me to write Erica's story.

I've seen the power of *promesas* firsthand. When my father learned he needed cardiac bypass surgery, my mother promised to say the rosary every day for two years, and when my uncle learned he had prostate cancer, he promised to visit the shrine in the valley once a month for a year. My aunt didn't make a *promesa*, but her prayers and her gratitude as we gathered to walk in her honor taught me, just as they taught Erica, that the most powerful medicines are hope and the love of family and friends.

Yours,

Diana López

ACKNOWLEDGMENTS

Many thanks to my agent, Stefanie von Borstel; my editor, Connie Hsu; and the whole team at Little, Brown. I am so lucky to have your enthusiasm and expertise on my side. Thanks also to Christine Granados and Carmen Edington, who helped me get those first chapters in tip-top shape, and to my Daedalus friends, whose writing advice continues to guide me even when I am alone with the keyboard. Finally, I couldn't do this without the encouragement of my colleagues and students at UHV and the support of my family and friends, most especially Gene.